SHADOW WARRIOR

MICHELLE DIENER

ALSO BY MICHELLE DIENER

Sky Raiders Series

Sky Raiders

Calling the Change

Shadow Warrior

The Verdant String

Interference & Insurgency

Breakaway

Breakeven

Trailblazer

High Flyer

Wave Rider

Peace Maker

Enthraller

The Class 5 Series

Dark Horse

Dark Deeds

Dark Minds

Dark Matters

Dark Class

Collision Course

Rising Wave Series

The Turncoat King

The Threadbare Queen

Fate's Arrow

Truth's Blade

THE STORY SO FAR

We last left Taya and Garek in Pan Nuk at the end of Calling the Change.

Taya had been taken to Luf, the capital of the Illian state of Harven, but she'd escaped and foiled a plan by the sky raiders to reacquire Luci and the other villagers from Cassinya who had been captives with her on Shadow.

Realizing the sky raiders were trying to get their prisoners back, she and Garek raced back to Juli, to find the Kardanx had in fact been taken, and then on to Pan Nuk to find some of their friends had also been snatched up.

After mounting a successful rescue, they returned to Pan Nuk, where they were attacked by guards sent to grab Taya under the instructions of Dartan, the liege of West Lathor's advisor.

Taya killed one of the guards, and afraid she doesn't have the control over her calling she thinks is possible, she decides to find the Iron Guard and ask them to train her. She feels the weight of the future of Barit on her shoulders. She has the power to bring down the sky raiders, if she can master her calling.

This dovetails with her and Garek's concern for Aidan, who went missing toward the end of Calling the Change. Vent, the guard master of Juli, thinks he's been taken by the Iron Guard.

They decide to set out to find Aidan and see if General Hanson, the leader of the Iron Guard, will help Taya master her calling.

Vent wants the Iron Guard back, as well. Their reputation as an elite force kept West Lathor safe in the past, and their loss makes the prospect of war with Harven and the two other Illian states Harven is in league with much more likely.

But at the start of Shadow Warrior, the most pressing problem is Aidan's disappearance, and Garek and Taya are determined to find him.

ONE

TAKING control of the city of Juli didn't seem to suit Vent.

He looked tired and older than he had a week ago when Taya had last seen him.

Garek landed the sky craft on the palace wall and opened the door for Juli's guard master as he walked across the parapet toward them.

"Vent." Garek leaned out to call a greeting and wave.

As Vent had imprisoned Dartan, the liege's advisor, on the charge of collaboration with sky raiders, and she and Garek were in a sky raider craft, Taya guessed Garek didn't want to give Vent's detractors any room to use this meeting against him. He was making it clear this sky craft was piloted by West Lathorians.

Vent obviously realized what Garek had done, because when he climbed the ladder to the cabin, his face was grim.

"Protecting my reputation, are you?"

"Can't hurt." Garek stepped back and grinned.

"I suppose not." Vent stared out at the large unit of guards lining the wall. "Unfortunately, I need all the help I can get."

"Any news of Aidan?" Garek went straight to the point of their visit.

Vent shook his head. "I've sent a team to look for him, but there's been no word."

"And the liege? How is he dealing with this new turn of events?" Taya thought the petulant, intoxicated ruler of West Lathor would most likely have been the most difficult hurdle for Vent to overcome. The liege's relationship with Aidan was strangely adversarial, given Aidan was a loyal son.

"He's lying in bed, in some kind of stupor. My suspicion is that Dartan is responsible for putting him there. I've got doctors trying to work out what might have been given to him, because Dartan is denying involvement.

"Truth be told, even those with no love of Dartan were probably happy to see the liege removed from active office. Now they no longer have to go through the motions of pretending to follow the edicts of a man who had a very tenuous grip on reality."

"It has to help you, too," Garek commented, and Vent shot him a dirty look.

"Yes, and it's lucky I've got proof the liege was like that before I returned to Juli, so his illness isn't a charge that can be laid at my feet."

Garek nodded, calm and unperturbed, and Vent scrubbed a hand through his short hair.

"I want Aidan back, and I want him back now."

"That's why we're here. We're going to look for him." Taya pushed away from the window.

"Why?" Vent scowled at her.

"Because he's our friend. He helped us when we needed it. Now we'll help him." She also wanted to speak to the Iron Guard, who Vent was sure held Aidan hostage, but that was just fortuitous synchronicity.

"Well, we've all established you don't report to me," Vent said. "I'm not going to stop you."

"No, you're not. But I'd like to think you'd help us. We need to know where Aidan disappeared and what news you've had from whoever you sent out to look for him."

Vent gave a grunt that must have been agreement because he took the map Garek handed him, marking a spot on it with a thin charcoal pencil.

"This was where he was camping when he was taken. You bring him straight back when you have him. Straight back." Vent glowered at them. "No side trips or visits home. We need him right here. I'll hold back the tide of unrest as long as I can, but we need a liege, and we need the Iron Guard, as well. Persuade them to come home. All will be forgiven if they would just swear allegiance to the liege again."

"Depends on how they've treated Aidan," Garek said. "If he's unhappy with them, he might not trust them anymore."

"General Hanson wouldn't be that stupid. She's a woman who knows how to play the long game." Vent dismissed the comment with a flick of his wrist.

"Depends on why they took him in the first place," Taya said.

Vent turned to her. "Well, let's hope, for all our sakes, they wanted to reforge the alliance and decided Aidan was a better bet than his father."

Taya hoped so too. She had a feeling she needed the Iron Guard, and it would be a great deal easier to get that help if they were all on the same side.

NEITHER OF THEM were familiar with the terrain.

Garek's lips twitched.

Before Taya had been abducted by the sky raiders, neither of them had been familiar with much of West Lathor. They'd been no further than the two cities in their state.

Now, they'd flown toward the stars, and he had been around the whole of the planet of Barit.

That didn't help now, though. The area between Juli and Gara-mundo, the path Aidan had been on when he'd disappeared, was full of low valleys, high peaks, and thick swathes of forest. Aidan could be anywhere below.

Taya stood beside him with the map Vent had marked up, working as his navigator.

"That looks like the place." She pointed up ahead. "There's a bend in the river that matches where Vent marked on the map, and it looks like someone's camping there. Maybe Vent's search party?"

Garek saw it, nodded in agreement.

He set down beside a fire pit, and they both climbed out the craft to survey the area.

There were definite signs that the fire pit had been used as recently as that morning. When Garek bent down to touch them, the rocks ringing the fireplace were still warm.

"You can see where they slept." Taya pointed to the flattened grass. "But they haven't left any equipment. Maybe they're gone?"

Garek shook his head. "Standard guard procedure, you take everything with you every day. In case there's a change in plan."

"So what should we do?" Taya stepped up to him, and he hooked an arm around her shoulders and drew her close.

She came willingly into his arms, fitting her head under his chin and sliding her arms around his waist.

They stood like that for a long moment, and Garek breathed in the fragrance of her hair and savored the feel of her, warm and alive, against him.

He liked being alone with her. Privacy was a rare commodity since they'd returned from Shadow, and it felt good to be in each other's company.

A movement on the other side of the river ripped him out of the moment.

She was so attuned to him, she must have felt him tense, because she stepped back, face lifting to his with a query in her eyes.

"Someone in the trees, on the other bank." He let his gaze sweep the area.

Taya turned and studied the thickly forested area herself.

After a few minutes, someone stepped out from behind a tree and walked forward, dressed in a Juli guard uniform.

He walked to the edge of the bank and looked over at them.

"Vent send you?" he called.

"In a manner of speaking," Garek confirmed.

"I recognize you both." The man gave a sudden, decisive nod. He half-turned back to the forest, stuck his fingers in his mouth and gave a sharp whistle, then jumped down into the river and waded across.

"It looked deeper," Taya said, as they watched him get up to his waist at the deepest point and then struggle up the bank to stand at their feet.

Garek put his hand down, and the man accepted, allowing himself to be heaved up next to them.

"Captain Savo," he said, introducing himself. "Juli Night Guard."

"Garek of Pan Nuk." Garek inclined his head. "This is my intended, Taya."

Savo gave them both a brief nod, then turned back to see if his team had followed him.

They were standing on the other side, as if waiting to see what sort of reception Savo would get before committing themselves.

"Your team seems nervous." Garek saw more than one of them eyeing the sky craft suspiciously, and a few more looking over their shoulders back into the forest.

"We are." Savo gestured the two men and three women over with a wave of his hand. "We've been here two days, and we're being watched. We can feel it. Saw it a few times, too. Just a quick movement out the corner of my eye. That kind of thing weighs on you after awhile. There's been a few of those come over, too." He pointed at the sky craft. "Flying low and careful, like they were looking for something."

His team splashed up behind them, and he turned his attention to them.

Garek offered a hand to one of the women, and she took it with a nod, and when she was up, turned to help someone else.

They seemed comfortable with each other, and behaved like a close-knit team, anticipating each other's movements and needs.

Garek's respect rose, not only for Savo but for Vent for creating teams like this. In Gara, a good team like this was almost an impossibility, with the way things had been run.

Maybe things would change, now Aidan had appointed Captain Nostra, formerly of the Juli Day Guard, as Garamundo's new guard master. She was someone he respected, and it would be interesting to see how the Gara guards adjusted to her after years under the old guard master, Utrel, and his partner in crime, the corrupt town master.

"So, you're here to help us?" Savo asked when everyone had been pulled up onto the bank.

They were all dripping water, and then one of the women blurred just a little and suddenly they were dry.

Garek looked over at her. "Water calling?"

The guard smiled.

"We're here to find Aidan." Taya gestured to the camp. "You obviously haven't had any luck?"

Savo shook his head. "As I say, we think we're being watched. Who's doing the watching, I don't know. Whoever they are, they don't want to be found."

"I'm hoping they'll be interested in investigating the sky craft." Garek scanned the trees as he spoke.

"Or it'll scare them away," Savo countered.

"Maybe." He didn't think so, but it was worth giving whoever was out there two reasons to pay them a visit.

"I think I'll let them know I'm here, waiting."

Taya caught his eye. "What are you going to do?"

"Get high enough for them to see me." He hadn't done this in a while, not since he was in Gara, walking the walls, and he had been meaning to try it again. He had grown stronger, had pushed his own boundaries so much since he set off to rescue Taya, he wondered how high he could go.

He called his Change, let the air coalesce at his feet, and then rose up.

When he looked down, it was to find Savo's team staring at him with mouths open. Taya stood with a hand shading her eyes as her gaze followed him upward, and a broad smile on her face.

Then he looked outward, spinning slowly to search through the trees in all directions for any sign of a camp or place where the Iron Guard could be hiding Aidan.

In most places, the foliage was too thick and he couldn't see the ground, but as he rose even higher, a glint of Starlight off metal caught his eye.

He saw someone perched high in a tree on the other side of the river—just a glimpse of their arm and shoulder as they took aim at him with a crossbow.

He gave himself one last push and flew up a little more as the arrow shot past his feet.

He dropped, letting himself free fall until he was near the ground and then giving himself a cushion so his landing was soft.

He could have stayed up longer, but if someone was shooting at them, he'd better keep some power in reserve.

One of Savo's guards ran back toward the group, the arrow clutched in his hand.

"Did you see them?" Taya asked.

He nodded. He had a very good idea which tree the shooter had been in. And whoever it was, they were very high up—it would take them a while to get down.

"Will you be all right here?"

Taya frowned as she nodded. "Why?"

"I'm going to destroy a bit of forest, now."

TWO

GAREK RAN TOWARD THE RIVER, and Taya held her breath when he jumped as he reached the bank, propelling himself through the air onto the other side.

As he landed, he went a little fuzzy around the edges, as if someone was shaking him so hard it was difficult to see him properly, and then he stepped into the inbetween.

One moment he was there, the next, it was as if he'd disappeared, but rather than being unable to see where he was going, trees began to fall, exploding into splinters or crashing to the left and right.

She stared in wonder.

She had never seen anything like it. He was literally opening a pathway through the trees.

"What's he doing?"

She realized Savo had been shouting at her for a while, and she turned to him.

"He's called his Change, and he's going after the person who shot him."

Which snapped her back to reality. If Garek was confronting the person who shot at him, then she would be there to back him up.

She ran to the sky craft, scrambling up the ladder, almost falling into the pilot's chamber and then running through to the back to get one of the slim wooden boxes that had been built for her in Pan Nuk.

She carried it out far more carefully than she'd run in, and got all the way to the river before she opened it up.

She pulled a set of knives out of the water that filled the box. They were as long as her forearms and wickedly sharp, and she slid them into the two sheaths fixed to her belt.

She jumped down into the river, which came up to her chest rather than her waist, waded across, and pulled herself, dripping, onto the other side.

She heard Savo call something to her, heard a splash behind her, but she ignored him, running down the corridor Garek had forged.

The trees had been pulverized. Flossy splinters crunched underfoot, and smaller dust particles floated in the air around her, making her sneeze.

Garek had told her more than once he couldn't use the inbetween near buildings because of the danger of destruction, but her imagination had come up with something much tamer than the reality.

The path he'd carved out turned left, and she followed it, turning the corner to find a solid wall of trees in front of her.

He'd stepped out of the inbetween here, and gone on without it— she could only guess because he hadn't wanted to overshoot his target.

She'd come to a halt at the sight of the undisturbed forest in front of her, and now she moved forward more cautiously, trying to make as little noise as possible as she entered the cool darkness of the woods.

It was as if there was no one here but the wind in the branches and the small animals and insects that scurried underfoot.

She stood still and closed her eyes, listening intently, and when she opened them, there was a man watching her from thirty feet away.

He stood between two trees, and he held something loosely in his hand she couldn't quite see. Something small enough to fit in his palm.

He tipped his head to one side, studying her with almost insolent thoroughness, but that was fine.

She studied him right back.

The sudden, shocking sound of a fight raging somewhere deeper in the trees had him turning sideways and looking toward the confrontation.

Taya drew her weapons when he moved, because there was no way she would allow him to come up behind Garek or join in a fight against him.

He stilled when he saw the knives.

"You're all the way over there," he said, voice low but loud enough to carry. "How are you going to hurt me with those?"

He took a step away from her.

"Stay where you are." She heard the panicked snap in her own voice.

"What if I don't?" He took another step, and she lifted both arms, elbows bent, hands back, ready to throw.

With a grin, he turned to face her and started walking backward, and she threw, aiming the blades, but calling her Change to propel them forward.

He smirked, concentrating on the knives, and with shock she realized he was calling his own Change, that he thought he could control the knives himself.

The moment he realized he couldn't, his smirk turned to panic, and he threw the object in his hand without aiming.

She changed the trajectory of one of the knives, intercepting what seemed to be a disc, and with a high-pitched ting, it flew off into the trees to her left.

The look of astonishment on his face almost made her laugh, but he was still a threat.

She stopped the flight of both knives, careful to keep them a few meters from him.

The last man she'd played this game with had died, and she shied away from the thought of doing it again. But for Garek's safety, she would.

"Who are you?" he asked. There was almost a reverent tone in his voice, but she didn't answer. There was no quick and easy answer to that question, anyway.

She started walking toward him again, steady and relentless.

"No closer." He brandished another disc, an almost curious look on his face, as if he wanted to find out how she would counter him a second time.

She ignored him, and with a quick grin, he threw the second disc, which she met with her knives again, crossing them over each other and knocking it to the ground.

He saluted her, and before she could uncross her blades and aim them at him again, he ducked behind the tree and disappeared from view.

She ran forward, calling her knives back, and kept them in her hands as she reached the spot where he'd stood, but he nowhere to be seen.

A sound behind her made her spin around, knives raised, to find Savo standing there, his face carrying a strange, unreadable expression.

He bent down and picked up one of the discs. "Looks like you found the Iron Guard."

———

THE ARROW CAME at him the moment the archer swung down from the tree, and Garek was grateful for every moment of his training. He dived low, rolled and came up running full tilt toward the shooter.

He had no weapon of his own beyond his body and the strength of his Change. He'd given back his sword when he'd left the Guards in Gara, and he hadn't chosen to acquire another one since.

Now he lashed out, knocking the bow from the archer's hands before he could notch another arrow. If he was Iron Guard, though, he wouldn't need the bow to propel the iron-tipped arrows, so to counter it, Garek used the last of his power, drained by the inbetween, to swirl the air around them, throwing up the dead leaves and other debris of the forest floor so it was a battle to see clearly.

"How," the archer grunted and leapt back to avoid a hit, "did you get here so fast?"

Garek ignored him. He focused on the way the guard moved, and grudgingly admired his style and form.

"Tell General Hanson I need to speak to her." He avoided a blow, and didn't strike back, even though he could have done so, to underscore his point.

"Who are you?" The archer didn't give anything away.

"Garek of Pan Nuk. Friend of Aidan of Juli. And the man who controls a sky craft."

The archer stepped back, hands up, and Garek did the same.

"I don't know who General Hanson is."

Garek shook his head. "The time for games is over now. We've got war on our doorstep from the sky and from our neighbors. Tell Hanson she needs to speak to me, and soon."

The archer's gaze flicked momentarily over Garek's shoulder, and Garek used the last, the absolute last, of his Change to jump.

A disc thudded into the tree beside the archer, embedded deep, and as Garek landed back on the ground, half-turning, he saw a second man with his arm drawn back to throw another disc.

He didn't think he had anything left in him, but he managed to squeeze out a final dust devil, swirling it around the newcomer so he was curtained in soil and leaves.

The man coughed, rubbing at his eyes, his arm lowering.

"You play dangerous games with people you might want to be friends with later." Garek shook his head at them, the headache from the overuse of his Change pounding spikes into his head and making his temper flare. "Tell Hanson, either she comes to me, or I will come to her. And neither of you will like it when I do."

"Did you destroy the forest?" The second man kept the disc at his side.

"I did." He held the man's gaze for a long beat. "Tell Hanson. Time is wasting."

He nodded, and edged around Garek until he reached the archer standing by the tree, and used a tool on his belt to retrieve his disc.

"If you wouldn't mind asking the other guard if she would collect the other discs, I'd appreciate it." The iron guard slid his discs into a pouch.

"Other guard?" The pounding in Garek's head intensified, and he felt a frisson of fear run down his back.

"The woman with the knives." There was something awed and a little too interested in his tone.

"If you have hurt even one hair on her head—" Garek stepped forward, and from the look on the two iron guards' faces, he was finding the inbetween again, even though it should be impossible in his current state.

They ran, and he stood for a moment, unable to move.

"Garek?" Taya's voice cut through the fog, and he turned to her, saw she seemed unharmed, and then went down like one of the trees he'd just destroyed.

THREE

GAREK FLICKERED in and out of the inbetween, and then turned as she called out, broke into the strangest smile at the sight of her, and then collapsed.

Taya ran toward him, knives out, and behind her she heard Savo and the guards on his team spread out to look for the two men they'd seen standing off against Garek.

She went down in a crouch, ready to jump up and defend Garek if she needed to, and brushed gentle fingers over his face.

"Just tapped out," he murmured, eyes closed. "Too much energy expended."

She bent over him in relief, resting her forehead against his for a moment, then looked up as Savo approached her.

"He burnt himself out," she said, looking up at him. "Can you help me get him back to camp?"

The sky craft was sitting there unprotected, a nice little gift for the sky raiders, should they come by. She could fly it now, Garek had shown her how while they waited for Quardi, Garek's father, to sharpen and finish off the shadow ore weapons they had made together, but it was still very much necessary to have Garek onboard to help with the take off and landing.

Savo nodded, and indicated with a wave of his hand for another of the guards to come over. They were a similar height, and they lifted Garek between them, getting under his shoulders, but after a few steps, changed their strategy and called another two helpers to carry him horizontal to the ground.

The trip back to the camp was done mostly in silence.

The pulverized wood, lying on either side of a clear, person-sized pathway, seemed to render the guards mute, and Taya took turns with them as they carried Garek carefully back over the river.

No one spoke, not even to discuss who the two men had been.

By the time Taya had Garek back in the sky craft, comfortable on the mats they'd brought from Pan Nuk to sleep on, and had taken some of their food out to cook on the camp fire, the sky had darkened almost to night.

The guards' banter died out when she dropped to the ground from the sky craft's ladder, and she forced herself forward when her inclination was to turn around, climb back inside, and continue watching over Garek.

She looked up at the sky first, just to make sure there was no sign of sky raiders. It was clear, and Taya hoped their close proximity to the wide river would help to confuse whatever systems the sky raiders used to trace their craft.

Water was a shield, and there was certainly enough flowing past the camp.

She set down the bag of flatbread to be warmed over the coals, and some carefully wrapped bobber. It was fresh, wouldn't last long, and there was more than enough to share.

Perhaps it was time to forge some allies.

"Garek and I came from Pan Nuk this morning," she said, looking over at Savo. "I've got enough bobber and flatbread for everyone."

Savo jerked his gaze to her in surprise. "That would be a nice change. We've only had one night here, last night, the rest of the time we were traveling from Juli, and we had to live on pack food, and you know how monotonous that gets."

She hadn't had pack food before; the dried meat, fruit and double-baked hard biscuits that were a staple for traveling guards. But she realized he thought she was a guard herself, because of the clothes she was wearing, and probably because she'd called her Change in the forest.

She lifted out the two bobbers, the birds already dressed with a spit stick through each of them thanks to Quardi, Garek's father, and two of Savo's team stepped forward to help her set them above the fire.

The other four guards, Savo included, drew nearer, sitting on the rocks and old tree stumps someone had set around the fire pit.

"So," Savo broke the silence. "This is Rig," he pointed to the big man who'd initially helped him carry Garek. "This is Fran and Ness," he pointed to the two women who'd rolled some logs close to the fire to sit on, "and then there's Yanni, and that's Elina." He waved his hand at the two who'd moved forward to help her.

"I'm Taya—"

They were nodding before she went any further.

"We saw you, the night you arrived back from Shadow with Aidan," Elina said, pushing back a short piece of hair that had fallen over her brow. "Garek, too."

"Didn't know he could do that, though," Savo said, looking across the river at the devastation Garek had caused.

"He'd told me what happened when he was in the inbetween," Taya confided, "but today was the first time I'd actually seen it."

"And when he rose up in the air," Rig said. "That I've never seen before, either. I call the air Change, and I've never even considered doing it."

"You should try," Ness said to him, leaning forward and hooking her arms around her knees. "You never know what you might be capable of."

"Ask Garek how he does it, and give it a try," Taya told him with a smile.

"What I'd like to know is, what Change do you call?" Savo watched her as he put his hand into a leather pouch at his side and pulled out the two discs the iron guard had thrown at her. He tilted them so everyone could see them in the firelight, and they were both deeply chipped, damaged on their rims in such a way that cracks spidered from the outside toward the center.

Taya took one with interest, turning it in her hands and holding it close to the fire to see better.

She'd seen shadow ore penetrate rock on Shadow, and the outer shell of sky craft, as well. It was satisfying to see it worked on iron and steel, too.

Looking at the damage done by her knives reminded her that she'd left them in the box on the river bank before she'd climbed into the sky craft earlier. Suddenly nervous about their safety there, she stood and walked over, put the lid on the box and carried it back to the fire.

"Why do you keep your knives in water?" Fran spoke for the first time, stretching out her long, lean legs.

"It protects them." She wasn't going to give them information that would allow them to damage the sky craft until she could trust them, and they were still a long way from that.

"What are they made of? I've never seen dark purple metal before."

Taya hesitated. "It's shadow ore. It's what we were mining for the sky raiders on Shadow."

"So you call this shadow ore as your Change?" Rig put out his hand, silently asking her permission to touch, and she dipped into the water and handed him a knife.

The less people who knew her Change the better, but this was a tight-knit team and they would have spoken to each other. Savo at least had seen her with the knives this afternoon. Possibly others, too.

"I think it's a type of earth Change. Just very specific to shadow ore. And I'd never have known I had a calling if I hadn't been kidnapped to Shadow."

Savo had leaned in to look at the knife Rig was holding, but his gaze snapped to her. "You only found your calling on Shadow?"

She nodded. "I discovered it there, because I was exposed to shadow ore every day."

Everyone absorbed that for a while, and Taya turned the bobber spits, so the fat dripped from them, and the aroma of roasting meat hung tantalizingly in the air.

"I've never heard of someone finding their calling so late," Rig said at last.

"I've thought about it a lot, how many people must have a calling but never encounter their element." Taya lifted the bobbers off the fire one at a time and placed them on the smooth, flat plates the guards had put near her. She carefully set the flat breads on the coals, keeping a careful watch on them. She looked up. "I've even wondered if everyone on Barit has a calling, and it is just that those who find theirs early call more common elements. After all, we're all people of the same place. Why shouldn't everyone call a Change?"

There was another silence at that.

"I've never heard that theory before," Savo eventually offered.

"I'm the living proof it's possible." Taya pulled her second knife from the water and used it to flick the flatbread onto a plate.

Rig helped her cut up bobber with the shadow knife he still held. "I would do a lot to get a knife made of this ore," he said when everyone had a piece and he handed it back.

"There were two statues in Kardanx that I saw when we took the Kardai who'd been captured back home. Both had shadow ore in them." Taya recalled the surprise and excitement she'd felt when she'd sensed what the two stylized trees were. "So there is a mine or a source of it somewhere on Barit."

Rig cast another, covetous look at her knife as she cleaned each blade carefully with an oiled cloth, and then tucked into his food.

They ate in a more companionable silence than they'd had before.

"Did Garek manage to tell you what happened between him and that member of the Iron Guard?" Savo threw a bone into the fire.

"No, but I assume he told them we want to speak to General Hanson."

"He did." The voice came from just outside of the fire's glow.

All the guards were on their feet and facing outward faster than Taya could react. She set her plate down next to the one she'd set aside for Garek, reached for both knives, and stood.

She would need to get quicker, learn to react faster.

Garek had begun teaching her, but she'd sensed a reluctance in him. He knew it wasn't something she enjoyed, and his natural inclination was to make her happy.

She'd let him set the pace, and she saw now she should have committed more fully to becoming a better warrior. He had taken his cues from her, and she had been holding back because she didn't want to become what she needed to be.

"Little girl in the middle, are you the one my sentry came back babbling about?"

There was something derisive in the voice of the woman who spoke, something belittling, and Taya's temper flared higher than the fire in front of her.

"I don't know, am I?" she asked, and threw one of her knives into the air, holding it still above the fire, where it was clearly visible.

There was a sound of surprise, a deeper-pitched murmur, and Taya saw from the way Savo shifted, he'd heard it too. There was more than just a single person out there in the darkness.

"Well, well." The voice still held a hint of dislike, but it was smothered over in surprise. "I see my sentry was right. What do you want?"

"I think we've established you already know what we want," Savo said, voice cool. "To speak with General Hanson."

"You are speaking to her," the woman said, and Savo shook his head.

"You run along and tell General Hanson that Captain Savo of the Juli Night Guard wants to speak to her. Tomorrow morning is soon enough."

There was silence, and Taya thought she sensed a tinge of shock to it. She called back her knife, slipping it into the sheath on her belt.

They all waited a minute, then another, and then finally Savo made a quick gesture with his hand and Rig and Ness drew long burning sticks out of the fire and moved around, to check if there was still anyone there.

There wasn't.

The Iron Guard had gone.

"I'm really glad that wasn't General Hanson." Taya's relief was almost overwhelming. She needed help from Hanson, and she knew she would find it difficult to ask for it if she disliked her.

She most definitely disliked the woman who had spoken to her tonight.

"I trained with Hanson for years in Juli, I'd know her voice anywhere," Savo said, sitting back down beside the fire.

"Do you think she'll come tomorrow?" Fran asked him.

He lifted his shoulders. "The General Hanson I knew in Juli would come. But the General Hanson I knew wouldn't have kidnapped the liege's son."

"Sometimes desperate people make desperate decisions," Taya said. And these were certainly desperate times.

FOUR

GAREK CAME AWAKE as he had when he walked the walls, instantly. Beside him, Taya slept on her side, fully dressed as if she needed to be battle ready.

She had left the door of the sky craft open, so the orange and pinks of dawn spilled into the cabin, lighting everything in a warm glow.

Next to him was a plate of food covered over with a cloth, containing two flat breads with roasted, sliced bobber between them.

He was starving, as he always was when he'd pushed himself too far with his Change, and he slipped quietly from the mat, took the food with him, and climbed down the ladder.

Savo and his team were camped around the fire pit, and two of them were up and standing guard.

They nodded to him silently, and one pointed up and then gave the guard signal for all clear. Taya must has asked them to keep an eye out for sky raiders, and he nodded back his thanks before walking toward the river to stare over at the other side. The path of destruction he'd made yesterday was shocking to look at.

He'd barely noticed it while he was in the inbetween, and he hadn't been conscious when he was brought back again.

He'd never deliberately done something like this before.

He held himself back in Pan Nuk because any destruction would rightly have been frowned upon, and in Gara it had been out of the question, surrounded as he was by walls and houses.

He'd carved a swathe through the trees, and while he would do it again, it made him uncomfortable to look at.

When he finished his food, he made his way down the bank and followed the narrow strip of beach on the river's edge around a bend to a clear pool created by a few rocks. He took off his clothes and jumped in, ducking completely under the icy water to rub at his hair and scrub his body with the soft, clean sand on the riverbed.

When he got back to the camp, with both body and clothes wet and clean, it had come to life.

Those who had been sleeping were up, stirring porridge in a pot on the fire, and Taya was climbing down the ladder with a towel and a change of clothes balanced on top of the box containing her knives.

He took the box from her and set it down, and she stepped into his arms without a word, hugging him close even though he was wet and dripping.

"You look rested." She leaned back to look up at him.

He brushed a hand down her cheek and nodded, and behind him, Savo cleared his throat.

"If you're going to wash, Taya, perhaps you can go with Fran, Ness and Elina. It's better to have safety in numbers."

The subtle rebuke to Garek for his going off on his own was clear, and Garek let Taya go and turned to face the Juli night guard captain.

"I'm very hard to take by surprise." He let his gaze shift to the destruction he'd wreaked yesterday.

Savo swallowed. "The rest of us aren't so lucky."

Garek nodded, and guessed Savo was used to making the decisions and giving the orders. A former guard who didn't answer to him would be difficult to accept.

He heard Taya open the box, pull out her knives, and then she brushed her fingers against his hand in farewell as she headed toward the three women on Savo's team who stood waiting for her.

The four of them went off in the same direction he'd gone earlier to wash.

"There a reason you're so nervous?" he asked Savo, taking a bowl from the stack beside the porridge pot and helping himself. The food he'd eaten earlier had barely made a dent in his hunger.

"We had a visit last night." Savo joined him, and blew on his porridge before he took a bite.

"Hanson herself?"

"No." Rig, the largest of the six guards, leaned forward to serve himself his own bowl of porridge. "Did you recognize the voice of the guard we spoke to?" He looked over at Savo.

The captain shook his head. "No."

"I think I did." Yanni sat down beside him. His hair was wet and his cheeks pink from a wash in the cold water of the river. "I spent all night trying to think who that voice reminded me of. I think it was Etta."

Rig drew in a quick breath. "Could be."

"Neither of you liked her?" Garek scraped the bottom of his bowl.

"She was arrogant. She could have been a good fighter, but she didn't try very hard. She frustrated me. She barely bothered to do her exercises, and half the time didn't come to training. But she walked straight into the Iron Guard. They're supposed to be the elite, and I certainly put my name in for consideration, but they chose her. I've never been able to understand it."

"They only take guards who call the iron Change," Garek said. "That's why she knew she didn't have to try, she probably has a strong calling."

There was silence as everyone stared at him.

"Is there such a thing as calling the iron Change?" Savo set his bowl down.

"Yes, it's the same as Taya can do, but with iron."

Savo stood, as if he couldn't contain himself. "I suspected. For years, I suspected. I asked Hanson straight out, and she lied to my face. Like Yanni, for years I saw some of my best recruits rejected by the Iron Guard over others who weren't as good, but they weren't random guards, were they?" He looked over at Garek. "They put the iron called in with the general intake so no one would suspect."

Garek shrugged. "I only found out the Iron Guard's secret after Taya discovered her own calling. I don't know how they ran things, but I suspect this is the way it's done in Nordra. I think the liege's wife set up the unit, and when she died, things fell apart."

"The Nordren steel." Rig murmured it, but not so softly Taya didn't hear as she walked back to the fire, wet hair twisted into a thick rope.

She nodded. "That's what Garek's father said when we worked it out. All the years they've talked about superior iron smiths, when really, they've just got people like me shaping their steelwork for them."

Garek filled the bowl he'd used and handed it to her, and she took it with a smile. Her nose was pink with cold and she breathed in the steam from the porridge with delight.

"You've done it?" Fran asked. "Shaped ore?"

Taya lifted one of her knives. "This is all a single piece. The smith smelts it and then when it's liquid, I call it, and shape it in the air. When it looks right, I drop it into water, and then the smith polishes and refines it."

Fran took it from her, rubbing a thumb across the smooth hilt. "How didn't we know this before?"

She shrugged. "I can only think it's because if more people knew about calling an iron Change, those who had the calling would be hunted and stolen away. They are a huge advantage for any army. As it is, Garek's father thinks he was approached by two traveling Nordren when he was a child because they thought he might call the iron Change. When they realized he didn't they left him alone, but if he had, he thinks they'd have abducted him."

"Watch out for the Nordren, they steal babies." Ness sang the line from the old Illian rhyme with a smooth voice.

"Exactly." Garek hadn't heard the story Taya just told. His father must have mentioned it when he and Taya were up on Shadow together, working as slaves for the sky raiders.

"That makes sense, that the liege would be afraid all our guards who call the iron Change would be poached or stolen when they're young by others." Elina looked over at Taya. "Now the surprise I heard from that woman last night makes sense. She was shocked when you threw up your knife and hovered it in the air. She thought you might be an undiscovered iron guard." Elina gave a smile that told Garek she didn't like the woman any more than Yanni did.

"If she hadn't been hiding in the dark, I think we'd have seen the shock was more because she tried to grab the knife from me with her Change, and couldn't." Taya's voice held the same sense of satisfaction as Elina's had. "I can't be sure, but my guess is she assumed it was steel, and that she was stronger."

"And then she couldn't move it even an inch." Fran chuckled as she spooned up porridge.

"Not because she's weaker, but she doesn't know that." Taya grinned back at Fran.

Whatever reservations Taya and Savo's team had had about each other yesterday, they were gone this morning, Garek saw. "You all really didn't like her."

"If it was Etta, and I think Yanni is right about that, then she was her usual rude self." Even Savo smiled a little at the thought of besting the arrogant guard.

"Captain, I think we have the visitor we invited last night approaching." Yanni and Rig had taken up guard duty while everyone ate, and Rig pointed to the wide path through the trees that Garek had made the day before.

Someone Garek guessed was General Hanson walked openly down it, with two deputies a step behind her at either shoulder.

"I'm surprised she only came with two," Savo said.

"My guess is she didn't, we just can't see the others." Garek looked around them, but the Iron Guard weren't considered the elite guard for nothing. He couldn't see any sign of them, but his gut told him they were there.

This wasn't going to be a friendly chat. This was going to be an ambush.

It just so happened that he and Taya wanted to be in Hanson's clutches. That didn't mean Savo did, though.

"I think it's going to get ugly," he murmured to the captain. "If I negotiate for you to go back to Juli when we get confirmation she has Aidan, will you take it?"

Savo looked over at him for a long beat. Nodded. "I need to get back and let Vent know what's going on. The city needs to know if Aidan is alive and will return. Otherwise the whole of Juli becomes unstable. The whole of West Lathor."

Garek nodded. "Then that's what we'll do."

"Let two of my team stay to help you." Savo waited for Garek's nod of agreement, then stepped away, gestured to Rig and Ness.

He spoke quietly with them and they both turned wide eyes Garek's way, then bent back to listen to their captain.

They looked up again, and each gave him a brief nod.

Garek nodded back, and then moved forward, to where Taya stood with Elina, Yanni and Fran.

The three guards melted back as he approached, and he guessed Savo had motioned them to come to him so he could explain the plan.

"What is it?" Taya asked.

He stood close to her, watching Hanson approach.

"I don't think this is going to be a simple negotiation. I think she's got her whole guard around us. Just the fact that we have a sky craft would make her bring more than two guards. If she was hoping to surprise us, she should have brought more people with her that we could see."

Taya lifted startled eyes to his. "And how are we going to respond to it, if this is an ambush?"

"We're going to go along with it, but under our own terms, if I can help it. Savo needs to get back and tell Vent what's going on, but he'll leave us Rig and Ness."

Taya turned her attention back to Hanson. "I hoped this could be friendly." She sounded forlorn.

"Maybe it can be." He watched the way Hanson moved, easy and confident as she neared the river bank, but she couldn't be unaffected by the destruction he'd wrought. Even he was astonished by it.

It told him she was good at keeping her feelings locked down tight.

That was fine. So was he, except when it came to Taya.

"Do we pretend she's gotten one over us?" Taya asked, turning to him again. "Or do we tell the truth?"

"The truth. She has no reason to trust us. We don't know what her history is with the liege. Things obviously didn't end well between them, and she has an agenda. We let her know we'll go along with whatever she wants for now if it means we find Aidan, unless it involves harm to either of us."

"And if she does mean us harm?" Taya's hands curled around the hilts of her knives.

"Then she'll regret it."

FIVE

GENERAL HANSON WADED through the river as if she was striding over land.

Taya had wondered whether she would stand on the other side and hold a shouted conversation, but she didn't hesitate when she reached the bank, she jumped down into the water and was across in less than a minute.

The man and woman on either side of her did the same.

They ignored Garek's proffered hand of help, and pulled themselves up the bank on their own.

Hanson's gaze flicked to the sky craft, and then focused on Savo, although Taya didn't make the mistake of thinking they weren't all being closely watched.

"Captain Savo, it's been a long time. What are you doing out here?"

Savo walked forward slowly, hands loosely at his sides. "You know why. Give Aidan back."

Hanson looked from him to Garek. "And who are you?"

"Garek of Pan Nuk." Garek stayed where he was, not moving

forward like Savo had, and Taya guessed it was because he didn't want to leave her side.

Hanson frowned. "That tells me nothing."

"Then you haven't had your ear to the ground," Savo said, surprising Taya with his tone. "You've been hunkered down, deaf and blind to what's happening in the country you swore an oath to protect."

Hanson reared back in shock, but Savo wasn't finished.

"Look at that," he demanded, pointing to the sky craft. "What do you think it took to get one of those? To learn how to use it?" He snorted in disgust. "And you come striding in here, asking Garek of Pan Nuk who he is, when it is he who should be asking you who *you* are. And I can tell him. A disgrace!"

The two guards with Hanson visibly bristled at his words, but Hanson herself went still, her features blank. She looked at the sky craft again, and then back at Savo.

"You're right, I have hunkered down. But I'm asking what you want, who he is, only because I can see it is relevant in connection to her." She pointed straight at Taya, and her gaze snapped to Taya's face.

Taya stared back into eyes that were a dark brown, in a face that was barely lined, although Hanson must be at least as old as Savo.

"And why am I so important?" Taya asked.

"Because my sentry commander and one of her team tell me you are one of us, but strong enough to hold your weapon against them. As I have never trained you, I have to assume one of two things, you're a Nordren or you're a lost talent."

"I'm not a Nordren. I'm from Pan Nuk in West Lathor." She wanted to say that she wasn't like them, but that would defeat the whole purpose of coming, because it was her similarity to them that made her think they could help her.

"And you come in a sky craft, with a guard who can do that," Hanson pointed behind her to the destruction of the forest, "and with one of the best guard teams in Juli. I know why Savo is here, but what's your role in this?"

"Aidan is our friend." Taya stepped closer to Garek, although she knew he would prefer a little more room to move if things went wrong, but she was making clear her alignment with him. "We're here to ask you to let him go. We're fighting two wars, and West Lathor needs a liege."

"West Lathor has a liege." Hanson's words were derisive.

"As Savo says, you appear to not have heard much news lately," Garek said.

Hanson barely glanced at him, and then she focused back on Taya. "If you're from Pan Nuk, I would have trained you. You have to be lying." It was almost as if Hanson was holding her breath.

"I'm not lying. The reason I never became a guard was because I only found my calling a month ago, and I—"

She cut off abruptly as Hanson staggered back at her words, and her two deputies stared at her open-mouthed.

"A month?" Hanson whispered. "Show me. Show me what you showed Etta last night."

She hesitated. Hanson still hadn't made her intentions clear, and she still hadn't admitted to having Aidan, but if this helped smooth the way . . .

She drew a knife and held it in her hand, looked straight at Hanson, and threw it in the air.

She let it spin end over end in place.

Hanson stared at it, eyes narrowed, and Taya wondered if she was calling her Change, trying to take control. She flicked her gaze back to Taya and crooked her finger. "Bring it closer to me."

A familiar fear and dread washed over her.

The memory of the night she'd killed because of her lack of control reached in and clamped a clammy, icy hand around her gut.

She could still see the deep cut in the neck of her attacker. She'd meant to keep him at bay, not slice his throat.

She shook her head, pulled the knife up and back, and caught it in her hand. "No."

The look Hanson sent her surprised her.

She expected to see anger or frustration at not having her order obeyed, but instead, Taya saw a woman whose eyes looked like they were haunted by ghosts.

"General Hanson."

The sharp call from Savo elicited a hiss from Hanson as she turned to look at him.

"Will you hand Aidan over to us or not?"

Hanson glared at him. "No." She extended her arm and flipped her hand so the palm faced upward, then curved her fingers as if she were holding an invisible ball.

The sound of people moving behind them made Taya glance over her shoulder.

Guards slid out from behind trees surrounding the camp, cutting off their escape through the forest.

"You can all come to my camp, and see Aidan for yourselves."

"Is he unharmed?" Savo asked, and the look she shot him was almost hurt.

"Of course."

Savo looked over at Garek, gave a nod.

"We won't all be coming to your camp; Savo and most of his team will be returning to Juli."

The Juli guards began packing up their sleeping mats as Garek spoke.

"Is that so?" Hanson looked over at her guards, who surrounded them completely, and then back at Garek.

"It is." Garek sent her an exasperated look. "Are you planning to kill Aidan or keep him forever?"

Hanson's lips tightened into a thin line, but she eventually shook her head.

"Then Savo can stop Vent sending more people out to look for him, and Vent can honestly tell the people they'll be getting their liege back."

Hanson looked unhappy, but she gave a nod to Savo, then looked over at the line of guards who blocked the path to Juli, and they stepped aside.

Savo stopped in front of Taya and Garek and gave a formal bow. "Look after my people." He jogged away, with Yanni, Fran and Elani in single file behind him.

Rig and Ness settled into place in line with her and Garek.

Hanson watched Savo go, looked over at Rig and Ness, but didn't say anything until they disappeared among the trees.

"So, can I assume you'll come without a fight?"

"It suits us to see Aidan again." Garek walked forward to the fire, picked up Taya's knife box, and she reluctantly dropped the knives into the water.

It felt wrong to be unarmed, surrounded by the Iron Guard, but she couldn't get into the sky craft any other way.

Hanson watched what they did with focused interest.

"Will someone be joining us, to show us the way?" she asked Hanson politely.

Hanson seemed to belatedly work out they were planning to travel in the sky craft. She stared at it. "I will."

There was a murmur of protest from the deputy to her right.

"You can come too, Kima, if you like."

Taya climbed the ladder, waited at the top to take her knives from Garek as he climbed up behind her.

He must have spoken with Rigg and Ness, because when she'd stored the box away and came back into the pilot's chamber, he was alone in the pilot's chair, starting the engines.

"They're keeping Hanson and her deputy waiting at the bottom until I'm ready." The grin he sent her said he was enjoying making Hanson cool her heels. Then he got serious. "You haven't asked her for help."

Taya lifted her shoulders. "I know. There is something going on with her. Her reaction to me is so strange, I didn't want to say anything until I understand more."

He nodded, the man who always had her back, and then walked to the door and leaned out, signaled to Rig and Ness below.

The Juli guards came up first, and then Kima, Hanson's deputy, and finally Hanson herself.

She guessed both Hanson and Kima had been ready to complain about being kept on the ground, but when they stepped into the cabin they said nothing, looking around in quiet shock.

"Which way?" Garek asked.

"How did you get this?" Hanson turned from the massive, rectangular window that dominated the front of the craft. "I didn't need Savo to tell me it was a feat, but now I'm inside . . . How?"

"He took it from the sky raiders while he was rescuing me." Taya spoke when Garek said nothing.

"You were a prisoner of the sky raiders?" Kima sounded disbelieving. "I haven't heard of anyone being rescued from them."

Hanson put out a hand as if to quieten her, and Ness shook her head.

"As Savo said, you've been under a rock then, because Garek didn't just rescue Taya, he rescued everyone they'd taken. It's the talk of the whole of Illy."

"Where did they keep you?" Hanson asked.

Taya pointed out the window, to where Shadow lay low on the horizon.

"Shadow?" Hanson's voice was quietly shocked.

Taya nodded.

"Who *are* you?" Hanson faced Garek, eyes intense.

"Just a guard from Pan Nuk," Garek answered.

"And you're from Pan Nuk, too?" Hanson glanced at Taya, and she nodded. "I'd like to know what's in the water there."

SIX

THE IRON GUARD camp was deep in the forest, but Hanson had found a clearing that must have been hit by fire a year or so before, and was far more open than the area around it.

As Garek scoped the area for a good place to land, he could see the fire had come up against a deep, wide stream and had burnt out, unable to cross, because the forest was almost choked it was so thick on the other side.

The camp was established enough that there were wooden huts instead of tents, and they had set up open-sided pavilions over all their fire pits, to make the smoke more difficult to spot for anyone searching for them, and to shield their fires in the event of rain.

He set the sky craft down beside the stream, but his gaze was on the waterfall that fell from a steep hill beside the camp. There was no space to hide the sky craft behind it, but the rocks at its foot seemed level enough and he thought he might be able to maneuver the craft close enough to the cliff wall for the waterfall to land on the ship's roof.

It would make the sky craft invisible to the sky raiders.

When he thought of how exposed they'd been yesterday while he'd been burnt out, he felt a deep, ugly fear.

They would have taken Taya, and he'd have slept through it.

"I'll go out first." Hanson was looking out the window, and Garek saw the few guards she had left behind in camp had surrounded them. They seemed hostile and armed. He stood from the pilot's chair, moving closer to the window to see better, and caught sight of Aidan, leaning against the wall of a hut, arms crossed, with an expression on his face that was a mix between hope and fear.

"Oh, yes, princeling, it's us." Taya's quiet comment forced a laugh out of Garek, because he'd been thinking exactly the same, and she turned to him with a wide smile.

He leaned down and brushed a kiss on her lips.

When he raised his head, he found Hanson watching them, and he couldn't read what she was thinking at all.

He sat back down in the pilot's chair and opened the door. "Go calm your troops."

Hanson poked her head out, calling an order to stand down, and Garek saw Aidan's face break into a smile.

He started moving toward the sky craft.

Hanson swung down the ladder, her deputy right behind her, and for a moment, the four of them were alone.

"What's the plan?" Ness asked.

"Don't trust anyone. If there is a decent chance we can all make it to the sky craft with Aidan and leave, we take it, but don't antagonize. And finally, Vent wants Hanson back, badly. The Iron Guard's reputation kept a lot of nasty people at bay, and those people are all too eager to attack now they think the Iron Guard is gone. Vent wants them for what their name stands for as much as anything. If we can bring them all back to Juli, so much the better." As Rig and Ness nodded, Garek leaned in a little closer. "And keep your ear to the ground. Be unobtrusive and listen. Let them forget you're there and find out what the hell Hanson is even doing out here."

"Garek?" Aidan's call silenced him. There was something almost panicked in it.

Garek powered down the craft and then joined Taya, Rig and Ness at the door.

Aidan stood, held back by two guards, while Hanson stood beside him, face dark with anger.

Garek didn't like the mood he sensed below. And then he caught sight of the archer who'd shot at him the day before.

He jumped out of the door, ignoring the ladder, and calling his Change a little to boost him, so he landed right in front of Aidan.

He ignored Hanson, ignored the weapons that were raised at him because of his unexpected move.

"Aidan." He extended his hand and gripped Aidan's forearm in the traditional guard's handshake.

Aidan's own hand curled around his arm, and then he pulled Garek in close and thumped his back with his free hand. "It's very good to see you, my friend."

"Likewise." Garek moved back, looked the princeling over. He seemed unharmed, but he was flippant when under strain usually, and Garek had never seen him visibly stressed before.

Whatever had been done to him here was not good.

"You tread a dangerous path," he said to Hanson, turning his head to stare at her.

She tried for a moment to pretend she didn't understand what he meant, but then gave a nod in agreement. "If he didn't keep trying to get away, but . . ." She sighed. "Why wouldn't he? We've abducted him. Any one of us would do the same."

Her admission sent a ripple of shock through the guards around her.

"The princeling is free to do as he wishes," she said.

"Even to walk off?" Aidan asked her, and his tone held a bitter edge.

"Even to walk off. Although I hope you stay, and we can deal on better terms than we have up 'til now." Hanson looked behind her, and Garek saw her focus was on Taya again, as she walked toward them, with Rig and Ness on either side of her.

"You brought Taya here?" Aidan seemed so horrified, Garek's gaze flew to his.

"As you can see."

Aidan shook his head.

"What do you think we'll do to her?" Hanson asked, and again, as he'd heard in her voice when she spoke with Savo, Garek thought he detected hurt.

"Well, let me think . . ." Aidan shot her a filthy look, but before he could continue, Taya had reached them, and she stepped forward and gave the princeling a hug.

She was wearing her knives, so Garek guessed the delay in her joining them was because she'd carried out the box and armed herself.

"You shouldn't have come," Aidan murmured into her ear.

Rig and Ness gave a formal bow, hands clasped in front of them, and around them, Garek heard the start of murmurs. But it was nothing to Aidan's reaction.

That bow was given only to one person in a sovereign state of Illy, and that was to the state's liege.

"Is Valtor dead, then?" Hanson asked.

Aidan's face was pale, and he said nothing, waiting for Hanson's question to be answered.

"Your father is gravely ill, and no longer capable of rule," Taya said, ignoring Hanson and speaking directly to Aidan. "Vent has declared you liege."

"Is it up to Vent to do such a thing?" Aidan asked, his voice thick with emotion.

"Dartan is under arrest, so yes." Garek heard the faint roar of engines in the sky, and looked up, heart suddenly beating faster.

"I need to move the sky craft. Aidan, now." He barked the order at the princeling, and then ran toward the ship. Aidan reached the ladder moments after he did, although his breathing was labored.

The moment he got inside, Garek started the engines and left the door open as he lifted the sky craft and skimmed it low over the stream, hovering it close to the ground under the fall of water, and then slowly lowering it down bit by bit.

It managed to sit surprisingly level once he'd fully set down.

He switched the engine off, and moved to the window, looked out to see Taya standing on the shore. Her head was tipped back, watching the sky, and eventually she turned to him and nodded.

The sky raiders were gone.

"Is it true?" Aidan asked, leaning beside him against the window and looking out over the camp. "Is my father sick, and Vent in charge?" He sounded tired and dispirited.

Garek nodded. "We think Dartan poisoned your father. We think he somehow did a deal with the sky raiders, the same way Harven's liege, Habred, did."

"What?" Aidan leaned back against the window as if he couldn't support his own weight. "Could he have been doing it all along? All those times my father seemed so off . . ."

Garek shook his head. "Maybe. Or maybe he saw your father's decline as an opportunity to advance himself."

Aidan sucked in a breath. "Whatever the reason, I need to get back."

"Agreed. That's something we have to work on from now onwards. But tell me what they've done to you. Vent wants Hanson and her guards back, wants them propping up the military strength of West Lathor again. But I am guessing if you won't work with them, that's not realistic."

"They haven't tied me up, or locked me away, but I've had two guards on me every minute since I've been here. And that's worn on me. Not a single private moment. When I saw that it was you—" He rubbed at his face. "I went a little crazy. Tried to run to the ship. I suppose I thought if I was fast enough, we could just fly away." He gave a short laugh. "Being stopped just flattened me, even though logically, there was no hope of my making it."

Garek reached out and gripped his shoulder. "Sometimes, the logic of a thing doesn't matter. And sometimes even illogical ideas work." He looked around the pilot's cabin.

Aidan looked around with him, and when he laughed again, he'd lost the bitter edge. "That's true enough, you crazy bastard. That's true enough."

SEVEN

TAYA COULD SEE Hanson getting more and more agitated, the longer Garek and Aidan remained in the sky craft.

It looked so strange, sitting with its back under the waterfall, the water foaming and tumbling over it.

"What's taking so long?" Hanson took a step closer to the water.

Rig and Ness shifted nervously beside Taya, as if unsure what to do, but she gave them a tiny shake of her head.

"He'll join us when he's ready."

"Your loyalty is to him." It wasn't a question, Hanson's eyes bored into hers.

"It is best you never forget that," Taya agreed.

"And I noticed—I'm sure everyone noticed—that new liege or not, your friend has no compunction ordering Aidan around."

Taya smiled. "There are things that Aidan is prepared to put up with to keep hold of the sky craft and the only person on Barit who can fly it. When Garek says to do something to keep the sky craft out of sky raider hands, his word is law."

Rig signaled to her, a guard signal that she didn't understand.

She'd have to get Garek to teach them to her, but the feeling of eyes on her gave her a clue. She turned and came face to face with the guard who'd thrown the discs at her the day before.

"I'm afraid your discs are damaged," she said.

His eyes widened with panic at her words.

"What's this?" Hanson asked, Garek and the sky craft forgotten for the moment as she rounded on him.

"She threatened me." The words were stuttered out.

"You threatened me, too," Taya told him, voice cool. "But it's the way your friend shot at Garek, completely unprovoked, that made me angry."

"How many discs, Linus?"

"Two."

Hanson sucked in a breath. "How many arrows did Valn shoot?"

Linus shook his head.

"Two," Taya told her.

"Where is Valn?" Hanson's words were a whip crack.

"He went with you this morning. So he's still on his way back . . ." He trailed off as Garek jumped down from the sky craft, and then Aidan jumped down after him.

Both of them were soaked through by the waterfall, and they climbed down the rocks and waded through the small, hip-deep pool below the falls.

Taya enjoyed watching Garek as he made his way to her.

He was magnificent.

His gaze caught hers, and he must have seen a little of what she was thinking, because he sent her a slow smile as he pulled himself up beside her.

"So, what now?" Aidan rubbed at his hair, longer now than Taya had ever seen it. "I can leave, just like that?"

"I'd like us all to have a little talk before that happens," Garek said. "If you can stand to?" He glanced over at Aidan, and the new liege pursed his lips and then gave a nod.

Garek slid a hand along her shoulder, gave her a gentle squeeze. She knew what he was asking. Did she want to ask Hanson for help in controlling her calling?

She did. But there were undercurrents here. So far, everyone had been strangely focused on her, and it worried her.

But the better she could control her calling, the better chance she'd have at helping defeat the sky raiders.

Everyone had suffered since the sky raiders came. Not just the villagers and traders, but the guards, too. Garek had lost two years of his life to it.

If there was a chance she could destroy them, she had to try.

"I have a request, as well," she forced herself to say.

"Then let's sit down and talk." Hanson swept her arm to a large wooden structure that Taya assumed was a meeting room.

For better or worse, it was time for everyone to lay their cards on the table.

"I KNEW IT!" Hanson slapped a hand on the rough wooden table after Garek had told her they suspected Dartan was a traitor.

Kima, the deputy who'd accompanied the general in the sky craft gave a nod. "You were right."

Rig and Ness said nothing, but this was the first time they had heard the story, and Taya could see they were deeply shocked.

"You suspected Dartan was conspiring against my father and you said nothing?" Aidan stood and braced his hands on the table.

Rig and Ness stirred, and Taya tensed in her own seat, ready for trouble. It seemed as if Aidan wanted to launch himself at the general.

"I knew he was up to no good." Hanson shrugged, her eyes cool. "I knew he undermined me to the liege, and I knew from the intelligence I was getting from other parts of Illy that the sky raider attacks on Juli were strangely off, far less than elsewhere, but it never occurred to me that he could be in league with them. How is that even possible?"

"They found a way to get to Habred. They used a trader to make the initial contact. How they spoke to either man after that, we don't know." Taya remembered the agony on the face of Gern Danaldi, the jail master in Luf, the capital city of Harven, when he told her what he'd discovered his liege had been up to.

"And Habred organized to deliver up some of his own people to the sky raiders in exchange for them keeping clear of Luf?" Kima shook her head in disbelief. "He's finished."

Garek shrugged. "Maybe he is, maybe not. The very idea is almost unbelievable, and since you've held Aidan, there's been no one to inform the Illian Council."

Hanson rubbed her temples with stiff fingers. "Now you have proof of two people in high places being complicit, it will be easier to convince the other lieges."

"True, but at least two other lieges on the Council are in league with Habred to invade West Lathor, so it's in their interests to back him, no matter what they believe." Aidan slumped a little in his seat. "And telling them about Dartan will just give them further impetus to invade West Lathor. They might even get Council approval to take us without a fight."

Taya realized he was right, and felt a dragging sense of disquiet. "We can't let them go unpunished."

"We won't." Garek met her gaze. "If it has to be out of the public eye, so be it, but there will be a reckoning."

"I'd like it to be in the public eye," Aidan said. "I'll see if there is a way we can do that. But Garek's right. No matter what, there will be justice."

"One way to strengthen our hand is to have you and your guards back, General." Garek crossed his arms over his chest. "Harven, Kadmine and Favre are poised to strike, and that's because they think

Valtor is a befuddled mess and because West Lathor has lost the Iron Guard."

Hanson tilted her head up to look at him. "You're very comfortable disrespecting the liege. And his son seems content to let you."

Aidan snorted. "That's rich, coming from the person who abducted the liege's son. But as it happens, Garek has earned the right to say whatever he likes. And he's right, my father is a befuddled mess, and he got himself that way. Dartan just used it to his own ends."

"So you'll go back, take over?" Hanson asked.

"I will."

"Perhaps, then, you'll finally read the document I wanted you to read when I first took you." Hanson pulled a thick wad of parchment from her coat pocket.

"I'll sign nothing, read nothing, until I'm free, I've told you that from the start. No contract is worth the paper it's written on unless the terms are freely agreed."

Hanson glared at him, and pocketed the contract again. "Then I'll tell you what I told him. The only way I will allow the Iron Guard to continue under the West Lathor liege is if the way we recruit to the Iron Guard changes."

"I don't know how you recruited in the first place." Aidan straightened.

"We sent out scouts pretending to be traders, and they went village to village, carrying iron pots and pans, and they found the children who may never have been around enough iron before to feel their calling. And when they found them, they stole them away."

"I thought that was the Nordren," Ness said.

"That's who we got our methods from," Hanson said. "From your mother, actually." She speared Aidan with a glance. "That's where I'm from, originally. She used her contacts to send some of us down to her, to start the original team." The smile she gave was humorless. "I was fifteen."

There was silence around the table.

"We ran the unit the same way things were done in Turn, the Nordren city she was from. Up until her daughter—your sister, Kalia —found her calling." She looked away from them all, out of the window, as if struggling with some strong emotion. "It was only then, when she thought about how she wouldn't like Kalia stolen away, that she began to feel bad about all the other women's children she'd taken through the years."

Taya looked across at Aidan, and saw his face was stricken. He didn't want to believe it, but he did.

Perhaps he'd seen something, or heard something, but he was not surprised.

"So for the last ten years, we haven't recruited a new guard. You won't find a single person in this camp under twenty-three, your sister's age."

"And when my mother died, you wanted to start recruiting again?" Aidan's accusation made Hanson flinch.

"No!" She scraped back her chair and stood, pacing to the window and then turning to face them. "I wanted direction. A new way forward. We had to recruit new guards if we were to continue, but I did *not* want to do things the old way." She blew out a breath. "And your father and Dartan, so nervous to lose us, told me that the old way had worked, and that I must start doing it again immediately."

"So you left," Taya said into the silence those words created.

"Yes." Hanson turned to her. "I left, rather than do things that way again."

Kima reached out a hand and lightly touched Hanson's arm, a comforting gesture, almost like a daughter would give a mother.

And maybe that's how she felt. If Kima had been recruited the way Hanson described, the same way Hanson had been recruited herself, then the general may well be the closest thing Kima had to a mother.

"And that is why you are so interested in me," Taya said, almost coming to that understanding as she said the words. "Because I wasn't taken and trained young."

"You could be the way forward for us." Hanson tried to keep her voice steady, and failed. "To have someone who calls iron, who has never been trained, never even knowing what they could do—"

"The only problem is," Taya looked her right in the eye, "I do not call the iron Change."

EIGHT

TAYA SAW the shock in Hanson's eyes. She opened her mouth to clarify, but before she could, Hanson was out the door, striding away through the camp.

Taya stared after her in shock. "Why . . .?"

Kima leapt to her feet and lunged forward. Taya stumbled back, and Garek was suddenly behind the general's deputy, hands hold her arms tight.

She struggled for a moment, and then slumped in defeat.

"What is wrong with you people? Don't you ever just ask questions? You have to always grab people and threaten them?" Taya felt like slumping herself.

Kima blinked.

"Let's go," Taya looked at Garek over Kima's shoulder. "This was a mistake."

"Wait." Kima closed her eyes, breathed in noisily through her nose, and then opened her eyes again. "The general's at the end of her rope. And to be honest, this isn't living." She waved her arm at the camp outside the window. "We're just scraping by. And the general knows we've endangered West Lathor by leaving the liege, but at the same time, her conscience wouldn't let her kidnap any more children. She was hoping you were an answer, a blueprint for the way forward, and when you said you didn't call iron . . ." Her gaze went to the knives that hung from Taya's belt. "Why did you say that when you clearly do?"

"Because this knife," Taya pulled one out of its sheath, "is not made of iron."

"That's why we can't grab hold of it?" Kima stepped closer. "That's why it won't budge, not even a tiny bit?"

Taya nodded.

"What is it made from, then?"

"It's made from an ore I can feel in the Dartalian Range, and which is found in abundance on Shadow. We called it shadow ore."

Kima held out her hand, and Taya handed it over.

"It's like a piece of wood. Stone sometimes has iron in it, but this is completely dead to me." She ran her fingertips over it delicately.

"Does it matter that Taya calls a different metal?" Ness wanted to know. "It's still metal, surely?"

"You're right." Kima handed the knife back. "I'll go talk to the general. Please stay a little while longer."

"Why should we?" Aidan's voice was rough with anger.

Kima looked him in the eye. "Because all the talk about letting you walk out here if you wanted to was a lie. The general never intended to let you go until she had an agreement. She hoped by making you think you had the freedom to leave, you'd stay and negotiate. But if you try to leave now, with the general off somewhere and not present to counter her own orders, my colleagues will kill you."

"I told you." Aidan glanced over at Garek. His voice dripped with disgust.

"They can try." Rig looked out the window, and Taya got the sense he was working out how far the sky craft was, and how many iron guards lay between it and the hut.

"We need the general's cooperation." Garek spoke slowly, and everyone turned to him. "If Kima can find her, explain to her what

Taya meant, then we might solve some of the problems facing us. If we go, we end the chance of the Iron Guard returning, and Taya leaves without any help in controlling her calling." He tipped his head at Kima. "Some of us may also be injured. Something I'd like to avoid."

Kima nodded. "This is the only empty building, so make yourselves at home. I'll go find the general."

"I need to be home," Aidan said quietly when she'd gone, his voice urgent. "I need to take up the reins my father has dropped."

"Agreed." Garek lowered himself back into his chair, and Taya sat down beside him. "But all that will do right now is give everyone a quick sense of relief. It won't change the danger posed by an invasion, it won't help us against the sky raiders. If we can spend a little time here, persuade Hanson to train Taya and come back with you, it will mean significantly more."

"Even though I see the logic of that, I just want to go."

Taya reached out and touched Aidan's arm. "As someone who was held prisoner myself, all I can say is I know the feeling."

He started, as if he hadn't drawn a parallel with their experiences. He gave a nod. "We'll give her a bit more time. But if it looks like there'll be no deal, we need to have a plan of escape."

They all leaned forward, and began doing exactly that.

NIGHT WAS FALLING, and Kima still hadn't returned.

Taya knew there were eyes on her and Garek as they walked hand in hand toward the sky craft, but she nevertheless enjoyed the sense of privacy the gloom afford them, away from Aidan, with his scowl, and the watchful, tense expressions of Rig and Ness.

"No further." The comment came from near the river bank.

Taya flinched, but Garek kept his stride even and she had the feeling from his calm that he'd known the guard was there.

"We need to get our mats and a change of clothes, as well as our food." He kept his voice reasonable.

The guard hesitated, and Taya guessed he didn't know how to deal with the request.

"You could be lying."

"We could, but Aidan is still here, as well as two other of our people." Garek gestured back to the hut.

They waited for a response and when they were met with more silence, Taya sighed. "Let me go, then. I can't fly the sky craft."

It was still light enough for her to see Garek look down at her, a scowl on his face.

She shrugged back at him. She was hungry, and she'd prefer a comfortable night on a mat to sleeping on the hard wooden boards of the hut floor. "You can hold my knives," she murmured, and handed them over.

He took them, but he was shaking his head. "Be careful."

"You're in shouting distance." She kissed his cheek.

"Just you is acceptable. But I'll come with you." The guard sounded as if he were quite excited about the idea. He whistled, and there was definite movement around them.

"Don't move," he said, and she guessed he was talking to Garek.

She walked forward, jumped into the shallow stream, and started wading across.

The guard fell into step with her, making far less noise. "So what happened between you and the general? Why did she leave so upset?"

Taya shook her head. "I'm not sure. I don't understand why myself."

He didn't say any more until they got to the sky craft. Taya climbed the ladder quickly, tapping the button to open it up, and pulling herself in.

The chamber lit up, and she moved through to the back, pulling the mats they had brought in a pile. They had spares, left over from when they rescued the Kardai back on Shadow, and when the guard stepped into the big back area, she handed him the pile and Rig and Ness's packs.

She picked up hers and Garek's and the smaller pack of food they'd brought with them.

It would feed the five of them for tonight, and perhaps tomorrow; after that, they'd have to eat whatever the Iron Guard were eating.

She cast a quick eye over the wooden boxes stacked to one side, but there were no leaks. Her weapons and the sky craft were safe.

"That's everything." She gave the guard a smile as he tried to balance the burdens she'd given him.

"I never thought I'd see the inside of one of these safely." He looked around. "It is beyond what I could have imagined."

She looked around with fresh eyes. Nodded. "The sky raiders are as clever as they are powerful and terrible."

She walked back to the pilot's chamber. "If you put the mats down, and climb down the ladder, I can hand them to you one by one."

He narrowed his eyes suspiciously, but he must have realized it would be the only way to get the mats down without dropping them in the river, so he kept Rig and Ness's packs on his shoulders and climbed down.

When they were both ankle deep in water, the sky craft shut up for the night, he looked upward.

"The water keeps the sky raiders from finding your craft?"

"It seems so. It's the best protection we know." She guessed they were all worried the presence of the sky craft would bring more craft down on them. It was a logical fear.

"How did you find it out? It seems such a strange thing to think of."

"It was something we learned on Shadow, when we were prisoners there."

He looked over at her, and in the very last of the light, she saw the skepticism that she'd been on Shadow on his face. She didn't try to change his mind. It would make no difference. He had no reason to trust her, and she didn't care what he thought.

"And what's your plan, besides stirring up the general?" His tone seemed to be more hostile, the deeper into the water they went.

Taya concentrated on the treacherous footing of the uneven stones on the river bed. "My plan is to defeat the sky raiders, and I'll put up with the rudeness of the Iron Guard if I have to in order to accomplish it."

Her words seemed to shock him into silence.

"What's your plan?" she asked him in return. "Hunker down here in the forest, or help West Lathor defend its borders?"

She reached the bank, and Garek was there to lift her up. He turned back and took the mats from the guard. When he'd clambered up beside them, Garek took Rig and Ness's pack.

"We aren't cowards." The guard's words were quiet.

"I never said you were," Taya answered. But she guessed, because he'd raised it himself, that deep down, he was afraid that's how the rest of West Lathor saw them.

The Iron Guard had ceded its place. Most people thought they had disbanded, and even though they hadn't, the way they were living, they might as well have done.

And that didn't sit well. With any of them.

NINE

AS EVERYONE in the hut stirred awake in the dawn light, Garek was forced to acknowledge their little band of outsiders had all managed to get a good night's sleep because they'd felt a certain safety in numbers. He'd far rather have spent the night in the sky craft alone with Taya, but that had never been an option with the Iron Guard.

Even if it hadn't, he knew Aidan would have objected to them being separated, and he was inclined to give his new liege his way at the moment.

Aidan's demeanor worried him.

The princeling had lost the confidence Garek had seen as an integral part of him, and if Aidan continued to hold that loss against Hanson, Garek didn't see how they could work together in the future.

He lay, propped up on an elbow, and Taya lay close beside him, her body touching his all the way down one side.

He looked down, found her studying him.

The look in her eyes said she also wished for privacy. Then she sent him a mischievous grin.

He grinned back, leaned down and nuzzled her neck, kissing under her ear and then her cheek, and lastly her lips.

"Enough of that." Aidan stretched on the mat next to them. "Let's do what we have to do and get going. I want to see the back of this place more than I wanted to get off Shadow."

Garek sighed. Rolled to his feet, and helped Taya up with an extended hand.

It was true, time was one luxury they didn't have.

Everyone woke and shared the last of the food, and Garek was surprised at how easy they were with each other.

When they stepped out of the hut to face the day, it was as a team.

They wandered to the nearest fire, and helped themselves to hot water and tea, waiting for someone to come for them.

It didn't take long.

Hanson and Kima walked over, and behind them came a contingent Garek recognized from the day before. The man who'd walked beside Hanson yesterday with Kima, and a group of three, including the archer who'd shot him, the guard Taya had fought with, and a woman who he guessed was Etta. The guard from Juli's guard training who Yanni had so disliked.

"Kima has explained what you meant yesterday." Hanson looked straight at Taya, no hint of apology on her face for walking away the day before. "I agree that it shouldn't matter which ore you call, the principle is most likely the same."

Taya crossed her arms and Garek could sense her hesitation. "I don't like being here." She watched Hanson closely. "You are rude, volatile, and unfriendly."

Hanson blinked at that.

"But I have a proposal. The ore I call is deadly to the sky raiders' ships. I can bring the ships down—I have brought some down already —but I could do better. Become stronger. I think you could help me. And you want to see what someone who's never been trained can do if they find their calling later in life. I think our objectives align."

Hanson opened her mouth, but before she could speak, Etta stepped forward.

"She could be anyone. How can we trust her? She could be from Kadmine or Harven, trying to discover our secrets."

Garek flicked a look at her, and Etta took a step back, eyes wide.

"She's from Pan Nuk. I confirm it." Aidan spoke, his voice soft, but full of authority. Garek thought his hands were shaking, and realized it was with rage.

Etta shot him a scornful look. "*You* confirm—"

"I take the liege's word." Hanson dipped her head, and Etta's mouth dropped open. It seemed the general hadn't gotten around to letting the guards who'd had to walk back from their campsite yesterday know that Aidan was now their commander-in-chief.

"Liege?"

"It seems hiding in the forest is a sure way to miss out on the latest news." Rig's rumble of a voice silenced the mutters from all around them.

"Abducting the future liege, or the liege himself—either way, it isn't a path to reclaiming your place in West Lathor." Aidan flattened his hands against his thighs and glared at the general.

She sent him a wry grin. "No. I was desperate. I wanted to return, to help West Lathor against the forces gathering against us, but at the same time, I wanted to honor your mother's wishes and my own sense of what is right." Hanson opened her hands and spread them in front of her, and she and Aidan stared at each other for a long, long beat.

Eventually, he nodded.

Hanson seemed to relax a little. "I accept your offer, Taya."

She held out her hand, eyes on Taya's knives, and Taya passed one over.

Hanson ran a light fingertip over the hilt. "These are well made."

"Garek's father and I made them together."

"You shaped them when the metal was liquid?" Hanson's gaze shot to Taya's face.

She nodded.

"How did you work that out?" Etta's tone was dripping with suspicion.

"Quardi, Garek's father, is a metalsmith. He understood the implications immediately when we realized what Change I called. He knew without doubt how the Nordren created such intricate metalwork. We tried it, and it worked. I suppose I'll get better with practice, but for now, I make the shape and Quardi hones it for me."

"Is this all you have?" Hanson tested the weight of the knife.

Taya shot a look Garek's way, and he met her gaze, leaving this as her call.

Eventually she shook her head. "There is more in the sky craft."

"I thought you said the ore destroys the sky craft systems?" Kima frowned.

"That's why we keep it in water. It seems to insulate it."

"What do you have?" Hanson seemed less interested in the details—Garek could hear the eagerness in her voice to get Taya in a training ring.

"Spears, arrows, discs for protection. The knives." Taya nodded toward the discs hanging from the general's own uniform. "I tried to remember what the iron guards were wearing in the paintings I saw in Juli."

Hanson chuckled. "Not much in those paintings is accurate."

Taya lifted her shoulders. "I had nothing else to go on."

"Well." Hanson took a step back. "Go fetch your other weapons, and let's begin."

Taya hesitated, then stepped around her, heading for the sky craft.

Garek fell into step with her, as did Rig, Ness and Aidan.

"Stop." Hanson's voice was sharp, and they all turned to look at her. "Some of you need to stay here."

Aidan shook his head, the look on his face stoic, but when he stepped forward to offer himself as what was to all intents and purposes a hostage, Hanson shook her head.

"Taya stays."

Garek looked Hanson directly in the eye. She had his measure, all right.

She might not be quite her old self, but she hadn't lost her edge. She knew he would leave Aidan behind if he had to. He would never leave Taya.

"I'm the one who knows which box is which," Taya said.

Hanson's lips thinned. "I bet your intended does, too."

Garek flicked a look at Taya, and she sighed. "Do you mind?"

Garek shook his head, but when his gaze met Hanson's, he made it clear he did mind.

A lot.

TAYA LANDED hard on the ground and rolled, coming up in a crouch.

The hollow, blunt spear of iron that had been thrown at her hovered in the air above her head. From its position, she guessed it would have struck her if someone—Hanson—hadn't called her Change and stopped it in midair.

Even if it had hit her, it wouldn't have done much damage. She had checked it carefully before the tests began, and so had Garek.

But even though she hadn't been hit, and would barely have been hurt even if she had, Garek glowered from the sidelines.

He didn't like the antagonistic nature of the tests, the hard physicality of them.

His attitude was probably only because she was the one being subjected to them. He must have endured much worse in his own training.

She straightened and walked toward Ness, who held out a cup of water to her.

"Were you tested like this as a guard?" She took the cup and gulped the water before waiting for an answer.

Ness hesitated, then nodded. "But only after I'd been in the guard for a good six months. The Iron Guard usually get their recruits sent to them after the first three months of general training. I think they're forgetting that no one arrives to walk the walls with the kind of experience they're testing for now."

"Problem?" Etta called. She was standing next to Hanson with a smirk on her face.

Taya turned to look at her. Debated her options. She didn't like people who spouted excuses, but equally, if this was going to work, they needed to be realistic about her abilities.

Eventually, she shrugged. "I've never been a guard, and I've never received any training. I gather the Iron Guard receives their recruits after at least three months in the general guard intake. I haven't had three months, and I haven't had any of the advice and training those who have a calling get in their villages before they arrive to walk the walls."

Hanson frowned at Etta, then walked across the open training area toward her.

Garek, who'd been standing opposite her, watching everything and everyone, moved to join them.

She felt a shiver in the air, the mirage that was Garek calling his Change without realizing it. She saw him flicker in and out of view, before he solidified as he reached her.

Hanson had seen it—and felt it—too. She sidled away from him, and Taya thought she saw a few guards raise their crossbows a little.

"You assume too much." Garek stared Hanson down. "You have lived as a guard for too long. Taya has never so much as run a training loop, let alone walked a wall."

Hanson obviously decided that it would be easier to talk to Taya than Garek. She ignored him and kept her gaze fixed on Taya's face. "You're right. I was stolen from my family when I was eleven. I have never known anything else. Everyone thinks the Iron Guard is recruited from the general intake, but they aren't. They've already spent years being trained by me and others under my command. They arrive to walk the walls as if they're genuine recruits, and then are funneled into the Iron Guard so no one questions who they are or discovers their secrets."

"Why do you keep it a secret?" Taya asked. "The Iron Guard would be even more feared if people knew they called the iron Change."

Hanson shook her head. "Two reasons. One, it would mean we wouldn't just have to keep an eye out for Nordren coming in and nosing around West Lathor villages looking for lost talent. It would mean we would have to worry about Kadmine, Harven, Dartalia and all the other Illian states doing the same. And second, it's much more frightening to not understand how someone does the things they do—aim so perfectly, throw with such force and precision—than it is to know it's simply someone's calling."

Garek met her eyes, and she could see he was still furious, and unwilling to give Hanson any leeway.

She needed to spend time with Hanson, and she knew she was too sensitive to Garek standing there, waiting for an excuse to react, to concentrate properly.

"Will you try to keep in mind I'm completely untrained? I'm physically stronger than I was before I was captured, because I did hard labor on Shadow, but I don't have the skills of a guard."

Hanson gave a formal bow. "I apologize. Garek is right, I assumed too much, and that makes me a poor leader. We'll adjust the program, and make sure we are careful with you." She turned to Garek at last. "Your intended is safe with us. You have my word."

Garek gave her a narrow-eyed stare.

"Why don't you use the day to fly over the border and check what Harven, Kadmine and Favre are doing?" Taya suggested to him. "It's a waste of your time to stand here watching me roll around on the ground."

The look he flashed her could have scorched.

She held out her hand and tugged him a little way away.

"Taya—"

She slid her arms around him and went up on tiptoe to reach his ear. "I can feel you scowling from the sidelines. It distracts me and makes me nervous that one wrong move from me, and you'll retaliate against my sparring partner."

She felt him tense under her hands, felt the sleek muscles in his arms bunch.

"I *will* retaliate."

She smiled against the skin of his neck. "I know. That's why I want you gone. I can take a little bruising in the cause of helping bring down the sky raiders. And you're scaring the Iron Guard."

He hesitated. "I don't want to leave you with these assholes."

"Hanson is too invested in the success of this, too guilty about leaving West Lathor to its own devices, to wish me harm. I'll be fine. Go and take a look at what's going on. Take one or two of Hanson's people with you. Maybe it will help persuade her to come back to the fold."

He leaned back to look at her. Gave a slow nod. Then he turned to Hanson.

"I'm leaving my intended in your hands. I don't think I have to tell you what will happen if she's hurt under your watch."

Hanson tipped her head to one side and gave a slow nod. "Where are you going?"

"I'm taking Aidan to check the border in the sky craft. You can send some of your unit to observe if you want."

At least three people stepped forward eagerly.

Hanson pointed to Kima, and then nodded to the other three. "Can they all go?"

Garek gave a guard signal that must have meant, let's go, because everyone who wanted to come smiled and then trotted toward the sky craft.

She reached out and grabbed his hand. "Be careful up there."

He pulled her close, kissed her forehead. "You be careful down here."

He gave Hanson a last, hard look, and strode away.

TEN

"I THOUGHT I HAD NO CALLING." Taya lined up her aim and threw her spear at the wooden target Hanson had set up for her. "Unlike Garek, I wasn't taken under anyone's wing and trained, and if you want to find people like me, understand that they will have lives that they've built outside of being a guard. I have my own business that I run. If I didn't know my calling could help defeat the sky raiders, I would not want to leave what I've already built. That is something you'll have to deal with. Free choice from your potential recruits. If you want them to consider their options earlier, you'll have to travel the villages looking for those who've just come through puberty and don't think they call a Change, and test them. Let them know before they make a decision on a trade or occupation that they have another choice."

Hanson grunted, squinting against the sun to check where the spear had hit, and then walking toward the upended tree stump which had been chipped a bit on the edges to make it look roughly like a person.

General Hanson tried to pull the spear out, and eventually had to put a foot on the trunk and haul at it before it came loose. She lifted it on her palm, testing its balance.

"You've used this before, to bring down a sky craft?"

Taya nodded. "Garek helped me, though. He propelled it harder than I could, and I aimed it."

Hanson nodded thoughtfully. "I've wished for a long time for more openness between the Iron Guard and the other units. If we had guards on our side who could call the air Change, we would be stronger."

"There is a synergy to cooperation like that," Taya agreed. "I saw it between my brother, who calls the earth Change, and Garek, and I've felt it myself with Garek when we've worked together."

"I'm sure the other guards would love to share in our glory."

Taya hadn't heard Etta come up behind her, and she turned quickly, in time to see the hard look in the guard's eyes.

Rig had remained behind, rather than going with Garek, and he took a step closer to her.

Taya gave him a quick shake of her head and she could see his reluctance as he came to a stop.

"Except we don't do what we do for the glory." Hanson's voice was cold, almost cutting, and Etta looked away.

"Given we have to go easy on her, Nori wants to know what test you want him to set up?" Etta kept her gaze down, but her tone was anything but respectful.

"I'll speak to Nori myself." Hanson strode off, her back straight as the spear she still carried in her hand.

Taya wondered whether she should call it back. Decided now was not the time to mess with the general.

"It's interesting to me that you keep mentioning how untrained I am, yet Yanni, of the Juli Night Guard, told me you were the worst recruit in his intake. He said you didn't try, didn't seem to care, and that everyone was astonished when you were accepted into the Iron Guard and they weren't." Taya was shorter than Etta, and she looked up at her. "Obviously none of them were ever going to get into the

Iron Guard because they didn't call iron, but now that the general has explained you had already been trained for years before you arrived in Juli to be part of the general intake, why did you pretend to be worse than you were?"

Etta smiled. "To mess with their heads. They were pathetic. They could barely hold a spear properly. Some had only ever used longbows, they'd never even seen a crossbow." She gave a short laugh. "But still, they thought they were little Stars in the sky. The look on their faces when I was promoted to the Iron Guard and they weren't . . ."

A sharp intake of breath had both her and Etta turning. Hanson stood behind them, and Taya felt a quick thrill of respect for the general being able to walk up behind them without making a sound. "You jeopardized the whole system in a petty power play?"

"A system you're trying to pull apart at the seams, remember?" Etta's thinned lips were a mirror of Hanson's own.

"I'm doing it at a level that will end it for good in an official way. You were just opening us up to being discovered by spies and mischief-makers."

Etta hunched a little, then shrugged. "What are we doing with her?" She flicked a venomous look Taya's way.

"We're going to see how good her control is." Hanson turned and walked away, obviously expecting to be followed.

Rig shot her a look and shooed her with his hands and she started after Hanson.

"Troublemaker." Etta hissed at her. "Been saving that little story, have you?"

Taya grinned, unrepentant. "I didn't expect Hanson to listen in, I just wanted you to know I'm not some helpless little village girl you can push around or play like you played Yanni and the other guards in your intake unit."

"They were never my unit." Etta had fallen into step with her, and she kept her voice steady. "I was stolen out of my bed when I was twelve years old. I've never seen my family again. I can't even remember where I'm from. My unit is the one I was forced to live with from that time onward. The general intake charade was a joke and I marked time there, bored out of my mind."

"I'm sorry about that. I don't think it should have happened to you, but why are you so hostile to me?"

"Because you got to live your life as you wanted to."

"They never would have taken me, even if they had come to Pan Nuk looking for recruits," Taya reminded her gently. "I don't call the iron Change."

Etta pulled away, walking a little faster.

"What would you have preferred to do?" Taya asked. "If they hadn't found you?"

Etta looked over her shoulder at Taya blankly, and then strode away.

Taya watched her go, feeling her annoyance and dislike of the woman morph into something closer to understanding and pity.

When she reached Hanson and Nori, the other deputy who'd accompanied Hanson the day before along with Kima, she saw the worry and sadness on the general's face as she watched Etta disappear amongst the huts.

"She's angry. My fighting against the way things are done has struck very close to the bone for so many of them. Forced them to confront the harm done to them, often by me. I'm both the guilty party and the force for change at once."

Nori made a sound of denial, and she glanced over at him, patted his arm.

"It's true. I deserve their anger, just as the person who stole me deserves mine."

Nori was shaking his head, and Taya noticed he was holding her spear in his hand.

"What do you want me to do?" Taya asked.

He sent her a look of deep gratitude for the change of topic.

"Can you lift this into the air?" He raised the spear.

Taya lifted it before he'd opened his hand all the way, and his arm jerked up. He let go, eyes wide, and he and Hanson studied it, hovering parallel to the ground.

"Can you make it vertical?"

She did that.

"Spin it?"

She had a few false starts, but she eventually worked out how to do it.

"Call it to your hand."

She pulled the spear to her, and enjoyed the little thrill that raced through her as her hand closed around it.

There was a spatter of applause as it did, and with shock she realized the training circle was surrounded by iron guards, with Rig standing directly behind her.

"How much shadow ore is in this spear?" Nori asked her.

"It's pure shadow ore. I separated it out myself."

She wondered what Quardi, Garek's father, had decided to do with the leftover slag. He was convinced it would turn out to be useful, and had decided to make a number of things with it to see what properties it had.

"That explains it." Hanson took the spear from her. "Your dexterity with it is exceptional. I don't think there's a person here who could do better with their weapon." She looked around the circle and no one contradicted her.

"Why is that?" Rig asked.

"Because pure iron doesn't make a good weapon. We have to mix it with other ores to make it harder and sharper." The person who spoke was the guard who'd thrown discs at her in the forest, Linus.

It sounded to Taya as if the Iron Guard would have had to develop more control than her, because they had less ore in their weapons.

"I'd like you to show me the control methods you teach new recruits." She looked around at the guards surrounding her. "I killed a man because I couldn't control my Change well enough. I never want to do that again."

"How did you kill him?" Etta asked, eyes glittering with malice.

"I was slashing the air in front of him with my knife, and I got too close. I slashed his throat."

"Your knife is that sharp?" someone asked, disbelieving.

Taya took out her knife. "Throw one of your discs into the air," she said.

Rig smirked, and Taya remembered he'd used her knife before, he knew how sharp it was.

Etta took out a disc and threw it directly at her.

She sent her knife straight at it, and by absolute chance, hit it dead center. The blade went through the iron disc like it was made of wood.

There was a moment of absolute silence, and Taya called her knife back. Rig stepped forward and while she held the knife hilt, he pulled the disc off the blade with a grunt.

"We should be mixing shadow ore with our iron," Nori said into the quiet.

"You'll have to find your own," Taya told him. "I need every bit of it I've taken from Shadow."

At his crestfallen expression, she relented a little. "I felt it in some metal in Kardai. I think they have access to it from somewhere."

"Unless they're also in league with the sky raiders," Hanson muttered.

Taya shook her head. "I felt it in some old metal sculptures in a rooftop garden. They weren't made recently." She gave a wry smile. "And the last thing the sky raiders would do is give up any shadow ore, especially not for decorative statues. It's the whole reason they're here in the first place."

Hanson accepted that with a slow nod. "It doesn't matter anyway. We have other things to think about than what would be nice to mix with our iron. Do you have small discs like this?" She fingered the discs that hung from clips on her uniform.

Taya nodded.

"Go get them." She leaned down and picked up a wooden practice dagger from a collection on the floor beside Nori.

Taya could see a place to slot a disc on the base of the hilt.

"That's how you train your recruits?" To maneuver the dagger with such a small amount of ore would be incredibly difficult she realized with a thrill of anticipation.

Nothing they'd done for her so far with regard to her abilities had been particularly challenging, only her physical fitness and guard training had been lacking.

But this . . . this looked like it would stretch her. And that's what she needed. Time was running out for them all, and she needed to get better fast.

ELEVEN

GAREK TRIED to focus on the job ahead, rather than worry about Taya surrounded by a potentially hostile guard.

"The general will keep her safe. That's why we've been stuck in that forest for the last five months. Because she didn't want to continue to do harm to lost talents like Taya." Kima had been watching him carefully since he'd taken off, trying to work out how to fly the sky craft, Garek was sure, but his face must have been more expressive than he thought for her to pick up what he was thinking so unerringly.

"And yet, there is a threat, just under the surface, that things won't go well for Taya if we don't come back." Aidan was leaning against the long, rectangular window of the craft. He didn't look over at them as he spoke, his gaze focused on the hills and valleys below.

Kima shifted uncomfortably. "She can keep Taya captive without harming her. You're perfectly fit, after all." She slanted a look at Aidan, but he was still ignoring them both.

Garek chuckled. "Not even Habred, the liege of Harven, could keep Taya prisoner, even when he locked her in the cells in his guards' barracks."

Ness, who stood on the opposite side of the window to Aidan, looked up with interest. "I heard part of this story when you were telling the general about Habred's complicity with the sky raiders, but what was Taya doing in Harven?"

"She was kidnapped by guards who knew Habred wanted her. But he didn't keep her long." Garek still felt a surge of satisfaction at that knowledge. He wondered what Habred was doing right now.

Panicking, at least a little, he was sure.

"With all due respect, the general is a lot more competent than Harven's liege," Kima said.

Garek looked at her for a long, long moment, felt the tension in the pilot's chamber ratchet up. "Good thing it doesn't matter, then, doesn't it?" He spoke quietly. "Because I'd never abandon Taya."

The breath everyone was holding was released, and no one said any more as he skimmed across the undulating landscape of northern West Lathor, toward the border.

After about an hour he was forced to climb higher as the Dartalian Range came into view, covered by thick white cloud.

He looked over at Aidan, but the princeling shook his head.

"No sign of sky raiders," he said. He'd kept watch constantly, and as soon as the others realized what he was doing, they'd been eager to help.

Garek lifted up, but tried to keep under the cloud cover, sticking close to the mountains. The high-pitched whine warning of their proximity to shadow ore began to sound through the craft.

He accelerated and rose at the same time, putting them in the cloud and blinding them all. The warning clamor continued until they broke free of the misty white into the bright blue of a Star-lit sky.

"What was that?" One of the iron guards who'd come along looked at him with wide eyes.

"There's shadow ore in the mountains. Taya says it isn't concentrated enough for mining—there are only tiny flecks of it in the rock—but it's enough to interfere with the sky craft, so a warning sounds when we get too close."

"This is not good for seeing what the Harven are doing." Aidan scowled down at the rippling sea of white.

"We're going in more or less the right direction, and maybe we'll get lucky and there'll be a break in the cloud." Garek had been over this range slowly and carefully when he'd been looking for Taya, and he'd been back since then to spy on the combined forces of Harven, Favre and Kadmine with Falk.

He had a good sense of where they were.

Everyone leaned against the window, foreheads pressed to the transparent material that was like glass, but far clearer and far stronger than any found on Barit that Garek had ever seen.

He moved as slowly as the sky craft would allow, almost drifting across what looked like a landscape of deep snow, with the occasional black peak of the Range poking through.

The cloud cover thinned a little as they reached the center of the range, forming and clearing and then reforming again as the winds blew and buffeted the craft.

Aidan gave a cry of discovery. "I see it. On a small escarpment surrounded by mountains."

Garek nodded. That was the place he'd found before.

"We need to go lower. It's hard to see." Kima put a hand on either side of her face as she bent her neck to get a better look.

"Can't go lower without the possibility of crashing." Garek circled the spot.

"And the cloud is moving in." Ness sounded disgusted. "There are a few buildings down there, and what looks like a training ground, but I can't see anyone."

"And it's gone." Aidan's voice was soft as thicker cloud rolled in, obscuring what little they could see.

"Anyone see troops?" Garek asked.

Aidan shook his head, his brows turned down in a deep scowl.

Kima suddenly laughed.

"What's so funny?" Aidan grumbled at her.

"How quickly we got used to being able to spy on our enemy from the air." She made a big gesture with her hands. "We're complaining we can't see better, and the cloud is blocking us, when it's amazing that we were able to come all this way in such a short amount of time, and try to see if our enemies are where we think they are. It would have taken us weeks without this sky craft, and even then, we'd have had to know where the camp was."

Aidan looked at her in surprise, and then gave a nod. "It is saving us time. But I wish we could have seen better."

Garek turned the sky craft around in a slow, lazy circle. "I don't think this is going to clear up soon."

Aidan nodded in agreement. "It's too thick. It looks like it's getting worse. We'll have to come back tomorrow."

As he finished speaking the whole craft shuddered a little, caught in a sudden crosswind.

Garek banked and then skipped the craft across the clouds, moving around a mushroom of black and gray that was growing out of the white near the edge of the range.

Kima was right, they had gotten used to the sky craft. It was a powerful weapon, and one he kept forgetting gave them an edge.

Unfortunately, they needed the edge, because in this fight, they were definitely the underdog.

TAYA SLID into the water just out of sight of camp with a tight gasp at the temperature, but also with a sigh of relief. It felt like she'd been under scrutiny the whole day, with as many guards as had free time following her training from the sidelines with avid eyes.

Just to be alone, and to know Rig was out there somewhere, making sure she stayed that way, even if it was just to dip her shivering body into the cold clear stream that ran past the camp, was bliss.

She quickly scrubbed the sweat of the day off her and was

hopping back into her trousers when she heard the shriek of the sky craft overhead.

She dressed faster, and found Rig almost vibrating with impatience when she joined him on the bank, his whole focus on the waterfall and the way Garek was maneuvering the sky craft back under its spray.

As soon as she joined him, they jogged along the river's edge and as she watched Garek's sure, skillful control of the sky craft, the weight of worry on her shoulders lifted.

He was safe.

She and Rig reached the curve in the river closest to the waterfall, and both of them jumped down into the shallow stream and began wading toward the sky craft.

"Stop."

The footing was treacherous—rocky and unstable—and Taya fell as she looked behind her at the person shouting.

Rig must have seen her come unbalanced because he reached out as she flailed her arms, and caught her just before she landed on some nasty looking rocks.

He hauled her to her feet, and they both turned to face the Iron Guard unit standing on the bank.

"You can't go to the sky craft. You have to wait for them to switch it off and come out." Nori's jaw clenched as he spoke.

"I keep forgetting we aren't allies, we're considered hostages." Taya couldn't erase the hurt in her voice. She'd spent the day in friendly and open discussions with most of the guard. She'd never once felt restricted, but that was all an illusion.

No one said anything as the sky craft powered down and then the door opened.

Taya didn't turn around to watch as Garek, Aidan, and the others waded through the water toward the camp, she kept her gaze on the guards lined up along the bank with weapons raised.

Rig did the same beside her and after a moment she felt the

warm, solid weight of Garek's hand on her shoulder as he, Aidan and Ness fanned out on either side of them, a solid line of defense.

"Put those weapons away, unless you actually plan to use them." Garek's voice was short.

She could feel the tension rise and then crest as Kima and the three other guards who'd spent the day in the sky craft stumbled through the shallow water, slowed to a stop, and then moved around them.

"What's going on?" Kima's tone had a sharp edge to it.

"She was going to meet the sky craft. I've got orders she isn't allowed near it while its engines are running and they can escape with her and Aidan." Nori's words were stilted and stiff.

Kima sighed and shook her head. "She was probably just going to greet them."

"Probably," Nori agreed. "And if she wasn't?"

Kima splashed her way to the bank, threw her hands up in disgust, and disappeared into the darkness.

The three guards who'd gone with her were stumbling a little as they struggled to carry something large between them.

"What the hell is that?" Nori snapped.

"Dinner."

There were a few whoops and others jumped in to help carry what seemed to be most of a levik.

Taya turned and slid her arms around Garek. "I'm glad to see you safe and sound." She rested her head on his shoulder, and let the relief she'd felt earlier reclaim her again.

He smoothed back her hair, and she felt his lips press against the top of her head.

Then he lifted her out of the water, swung her into his arms and carried her up the bank. "All good?"

She nodded, and he glanced over at Rig.

"No trouble." Rig agreed as he scrambled up behind them.

"Hanson was personally involved all day." Garek set her down and Taya shook out arms tired from repeated throwing. "It was helpful."

"But . . .?" Garek had heard the hesitation in her voice.

"I'll tell you when things are quieter." She meant when they weren't out in the open, surrounded by the Iron Guard.

They moved to the hut they'd been given, and with delight, she and Rig discovered they had a share of the food the sky craft crew had bought on the way home. Garek had brought the sky craft down at a small village on the way back, and once the villagers had gotten over the shock of West Lathorians in a sky raider ship, they'd sold them a butchered levik, fresh bread, and fruit.

Garek had taken a levik leg for their little group, leaving the rest for the camp.

"Did you tell the villagers they were in the presence of their new liege?" Taya asked Aidan as she helped Garek turn the leg over the flame.

She grinned when he nodded.

"There's never a down side to making it known I'm the new liege. And to showing the world we've taken a sky craft. That we're fighting back." Aidan lifted his shoulders. "That whole valley will know the news by now, and any merchant who comes through that way will, too."

"Did you see anything interesting?" Rig asked as he flopped down beside the little fire pit they'd taken over near their hut.

Taya knew he would have loved to have gone in the sky craft today, instead of spending his time on the sidelines, watching her try to throw a wooden knife over and over again without using her hands.

"The weather was bad," Ness told him, and Taya detected a conciliatory tone in her voice. "The clouds covered most of the range. We caught a glimpse of their camp but no details and eventually we had to turn back."

"We'll have to go back tomorrow." Aidan was crouched beside the fire, chewing on a piece of fruit.

"I wonder if they're still there," Garek said. "When Falk and I patrolled that camp two weeks ago, training exercises were going on in the yard, but today I didn't see anyone in the quick window of visibility we had."

"Me, neither," Ness agreed. "Hopefully the weather will be better tomorrow."

"What's the situation here?" Aidan had found a comfortable spot to sit, and he looked at Taya over the tops of his knees. "Will Hanson let us go?"

She shook her head. "I would have said yes before that little scene when you arrived this evening, but that showed us all the truth. They weren't prepared to let Rig and I get anywhere near the sky craft while its engines were running."

"And your progress?" Garek was watching her over the leap and crackle of the fire between them as they turned the levik, and his eyes gleamed in the firelight.

She shrugged. "It seems my control is naturally better, because my weapons are made with pure shadow ore, whereas their weapons are made of iron mixed with other ores. But because they've had to compromise on that, they're actually more precise than I am. They've had to grow stronger because they're carrying around extra weight which they can't control."

"What does that mean for you?" Aidan asked, and she could see his mind working as he filed the information away to use later.

"It means they had a lot to teach me today about control. It was hard work, and while I didn't do badly, this is not something that I'm going to excel at overnight. It's going to take practice."

"What's wrong with that?" Ness sat cross-legged beside her.

"We don't have time for me to train and study for weeks, which is the minimum time to get really good at controlling my weapons with the kind of precision they have." She twisted her lips in a wry smile. "The sky raiders need to make a move. They've lost their slaves on Shadow and they'll have to decide whether to replace them or come up with an alternative plan. Every day they delay, their sky craft deteriorate more. They have to be decisive. And I have to be ready when they make their move."

"What do you mean, their sky craft are deteriorating?" Ness asked.

"The metal the sky raiders use corrodes fast in our atmosphere. Faster than iron. At some point, the sky craft will be too dangerous to fly, and it'll disintegrate to a rusted hull." Garek didn't sound that sad about it.

"So if we want to use it to help in the fight against Harven, Kadmine and Favre, we have to use it soon." Rig rubbed at his forehead.

"If it's any consolation," Garek told him, "that won't be a problem. I can't see Habred and his cronies waiting much longer, especially if someone has given them the news that Valtar is confined to his bed and Aidan is missing. It's too good an opportunity for them to miss."

Ness wrapped her arms around her knees. "We really need to get out of here, don't we?"

Garek nodded. "Whether the general likes it or not."

"And I don't like it." Hanson stepped out of the shadows.

There was a moment of perfect silence.

Eventually Garek rose up from his crouch. "Soon your problem will be about far more than how to train Iron Guards, or the perfect way to do something. Soon, it'll be about fighting for West Lathor's independence. And you'll have to admit to contributing to the conditions that make it perfect for Harven to attack."

Hanson stared at Garek, then inhaled through her nose. "All Aidan has to do is commit to a new recruitment plan that we can all live with."

Taya turned to Aidan. "Why won't you? It has to be the right thing to do."

He glared at her. "I refuse to sign anything while I'm a captive. That is not the sign of a strong leader, and it's not something I'm prepared to do."

"Trust your new liege, then," Taya said, standing to address Hanson. "Let him go."

"Trust him?" She shook her head. "I don't know if I can." She turned on her heel and stalked into the night.

Taya shook her head, and then caught Garek's eye.

She could tell from his thoughtful expression that he was thinking of a way to solve the problem.

If it came down to that, she had a feeling neither Aidan nor Hanson would like what he came up with.

TWELVE

THE FOOD GAREK and the others had bought the day before had clearly lifted the mood in camp.

The whoops when the guards had handed the levik up the river-bank the night before had led to laughing and some singing late into the night. Nothing like the quiet, almost dour behavior they'd noticed on their first night here.

The guards had put on a display of skill, flexibility and strength in a dance of throwing knives and discs, where they threw, ducked and jumped in a complex pattern that promised injury if anyone got their moves wrong.

So it was to happier, more relaxed faces that they woke the next morning.

An army marched on its stomach, after all, and Hanson's people had been barely surviving out here. They were ready to go home, he could feel it. And soon, if Hanson didn't relent and let them all go back to Juli, she'd have a riot on her hands.

Between them, Rig and Ness had agreed to a swop, so Rig would come with him today, and Ness would stay.

Taya had argued that it didn't matter if either stayed, one Juli guard couldn't do much against the eighty strong Iron Guard.

That was true, but it was also true that sometimes, all you needed was one person to have your back, and Garek wasn't prepared to leave Taya friendless while he was flying over the Dartalian Range.

Aidan wouldn't, almost couldn't, stay, and Garek was afraid to put him in too close proximity to Hanson in case they both said things neither could come back from.

Aidan may be the new liege, but West Lathor needed the Iron Guard, even if for nothing but its reputation. If Aidan could come back to Juli with Hanson and her troops in tow, it would cement his power. And right now, they needed to have a visible, strong leader almost more than they needed to start preparing for war.

"What are you thinking?" Taya had her knives hanging from her belt, a strap of leather ran across her chest, holding a quiver of spears on her back, and she had hooked the circles of shadow ore to her special jacket. They tinkled and chimed as she moved toward him. She held a crossbow loosely in her hand, and he wondered for a moment where the arrows were.

She looked loaded down for violence, and it was almost hard to watch her approach him.

Seeing her like this made him feel he'd failed. She was not a warrior. She'd been the only one who'd ever seen him as more than a warrior himself; she'd been his place of peace, of quiet joy and long, lazy afternoons in the sun.

She had seen him, the person beneath his bulk and strength, and the outsized power of his calling.

And he had seen her.

And she was not this person who approached him. And yet, she had to be.

For that alone, he vowed as he held out a hand to her, he would destroy every last one of the sky raiders. He would smash them down and watch them claw at their throats as they suffocated to death in the place they should never have invaded.

"Shh." She had been looking straight at him, and as she reached him, she let him take her hand in his, and brushed the other down the side of his face, as if comforting him. "It will be all right."

"Yes." He would make sure of it.

"Are we going?"

Kima's call had them both turning to face her, and Garek drew Taya close for a quick, one-armed hug.

"The weather is clearer today. I think we should see more." Aidan joined them, hair wet from a quick bath in the stream.

Garek nodded. "Any sign of sky raiders in the night?"

Kima shook her head. "The guards heard the whine of engines, but it was far to the south, toward Juli. They didn't come directly overhead."

That was worrying in itself. With Dartan, the liege's treacherous advisor, unable to contact them, perhaps the sky raiders had decided Juli was fair game after all.

"We need to go back to Juli. Soon." He looked straight at Kima as he spoke, and after a moment's hesitation, she nodded.

"The general knows it too. But without a signature from the liege . . ." She glanced over at Aidan with dislike.

"I will not sign anything under duress. That is not how to start my rule, and Hanson knows it as well as me."

Kima shook her head and looked away, and Garek wondered how long this little tug of war could continue.

"You need to sort it out soon." He looked between Aidan and Kima as he spoke. "Or I'll sort it out for you."

Aidan sucked in a quick breath of outrage, paused before he spoke, and then gave a quick shake of his head. "You have no choice now, you understand. You will be my general."

"Why is that?" Kima asked, and Garek could hear the genuine curiosity in her voice. "He orders you about as if he were the liege, not you."

"Because he'll never tell me what I want to hear. Quite the opposite." Aidan gave a small grin.

Taya laughed, and the sound of it, the sweet, clear sound of it, so like the laughter she'd shared with him before he'd gone to walk the walls of Garamundo, lightened his mood.

Under the weight of the weapons she carried, she was still the same Taya. And if he had anything to say about it, she would lose the burden of them as soon as possible.

"THEY'VE DEFINITELY GONE." Kima peered out as Garek made a slow pass over the camp in the cloudless blue sky.

It wasn't much of a camp anymore.

The few permanent structures they'd built remained, but most of the quarters had been tents, and they'd been taken down.

There was no one left below.

"Which way would they go?" Rig leaned against the window, where he'd been since they'd set off from camp this morning.

"They must be headed for West Lathor, and they'll have a few choices with regard to route, but if they're trying to be sneaky about it, they'll go west through the mountains of Harven and come in through the foothills directly into West Lathor. If they want speed, and don't care who sees them, they'll go east and cut through the bottom part of Dartalia, over the thin strip of Favre, and onto West Lathor's north east escarpment," Aidan said, then lifted an eyebrow as Garek turned east. "You think Dartalia?"

"It'll be easier to check if they have gone that way. We can get lower without the mountains." Garek gave a slow, satisfied smile. "And it'll be very good for us, if they have."

"Why's that?" Kima glanced over her shoulder at him. "Dartalia must be involved in Harven's plan. They wouldn't go through there without permission."

Garek's smiled deepened. "They originally had an agreement with Dartalia that it would stay neutral and not interfere, but things have changed since that agreement was put in place. Habred, the liege of Harven, knows it, too. Susa, Dartalia's liege, has informed him she's now a confirmed ally of West Lathor. I was there when she wrote the missive."

Aidan stared at him, mouth open. "How? How did that happen?"

"When Taya and I were explaining things to you earlier, we glossed over some of what happened in Luf. The thing is, I met Zek there." He glanced over at Kima and Rig to explain. "Zek is a Dartalian trader who was one of the prisoners we rescued from Shadow. His liege was grateful to us for returning him and his fellow traders to Dartalia when we came back from Shadow. She decided the neutrality treaty she had with Harven could no longer stand, given the help we'd given her citizens, and she sent Zek to Harven with the message.

"Before he could pass the missive along, though, he and I were attacked by some of Habred's guards, and Zek was badly injured. I flew him and the diplomats with him back to Dartalia.

"When Zek told Susa the full story, she not only withdrew any neutrality agreement, but upped the stakes and aligned herself with us."

"Why would she do that?" Kima asked, voice a little hushed. "Just withdrawing neutrality would have put us in her debt."

"Two reasons. She had already decided to withdraw from the agreement, but Habred hurting Zek pushed her to making things even harder for him. Also, we have this," Garek waved his hand around the interior of the sky craft. "Zek is all too aware of its power and the opportunities it presents."

He thought things through a little. "When I see her again and tell her what we now know about Habred, that he's been cooperating with the sky raiders . . ." He remembered the steely resolve in Susa's dark eyes and shook his head. "My guess is that her own economy has been hard hit by the sky raider raids, because so many Dartalians are traders. If what Taya's friends in Luf say are true, then Habred has a deal where the Dartalian traders have their goods stolen from them after they've spent their money in Luf, not before."

He imagined what the tall, grim leader of Dartalia would make of that.

Aidan blew out a breath. "This is . . . very good news. We have an actual ally."

"The best news I've heard in a while." Rig was grinning with delight.

"There they are." Aidan pointed down below, and they all saw a line of guards walking single-file down a narrow track toward the low hills on the southern-most border of Dartalia, to the east of the mountains.

Garek carried on, following the path, and after a minute or two, they found more guards stretched along a long river, watering their zanir and resting in the afternoon Star's light.

"There aren't as many as I thought," Kima said, but her mouth snapped shut when they followed the curve of the river and found the bulk of the army setting up tents in a relatively flat field hidden amongst the softly rounded hills.

Garek shot past them, banking slightly to the left so they could see what was happening below more clearly, and then they were over the valleys and cascading escarpments of Favre which led down into West Lathor.

"Go back?" he asked.

"Do you think they realize it could be us, or will they think it's sky raiders?" Rig asked.

"Depends how much Habred has told his allies. We don't know whether he's come clean with them and let them know we aren't as helpless as we once were. He may be afraid that if he tells them, they'll back out."

"My guess is he'll pretend it's all news to him when we do engage them with a sky craft," Aidan said, cynicism twisting his lips.

Garek gave a short nod. He'd take the same guess.

"Garek?" Rig had been straining his neck to look back as much as he could.

"Hmm?"

"Real sky raiders."

Garek spun the sky craft around, pulling on his Change to do it, and there, hovering above them, was a massive ship, far larger than any he'd seen so far flying around Barit.

The only one he'd seen that was bigger was the sky raiders' mothership.

There was a hissing sound from under his hand, and he jerked it up with shock.

"Will . . . you . . . land?" The hissing turned into words, stilted, as if the speaker was uncertain of the accuracy of what they were saying.

Aidan looked at him with wide eyes.

Garek studied the ship in front of him.

He didn't think it could be from the mothership.

He'd seen all the craft stored in its hanger, and there was no room there for something this size. It hadn't been anywhere to be seen on Shadow, either.

He flown there twice, and he would have noticed something this big.

Besides, it was pristine. Its metal shell hadn't yet been touched by the corrosion even a few days caused on Barit or Shadow.

It was also the first time the sky raiders had ever tried to talk to him. He wondered now why they hadn't tried before.

"Can you hear me?" he asked, and had a sick, sinking feeling. What if they had always been able to hear everything that was said in the craft?

There was no response, and eventually he decided he needed to press something to respond. Something he had no idea how to do.

He banked and looked for a suitable flat space that would fit both ships.

"Is this wise?" Aidan's gaze had swung back to the sky craft, and his hands were fisted at his sides.

"They could shoot us out of the sky if they want. They obviously want to talk. I'd prefer that option, because something tells me their ship is a lot faster than this one."

Aidan looked back at him, gave a slow nod. "You think they want to talk us over to their side, like they've done with Habred and Dartan?"

Garek shrugged as he dipped lower and aimed for the field below. It was far enough into West Lathor to be out of the sight and reach of the combined army behind them, and far from any village that he could see.

"I'll keep the engines running." He stood, walking to the door as the big craft landed a little way away from them.

"I'm coming," Aidan's tone didn't brook any argument.

"I want to see what they look like. I'm coming too." Rig didn't sound like he wanted to back down, either, and Kima simply started walking toward the door.

Garek sighed. "Then everyone be prepared to get back up the ladder and inside at a moment's notice. I'll leave you behind if you take too long."

Rig and Kima gave a nod of agreement, but Aidan glared at him, and he couldn't help but grin at the princeling. Better that the new liege assert himself as a leader than accept orders, but in this instance, Garek planned to do the talking. He was the one who could fly them away, after all.

He touched the button to open the door, and swung his leg out to go meet the first sky raiders to ever ask him to talk.

THIRTEEN

TAYA WAS IMPROVING, but she was a realist. There was no way she'd get to the Iron Guard level of control in a few days.

She was embarrassed to think she'd assumed she could.

Back in Pan Nuk, it had seemed a good solution, a way to take control after the horror of killing someone she never meant to kill.

But the reality was these guards had trained for years, and there was no easy way to becoming as adept as they were.

Hanson was getting much more out of their deal than she was. Taya could see her satisfaction at Taya's slight improvement.

"Did you think someone who was brought in at my age wouldn't be able to learn?" she asked.

Hanson shook her head. "No, I thought . . . I believed . . ." She gave a sigh, started again. "Obviously, anyone can learn if they put their mind to it and have the calling."

"And?"

"And you've shown me that a lot of the commonly-held wisdom is wrong." There was a bitterness in the way she spoke, and Taya wondered what the true story was. What had Hanson been told that she'd found to be a lie?

Hanson was staring at her again. "How do you feel when you call your Change?"

Taya thought of the blood-fizzing, hair-crackling shiver that gripped her every time she reached for shadow ore. "Like it's exactly what I should be doing."

Hanson nodded. "I was afraid that sensation was confined to those who'd felt it from adolescence. But you've shown me otherwise."

Taya nodded. She looked at the straw target she'd been throwing spears at. Her spears were close to the central target, and her control was indisputably better than it had been yesterday. They'd had to adjust the slot at the base of each spear, because the shadow ore discs she and Quardi had made were smaller than the standard iron discs the Iron Guard wore.

"This is helping you, Taya—" Hanson must have picked up on her disappointment with her progress, but she cut off what she was going to say, and Taya followed the direction of her gaze.

Two of the guards emerged from the trees, running in silence, and as soon as they realized they had been seen, they began signaling in the same way she'd seen Garek do.

"A new group of guards from Juli," Hanson said, her surprise evident.

"Savo can't have gotten back yet, it's at least three days on foot." Taya shaded her eyes to see better.

Hanson nodded. "Perhaps Vent sent another group out, and they missed Savo." But she didn't sound sure. She sounded suspicious.

Taya said nothing. She had no idea what this was about.

Hanson made a hand signal, and Etta was suddenly there.

"Put Taya and Ness in a hut and guard them." Hanson sent Taya a quick look of apology. "Sorry, but until I know what's going on, you'll have to be a prisoner for a while."

She ran toward Nori, and Taya watched them bend their heads together, talking softly.

"Another unit from Juli?" Ness was suddenly beside her, and

Taya looked at her with surprise, then remembered Ness was a guard from Juli herself. She'd understand the hand signals.

She nodded. "That's what Hanson said. Maybe Vent sent another group off after we spoke to him. And they must have missed Savo coming in the opposite direction."

Ness nodded, but she looked disturbed herself. "The only reason Vent would have done something like that was if things were going seriously wrong."

That was Taya's worry, too. It might have been all Vent could think of to do if it was getting harder to control the crowds demanding to see Aidan.

There was a power vacuum in West Lathor, and it had to spell danger for everyone.

"This way." Etta's voice, hard and sharp, even when lowered almost to a whisper, jolted Taya back to her surroundings. She'd forgotten Etta was even there.

Etta grabbed her arm and began marching her toward a small hut, and Taya didn't struggle. She saw Ness's mouth form a thin, angry line, but the Juli guard fell into step.

"It's not necessary to drag her," she said, not bothering to lower her voice.

Hanson glanced over at them, and Etta dropped her grip, as Ness must have known she would.

Taya didn't dare meet Ness's gaze, because that surely would have enraged Etta even more.

"Play your little games, but you're still the prisoners here." Etta wanted to shove her into the hut, Taya could see her hands clenching reflexively at her side.

She climbed the three step wooden ladder up into the dark, smelly space, and and realized this must have been where Aidan had been kept before they'd come.

No wonder he'd been less than happy about his stay here.

"This is disgusting." Ness put her hand up to her nose.

Even Etta seemed a little surprised at the state of the place.

There was no bed, but there was a rough pallet made from springy, thick bush branches covered over with a thick fabric. It became obvious the smell was coming from food that had been left in the hut, and had gone off in the last two days.

Without asking permission, Ness picked up the rough wooden plate it was sitting on and threw it out of the door.

Taya lifted the wooden board that covered the window away and a cool breeze began to flow through the place.

"He must have been eating when you arrived the other day, and no one's been in here to check the place since then." There was a defensiveness to Etta's voice.

Of course, she didn't just see herself as a Juli guard, but as the elite force of the land. And this would not pass muster in any military barracks.

"It's not exactly the Guard House, is it?" Ness said, echoing Taya's own thoughts.

"No," Etta said shortly. She looked like she wanted to say more, but she shut her mouth with a snap and looked out of the window.

"You going to talk to the guards Vent has sent?" Ness asked. "Find out what's going on?"

Etta glanced at her. "I don't know."

"If you don't, you're all more idiotic than I thought." Ness let her scorn show through.

Etta bared her teeth in a silent threat of violence, her gaze never leaving the view out of the window.

There was a scream. It rose up, and then cut off sharply.

Ness shoved Etta out the way to look, and Taya heard the tiny sound of fear Ness made at the back of her throat before she spun around and ran out the door.

Etta ran after her, leaving Taya free to go to the window herself.

Ness made it around the side of the hut, and ran toward a small group of Iron Guard, screaming a kind of battle cry as she went.

Some of the guards in the group turned to her in surprise, and Taya caught a glimpse of someone on the ground.

She slid onto the window sill and then dropped to the ground behind Etta, who was racing after Ness.

Etta had left her armed.

Taya fingered the knives at her hips. Her spears were on the ground near the training area, but she also had her fine needles, worked into the sleeves of her shirt.

She increased her speed as Ness reached the group and threw herself to the ground, bodily blocking whoever lay there from the other guards.

Etta slowed, and then sauntered up to the others, now she knew one of her charges wasn't trying to escape.

Nori asked her something in a quick, curt voice, and Etta turned back to the hut, insolent, and then went still at the sight of Taya coming toward her.

Taya gave them all a smile. She stopped when she was far enough away for her to feel more or less confident in the control of her calling, but out of physical reach of the guards.

"What's going on?"

"They hurt Damin, who is a Juli guard. One of their own," Ness spat.

"Badly?"

"It's just a minor injury." Hanson was dismissive. "What I want to know is how many of you there are, and where you are camping?"

Damin hunched over himself, refusing to speak.

Taya blinked. She *knew* him. "Aren't you one of Captain Nostra's people?"

He looked up with shock.

"Well, she's Guard Master Nostra now," Taya said. "Have you come from Gara?"

"Taya of Pan Nuk." Damin spoke slowly. "Are these the people who abducted you from your village?"

She shook her head. "No. I got away from them some time ago. I came here to get Aidan back, because he was caught on his way from Gara to Juli by this lot, just like you."

Damin looked around at the guards, obviously wanting to speak but not wanting to reveal anything in front of enemies.

"You can speak. Let's make them feel the full burden of their guilt. Did Nostra send you for word on Aidan?"

Damin nodded. "There are rumors he's been taken and killed. That the liege is dead, too. That West Lathor is leaderless."

"He was taken," Ness said bitterly, looking Hanson in the eye. "But not killed."

"Things are getting out of hand now, General." Taya stood with both feet planted a little apart. "It's time to pick a side."

Hanson waved a hand at the guards around her. "I have picked a side."

"Then to keep their country free and their lives safe, you will have to give way. You thought you were dealing with the princeling, but you're dealing with the liege now. And he can't capitulate to you." She fingered the hilt of her knife. "I give you my word, I will convince him to agree to your new recruitment methods. But even if I'm unable to manage that, after this battle is done, you can refuse to continue to recruit new guards. No one else can do it but you and your team. Simply stop."

"I didn't think I could, before I saw that you are perfectly sane and fine. For years, we were told if a child Called a change and didn't find his or her element, they went mad."

"No. They live a perfectly normal life." Taya lifted her hands. "They do other things."

There was silence for a long time. Eventually, Hanson made a signal with her hand and Damin was released.

"Go see to his wound," she said to someone next to her. "And everyone else, start packing up. We're going back to Juli."

FOURTEEN

GAREK KNEW they were in danger.

There was something in the silence as they stood before the massive sky craft that told him they were being viewed down the sights of some sort of weapon.

Aidan made a movement, a quick, almost involuntary flinch, and then a door opened and a figure climbed out dressed in the same dark blue suit Garek had seen the sky raiders wear before.

He or she came alone.

It strengthened Garek's belief he and everyone around him could be killed in an instant.

"They're smaller than I thought." Rig spoke quietly, and Garek guessed most people thought of the sky raiders as monstrous. They were taller than the average Baritan, but nothing like the hulking beasts of the legendary shadow pits, which is how most people spoke of them.

Their faces were truly frightening, with long incisors and cold yellow eyes, but Garek had seen the panic on those faces as they'd died, the fear in those eyes, and he had come to understand they were not much different to the people of Barit.

He moved forward to meet the sky raider, and they both stopped when there was about five feet between them.

"Tell your friends to stay back." The hiss was chilling, but Garek knew it wasn't the sky raider's actual voice, it was some machine that translated his own language into Illian. Taya had told him of the moment when she'd realized this, and how it had helped her get over her fear of them.

He glanced behind him, saw Aidan had already started following behind him, and Ness and Rig had moved forward a little, too.

"One of them is a leader of our people. He needs to come closer, but the other two will stay back." He jerked his head at Aidan, then faced the sky raider again.

The sky raider's helmet went from a dark, polished surface to transparent, clearing away like clouds before a strong wind.

Garek looked straight into hard, curious eyes. There was a look on the sky raider's face that said he wasn't happy about Garek's refusal to obey orders, but he was going to let it go.

He waited until Aidan stood just behind Garek's shoulder before he spoke.

"You have one of our ships."

The way it was spoken, Garek could hear the question in the tone, and felt a little frisson of interest.

"I stole it from the mine on Shadow," he said. "I'm surprised you don't know that."

The sky raider cocked his head. "Shadow?"

Garek pointed upward, to where Shadow hung, blue and grey in the afternoon sky.

The sky raider turned to look at it. "What was the ship doing there?"

"There's a mine there. A shadow ore mine. I understand that is why your people are here."

"What if I were to tell you that we are not the same as those people, the people you stole that ship from."

Garek looked at him for a long moment. "I would say that's very interesting."

"What I find interesting is how you got up there to steal a ship at all."

Garek hesitated, but if this was a different group, the risk of laying things out would be worth it. Very much worth it.

"The others like you stole many of our people to go work in the mine for ore. I knocked one of your small little ships out of the sky, and I used it to go and rescue them. And to bring them back I needed a bigger ship, so I took this one."

The yellow eyes blinked. "Why did they take your people?"

"Because they can't go into the mines themselves. The ore affects your machines and it even affects the suit you are wearing now. Stops it working so you suffocate and die." He let the knowledge of that show on his face, so the sky raider had no doubt that he had seen that happen with his own eyes.

There was something in the eyes that looked back at him, a fierce light that said he understood Garek's point, and that Garek would find it difficult to do the same to him.

"I struggle to believe that you brought down one of the fighter craft to make your original trip. You don't have the technology." Perhaps the sharpness and insult in that statement, even over the translated hiss, was because the sky raider didn't care for the threat that Garek had made.

There was no way Garek was going to go into his calling and so he shrugged. Gestured back to the sky craft. "And yet, the mine on Shadow no longer has people working in it, and I have a sky craft."

The sky raider watched him, unblinking, for what felt like a long time.

"Why do the others like us want this ore? Did your people work that out?"

Garek frowned at him. "I've already said. Because it renders your systems unusable. We assumed the problems with it were also the reason it was valuable. You can use it against each other."

The sky raider's eyes widened in sudden surprise. He looked back to the big ship behind him, a reflexive movement, because Garek was sure they were talking to him inside his helmet.

Then he looked sharply upward, and Garek lifted his gaze as well. Saw the familiar glint in the sky.

"Friends?" He demanded of the sky raider.

The sky raider shook his head. "But we can deal with them." There was an arrogance in his voice.

Garek took a step back, head still tilted up. The sky craft coming closer was one of the smaller fighting craft. The sky raiders had to be getting to the end of their supply of them and he wondered how many they had left. He and Taya had together destroyed four of them.

It must simply have been on patrol, and stumbled across them, because surely it didn't think it could attack the massive ship on the ground in front of him.

Its white lightning could still kill or hurt him, though, no matter its size.

"Get back in the sky craft," he called to the others, and turned and ran himself.

"There is no danger—"

Garek ignored the sky raider's call. His blue suit might protect him, but Garek knew all too well the pain of white lightning.

Kima and Rig reached the ladder first, swarming up it, and Garek gave Aidan a boost, calling his Change to throw the princeling up to the top of the ladder, and used his calling to propel himself up, as well.

They were in the air and moving by the time the fighter craft swooped down.

The sky raider he'd been speaking to took a defiant stance, staring up at the fighter.

It swooped overhead, dipping low, and then turned around for a second run.

There was something in the way it did that that made Garek

move back further, still close enough to observe, but effectively leaving the field.

The fighter skimmed over the top of the big sky craft as it came back in, and Garek saw something fall from it.

He caught a flash of something dark and small which struck the big craft on the roof.

For a moment, nothing happened, and then the world lit up.

The light was blinding, ultra white, searing his eyes so when he closed them he saw nothing but bright lights sparking behind his eyelids. The low, deep thump of the explosion came next, rattling his very bones.

For an instant, there was no air.

The sky craft dropped, and then wobbled as the air came rushing back, and Garek moved them up and back even further and higher than they'd been before.

The big sky craft was gone.

Aidan made a sound, a gasp of disbelief, but Garek barely glanced at the wreckage. He looked for the small fighter craft, and found it very easy to find.

Black smoke poured from one side of it, and the small craft flew at an angle.

The familiar whine had been replaced by a higher pitched sound.

"They misjudged the power of their weapon." Kima was watching it, too.

The craft disappeared amongst the hills ahead.

"Whether they survive or not, that's another of those fighter craft that's damaged." Garek liked that.

"Look." Rig pointed down to the ground.

The sky raider lay on the ground. By some twist of fate, he looked unharmed, but he lay too still for that to be true.

Garek brought the sky craft forward and landed beside what little remained of the original ship.

He jumped down without bothering with the ladder, and crouched beside the sky raider.

The helmet seemed untouched, but when he got closer, Garek could see chunks missing from the suit itself, and he knew the sky raider was going to die. The air the suit circulated would have escaped and the air of Barit was poison to him.

The sky raider turned to look at him, moving his arm, and Garek saw it was more than just lack of air that was killing him. His whole side was slashed open by debris from the ship, and a massive piece of metal was lodged just below his ribs.

"That was . . . the shadow ore?" He could barely whisper the words, the hiss of his translator making the words almost indecipherable.

"I think so, yes."

"We need to speak to you . . ." He paused, then caught Garek's gaze again. "Behind the planet you call Shadow." The sky raider drew in another breath, as if to say something else, but instead, he went still.

"Is he . . .?" Kima crouched next to him.

"Gone." Garek looked to where the smaller sky craft had disappeared.

The more expensive it was for them to stay here, in terms of people and equipment, the less likely they were to return.

He didn't make the mistake of thinking the new group would be any better than the first. It might help West Lathor's cause for now for there to be two opposing groups, but if the sky raiders saw benefit to staying on Barit and Shadow, he didn't see them retreating just because the people of Barit didn't want them here.

"What now?" Rig was looking at the almost vaporized remains of what had once been a huge ship.

"Now, we go tell the Dartalian liege that there are foreign troops on her soil."

Aidan moved his arm, encompassing the destruction. "What about this?"

Garek shrugged. "If this wasn't their main ship, and they're not all gone now, then at some point we need to speak to them again."

"Do they want to ally themselves with us?" Kima asked. "Like the others have done with the Harven?"

Garek shook his head. "It's likely they just want to know more about shadow ore. And if the ship that was destroyed was in some kind of contact with its mothership, then they've just seen for themselves how powerful it is."

"I didn't know it was this powerful, and I've seen Taya take down ships with it before." Aidan spoke quietly.

Garek agreed. "I think it's safe to say the sky raiders have found a way to make it even more lethal."

FIFTEEN

IT WAS a three hour journey to Valian, the capital of Dartalia, and Garek found it quickly because he'd been here twice before.

When they came in to land, it was to the same calm, alert but not aggressive guard unit that had met him last time.

"Welcome." Susa's general, Dix, greeted him with a smile as they climbed out of the sky craft and made their way toward the small group. Her blonde hair, a darker gold than Taya's, was braided in an intricate pattern, and her warmth was genuine.

"We have news from the border." Garek had made a promise last time he was here that he would share what intelligence he could with Susa.

She had immediately seen the uses of the sky craft and what flying over the surrounding borders could tell them, although he guessed she would not have anticipated an invasion of her territory.

"Who are your friends?" Dix asked. She still had the friendly smile on her face, but he realized she would not let him near Susa without first knowing who would be coming with him.

He nodded to her in respect. "This is Aidan, the new liege of

West Lathor. Rig is part of Juli's Night Guard and Kima is a lieutenant in the Iron Guard."

There was a sudden hush.

It occurred to Garek that between them they represented the full strength of West Lathor. There was perhaps no better envoy to speak to Susa, even if he had planned it carefully.

Dix sent him a quick, searching look, and when he said nothing more, gave a decisive nod.

"Welcome," she said again, this time bowing slightly to Aidan. "Come with me."

She flicked her hand and four guards broke away from the group, boxing them in as they walked into the low, sprawling palace.

Dix took them to the big, comfortable room Garek had been in before when he'd brought Zek back from Luf with an injury.

"Is Zek recovered? Is he here?"

Dix paused in the doorway, clearly on her way to alert her liege. "He's here. I'll tell him you're visiting."

She disappeared, leaving the guards behind to watch them, but there was no real sense they were being treated as a threat—it was more caution, and that was something everyone could understand.

Aidan being with them had something to do with it.

As the liege of West Lathor, he was presenting himself with minimal guards, although powerful ones. It would have been a good move, if they had come officially.

That it had worked out in their favor was just luck.

Susa played no power games—there was no waiting.

Zek arrived in less than five minutes. He was looking much better than he had the last time Garek saw him, his stab wound had obviously healed well.

He slapped Garek's back, and then bowed to Aidan with a grin. "I hear congratulations are in order."

Aidan grinned back but before he could reply, Susa walked in with Dix at her side.

Aidan stepped forward and bowed as elegantly as the princeling he was.

"Peace to your house and your state," he said.

"And to yours." Susa looked extremely satisfied, and Garek recalled her telling him last time that she hoped Aidan would step up as liege soon.

"You bring an interesting entourage," Susa said, and Aidan slid a look at Garek and then simply nodded.

"These are interesting times."

"Did you find Taya?" Zek asked Garek, and because that question was asked before any others, Garek gave a bow himself.

"I did. And she came across information that will interest you. But my suggestion is that we tell you all the news we have while we travel to the far south of your border in the sky craft."

Susa frowned. "Because?"

"Because you have trespassers."

Susa looked at him, then glanced at Dix. "How many of us can you take?"

"Eighty, if you want to take that many."

Susa and Dix exchanged another look.

"Get twenty, with tents and provisions, for now." Susa said, and Dix stepped out of the room.

"What will I find when we get there, Garek of Pan Nuk?"

"Three armies, using your territory as a crossing point to get into Favre and then on to West Lathor."

There was silence for a beat.

"Three armies?"

Garek nodded. "You know who they are."

"I do." Susa tapped her lips, looking toward Aidan. "You confirm this?"

Aidan nodded.

Susa sighed. "Zek, draft a missive to the council. The sooner it goes to them, the better. We might as well get those wheels rolling now."

The merchant, who Garek had come to understand was far more than just a trader for the state of Dartalia, walked to where a large desk was pushed up against a wall, and began pulling out parchment and pen.

"Have you sent word to the council, too?" Susa turned to Aidan.

Her eyes widened with surprise at the shake of his head.

"We came straight here after we saw them. I haven't been home." Aidan only spoke the truth, but Kima shifted uncomfortably at his words.

"Would you like to do it now?" Susa asked him. "Zek can arrange for your missive to go with ours."

"I would be very much obliged." Aidan clasped both hands together, and obviously much pleased, Susa led him to another desk and gave him what he needed.

"Your boss needs to change her methods soon, or there won't be anything worth saving." Garek spoke softly to Kima, and she gave a nod of acknowledgment without looking at him.

Although she couldn't have heard him, Susa turned in Garek's direction when Aidan was scribbling his formal protest to the council.

"Which of your companions is from the Iron Guard?" she asked, her eyes bright with interest as she looked Rig and Kima over.

Kima stepped forward, clenched fist over breast. "Respect to your house."

"Thank you." Susa looked at her carefully, and Garek knew she was seeing the worn clothing, the missing iron discs where they'd come off the uniform, and the gauntness in Kima's face. "You have been on assignment?" she asked.

Garek realized she thought the Iron Guard had been on reconnaissance, spying on Harven, Kadmine and Favrean troops in the mountains.

Kima looked up. "The most important assignment of my career."

"Ah." Susa looked over at Garek. "It is a pity the rumors of the

Iron Guard's disappearance was attributed to them abandoning their liege, rather than putting themselves in danger for him."

Garek lifted his shoulders. "I didn't know the truth of what happened myself until a few days ago."

Susa said nothing more, but Garek could see her realigning her thoughts, rewriting everything she'd heard.

It was to West Lathor's benefit, and he felt no guilt in misleading her when it came to the perceived strength of his state.

And the Iron Guard *were* back. He would make sure of it if that became necessary, but he didn't think it would.

General Hanson had a deep, big heart. It was why she hadn't abandoned West Lathor, even when it looked like she would never get her way. She wanted to save her people, even at massive risk to herself.

"I'm done." Aidan walked over to them, and Garek could see the wariness in his eyes as he realized Susa had been speaking to Kima.

It wouldn't do at all for the Dartalian liege to learn that he had been imprisoned by one of his own generals.

"It's best we leave as soon as possible," Garek said, and his tone obviously relaxed Aidan, because he offered Susa his arm.

The Dartalian liege took it with a graceful nod of her head.

The picture of unity wasn't lost on Garek, or anyone else in the room.

Aidan did diplomacy well.

And diplomacy, and some old-fashioned friendships, were what they needed badly right now.

GAREK SET the sky craft down where Susa instructed him to. A narrow valley, which looked to be the only viable way out of Dartalia into Favre.

It was the perfect spot to stop the army they'd flown over half an hour before in its tracks. Except . . .

He looked at the twenty guards jogging down the ramp at the back of the sky craft, and, under Dix's instruction, setting up a thin line of resistance.

"It's symbolic, for now." Susa had obviously seen the look on his face. "Whether I have twenty or two hundred, they have many, many more."

She had been shocked at how many where in the combined army. She'd gone quiet, and then she and Dix had shared a long look, when they'd flown over the troops. She'd directed them to this spot in a soft voice, although there was no weakness there. If he were to guess, he would say it was fury tempered with control.

"I don't want to wait for them to get here," she said when the guards they'd brought began setting up camp.

"It will take the armies hours to reach this point," Aidan agreed.

"I'm eager to talk to whoever is leading this army. And then, if it isn't too much trouble, I'll ask for one more ride to Valian to get more troops for this bottleneck. By then, we'll know if we need to ask West Lathor and our other allies for aid, or not."

There was something grim and determined about her words.

"West Lathor will be with you to the end," Aidan said.

That there was no down side in this for West Lathor need not be said. It was true, but Aidan's words were welcome anyway.

It was almost as if the offer of support was all Susa needed to stand a little taller.

"I've had my problems with Harven, but Kadmine and Favre have never given me cause to doubt them until today." She straightened the cloak she'd thrown over her clothes, which resembled a modified, but still practical, guard uniform.

"You should have more than just me to guard you when you meet them," Dix said, glancing out at the twenty guards outside with a frown.

"It will be our honor to provide a guard," Rig said, and after a moment of hesitation, Dix gave a nod.

It seemed her assessment was good enough for her liege, because Susa nodded, too.

"It would be my honor to accept."

Garek lifted the sky craft back into the air. He ignored the front troops, the advance parties, with their small units of six or less guards, all riding zanir.

He skimmed low over them, making them duck for cover, and followed the contours of the landscape until he came to the main body of the column.

"There's a good place to set down," Aidan said, and Garek could just hear the suppressed excitement in his voice.

He knew the value of theatre, did the princeling. And they would be making quite an entrance.

As instructed, he landed on the flat field in front of the army.

They came to a halt, and he saw a line of archers had formed at the front of the column, crossbows raised.

They rained arrows down on the craft.

He waited it out.

One . . . two . . . as the third wave hit and glanced harmlessly off the outer shell of the craft, he shook his head.

"Might as well waste their arrows," he said, and saw Kima give a quick grin. "Would you like to help me make a point?" he asked her.

She seemed both surprised and intrigued. Gave a nod.

"We won't be long." He turned to Susa. "Could you write a short request for talks, if you have any parchment?"

Susa said nothing, although her eyes were bright with interest. She had brought a small satchel with her, and she quickly crouched on the floor of the craft, took out a piece of parchment and wrote a few lines.

He looked over her shoulder and suppressed a laugh at her wording. He wished they were close enough to see the face of whichever general received it.

She handed it to him, and he gave it to Kima, just catching Aidan's grin as he stepped out of the craft and dropped to the ground.

He waited for Kima to step onto the ladder.

"Wait there," he called before she started down it. "Can you see the column's front shield?"

She nodded.

He threw up one of the arrows that had landed on the ground, and she caught it easily.

"Stab the message onto the arrow, call your Change and throw it at the shield."

She shook her head. "My control is excellent, but I can't get it that far without a bow."

"You have me instead of a bow."

She frowned at him and then shrugged, and he could see her focus on the shield up ahead. It was decorated with metal plates depicting the units of the column and they gleamed in the Star's light, but it was mostly made of wood.

"Ready?" she asked him.

He nodded and she threw, her face fierce with concentration. He called his own Change and propelled the arrow forward. It wobbled a little as she reacted in surprise at the touch of his calling with hers, but she recovered well, and when it hit the shield dead center with a crack audible even to their ears, she gave a short, low chuckle.

They shared a look, hers of appreciation.

"That's what Taya was talking about? When you helped her?"

He nodded.

Aidan stuck his head out. "They've raised the peace flag."

Garek saw they had. "Let them come to us. I'd rather be close to the sky craft, in case we need to go in a hurry."

It seemed everyone agreed with that. They all climbed out of the craft and ranged themselves in front of it as six officers approached on zanir, the saddles brightly trimmed in unit colors.

Aidan stood beside Susa, with Rig and Kima on either side of them. Garek stepped forward, positioning himself a little in front and to Aidan's right, Dix took up her place in line with him at Susa's left.

The zanir were coming in fast, and their riders showed no signs of reining them in.

It was either an attack or it was an attempt to intimidate.

"Dix." Garek glanced over at her. She had drawn her sword, and was holding it with both hands. "What Change do you call?"

"Earth."

He had thought so. Had seen a few things that made him suspect. "See that point there, were the grass ends. Throw dust into the air."

She looked at him for a moment, curious, and then did it, and Garek easily called his own Change to meld with hers and keep the soil suspended in the air to create a swirling barrier.

It looked as if a wall of red dust boiled up out of the ground to bar the way.

The zanir reacted, rearing up in panic, and the officers riding them had to slow, and then bring them to a stop to calm them down.

When it seemed they were going to stay where they were, Garek pulled back, and so did Dix.

A little of the dust hung naturally in the air for a moment, and then cleared.

There was a long silence.

Eventually one of the riders moved forward slowly.

Garek saw the moment when the seal of Dartalia, which formed the clasp of Susa's cloak, caught his eye.

He came to a stop again.

He'd planned to take the bluster and arrogance route. Garek saw it in his posture and on his face. But the official seal stole the wind from his sails.

"You would run down the liege of Dartalia on her own land?" Susa asked him coldly. "You would dare?"

Garek hadn't looked her way while he'd been creating the wall of dust, but now he heard the icy fury in her voice. She had not liked the intimidation tactic. She had not liked it at all.

"No." The rider looked behind him, and two of the remaining five walked their zanir forward to join him. "We thought . . ."

"What did you think?" Aidan asked. "You raised the peace flag. Does that mean nothing to the people of Harven, Kadmine and Favre?"

The rider shook his head. "We thought you were . . ." His gaze lifted to the sky craft behind them. "How did you come by a sky raider's ship?"

"I'm assuming one of the three of you is from Harven?" Susa looked at them with such a gleam of righteous anger in her eye, they all shifted uncomfortably. "But please, before you go any further, I am Susa, liege of Dartalia."

"I am Commander Laman of Kadmine." The man who'd come forward first touched his fingers to his brow, in the way Garek had heard the Kadminians used as a salute.

"I am the commander of the Favre forces, Selene of Ufolo." The woman between the two men dipped her head.

There was silence from the last man, and Laman and Selene looked left.

"Calvin?"

He cleared his throat. "Commander Calvin of Harven." He nodded to Susa. "I had heard the West Lathorians had a sky craft, not the Dartalians."

There was a stunned silence from his two allies.

"That is right, we do. I am the liege of West Lathor," Aidan said with a smile. "Aidan of Juli."

"The liege?" Laman wasn't fast enough to hide his surprise and shock. "I had heard . . ."

He trailed off. His face had gone pale, and Garek caught his eye, gave him a slow, knowing smile.

Yes. We know what you're up to. We understand exactly what is happening here. The element of surprise you thought you had was never there.

"Enough." Susa kept her voice even, but Garek could hear the undercurrents of outrage. "What are you doing on my land without my permission?"

"It was my understanding that we did have your permission?" The commander from Favre's statement trailed off into a question at the look on Susa's face.

"Not even the neutrality agreement I had with Harven, which I withdrew from some weeks ago, contained any agreement to allow three armies to cross my border."

"We're nearly out of your territory anyway." Calvin's voice was cool and reasonable. "Allow us to proceed into Favre, and we'll be gone from your lands by tomorrow afternoon at the latest."

"I don't reward gross breaches of trust." Susa drew herself up. "Turn your troops around, and go back the way you came. And I will warn you, the full council has already been informed of this."

"And if we don't?" Calvin asked softly.

Garek readied himself to call his Change and squeeze the air from the bastard's lungs, but Susa laughed.

"Really?"

"We were given assurances—" Laman looked from Susa to Calvin. "We were told that we had your permission." He sounded slightly recalcitrant, as if he suspected Susa had inconveniently changed her mind.

"What document was shown to you?" Susa asked him, and while she seemed perfectly reasonable, Garek noticed her hands were fisted.

"None, but the assurances came from our own generals—" Selene cut herself off, realizing the tricky territory she had stumbled into.

"You will turn around and go back the way you came, and you will do it now. And your lieges will pay reparation for the harm done, and all our treaties will have to be renegotiated."

Selene stared at her. The repercussions seemed only now to be sinking in.

"Can at least my troops cross back into Favre?" Selene asked.

"Where did you come in from?" Susa asked.

Selene paused, as if unsure whether to say.

"They came in from Harven," Garek said. He pointed to the mountains. "From a camp up in the Range."

"And how did you get to that camp?" Susa asked.

Selene glanced at Laman.

"The Favre troops came into Kadmine, marched north with us on exercises, and then we entered Harven from the far north and worked our way down through the Dartalian Range on the Harven side." Laman's gaze didn't waver.

"That would have taken, what, a full month?" Susa asked.

They said nothing.

"If I find out Favre and Kadmine used this corridor to get into Harven, before using it to come back again, there will be more fines." Susa lifted her hands. "And now, turn your zanir around and leave."

"You're being unreasonable." Calvin moved his zanir forward a step or two. "Let us pass through to Favre. It'll be faster."

Of course, if they had to turn around and go back to Harven, it would take them at least another week to make their way into West Lathor, and they would have to do it through the inhospitable mountains, rather than the valleys of Favre. There was no way they wanted to turn around.

"I'm being unreasonable?" Susa crossed her arms over her chest. "You invade my state, and call me unreasonable?"

"We are not turning around." Calvin made a chopping motion with his hand. "And it doesn't seem as if you can stop us. We'll leave, but it will be south, through the valleys, and we will pay whatever reparations the council decides."

"You'll pay," Susa agreed. "But you will not go south. I have an army gathered in the Corridor already to stop you. Do you think the foreign commander of another state's army can give orders to a liege on her own soil?"

Calvin seemed to blink, as if he had forgotten who he was speaking to. "I apologize for any offense, but we need to go south, and we will. As fast as we can."

"No." Susa stepped forward. "Be gone." She pointed behind them, in the direction they'd come.

Garek wasn't sure what Calvin planned to do, whether it was to strike her down, or simply bump past her, but he surged his zanir forward, straight at her, and Garek reached out with his Change, and took the air from his lungs.

The Harven commander lifted his hand to his throat in a panicked, jerky movement, gasping, and fell off his mount as he clawed at his throat.

Dix walked up to him, skirting him as he flailed about, and her gaze lifted, and met Garek's. She gave a nod.

Then she lifted her sword and swung it down against his neck.

"You are here to declare war on Dartalia?" she asked Laman and Selene. She flicked her sword up, dripping with blood, as she spoke.

They both backed their zanir away. Garek could see the shock on their faces, the trembling of their hands on their reins.

"No. Calvin was too focused—" Laman must have suddenly remembered why it might not be a good idea to say what Calvin had been focused on. He stopped mid-sentence. His gaze went beyond the sky craft, toward the south.

It was starting to sink in that they were not going to get their easy run into West Lathor. And that far from it being a surprise, West Lathor already knew they were coming.

Selene sent a quick, nervous glance toward Aidan, then back down to Calvin's body. She swallowed. "What happened to him? Why was he choking like that?" Her voice was a little off-pitch.

Dix gave her a cold smile. "He attacked my liege. That's what happened to him."

"Do I have to tell you again?" Susa asked them, her eyes on them, not the body of their colleague. She stepped forward. "Go. Now."

There was a moment of silence, and then they wheeled their zanir around. They reached the other three officers at a walk, but by the time they were halfway back to their troops, they were at full gallop.

SIXTEEN

THERE WAS A FINE, arched spray of blood on Dix's cheek. It stood out on her pale skin, and made the blue of her eyes even brighter.

She was in sharp contrast to her liege. They strode together toward Garek in perfect step—Susa with her dark skin and her brown hair and eyes a foil to her golden-haired, pale-faced general, and it was clear there existed between them a rapport that needed few words.

"I would like us to have that same understanding between us." Aidan spoke quietly in Garek's ear as the two women reached the ramp at the back of the sky craft and stopped to look behind them.

Susa's palace lay glowing softly in the early evening light, windows lit with warm golden lamps. Sixty guards emerged from one side of the building in tight-knit units of ten.

Adding them to the twenty already securing the Corridor would not stop a determined army of three states, but Susa wanted a better show of force.

"They will turn and go back," Aidan said to her.

"What makes you say that?" Dix asked.

"Calvin's death brought home to them that they are not on their own ground. That they are committing a crime by any standard of the laws of Illy, and that there are further repercussions to pushing on. They are also aware that they have either been lied to or given incorrect information, because I don't think they were lying when they said they believed you'd given your permission. They're wondering now if they're going to be sacrificed afterward in whatever apology their lieges make to you. That you will be told they were acting without orders."

"I agree, but I think Selene and Laman will think about it for a bit first." Garek motioned to the guards gathered behind their liege, and they began to walk cautiously up the ramp. "They'll spend tonight huddled in their tents, arguing, and tomorrow, they'll pack up and go." He looked at the guards standing uncomfortably against one wall of the sky craft. "We can fly low over them on the way to drop these troops off in the Corridor. It might remind them that we are not as impotent as they think."

"You think they'll understand it's us, not the sky raiders?" Dix looked thoughtful.

"Selene and Laman will at least get a little fright, and it will focus their thoughts."

"And if they don't turn. If they choose to forge ahead and make for the Corridor?" Susa looked at her guards.

"Then we'll fight," Dix told her. She sounded quite satisfied with the idea, and certainly, none of the guards looked unhappy, either.

Susa exchanged a look with Dix, and what she saw there must have convinced her, because she gave a sharp nod. "So be it. I will contact the Council again, and call them to me. Garek, I know you cannot say when you will have a chance to return this way, but if you can come, I will be grateful for news, and to share my news with you."

"We'll try," Garek told her, and walked into the pilot's chamber to start the sky craft engines, leaving Aidan to take a more formal leave, liege to liege.

Night had fallen, and he still had far to go before he returned to Taya.

"YOU ARE VERY WORRIED." Ness put a hand on Taya's arm, interrupting her pacing.

Darkness had fallen a long time ago.

Garek must have encountered some trouble, there could be no question about that. The only question was whether he'd managed to get out of that trouble or not.

At her look, Ness dropped her hand.

Taya sighed. This wasn't Ness's fault. "How is Damin?"

"He'll be all right. Last time I checked, he was asleep in the hut. I'm glad you refused to go with the Iron Guard. I don't think he'd have been able to march today." She looked around the deserted camp. "I'm glad to be rid of them."

Taya hugged herself. "I can't say the same. They were stolen as children. They have a right to look for justice, and they're not even seeking it for themselves—they're trying to help those coming after them. I have to respect that." She bent and threw another log on the fire, the only one lighting the strangely forlorn camp.

She stirred the flames with a long stick and looked over at Ness.

"You'll have to work with them when we get back to Juli. It's best we put what happened here aside and move forward."

Ness's lips thinned, and Taya guessed it would take her a while to forgive and forget. Damin's injury wasn't too bad, but Ness had been angrier than he was about it, not to mention the way they'd held Aidan.

She hoped the rest of the guard at Juli would be more welcoming. Vent would be, she knew that.

He'd get down on his knees and kiss General Hanson's boots in gratitude to have her back.

She poked at the fire with the stick again, and then everything in her soared at the sound of a sky craft overhead.

She spun, jumped a log, and was on her way to the river before it had even passed over, but she stopped when it came in low, turned just beyond her sight over the trees and came back in.

There were no lights on it, and it was hard to see in the darkness, but the engine noise told her it had landed on the flat area beside the river in front of her, not in the water itself like usual.

A light, tingling sense of worry ran down her arms.

"He can see there's only one fire," Ness said. "He probably wants to know what's going on before he does anything else."

She relaxed. Of course.

She moved forward, and took two steps before she remembered she had her knives on her hips. She would have to set them in their water bath before she got too close to the sky craft.

She turned back, and at Ness's frown, took out the knives and wiggled them in the air in explanation.

Ness nodded, and passed her, jogging with a spring in her step toward the craft.

As Taya got to the fire, a soft spill of light behind her told her the pilot's door had opened.

She ran the last few steps to the boxes laid out beside the fire and slid the knives into the correct one.

She rose up and turned back, but the light from the open door of the sky craft was gone, and apart from the low, red glow of the fire behind her, it was absolutely dark. Clouds obscured even Shadow itself tonight, and she strained her eyes to see what was going on.

There was no conversation, and she thought Ness would at least be chatting to someone by now. She took a few steps forward.

"Ness?"

A light suddenly blinded her, coming not from the sky craft, but from ground level. Too bright, too clear, to be from Barit.

Her heart spiked.

Sky raiders.

She shaded her eyes, protecting them, her hands going to her hips, closing over nothing.

She had just put her knives away.

With a hiss, a sky raider was in front of her. She only saw his boots and his legs to his knees, but then the light attached to his suit pointed downward, and at last she could look up.

He had Ness in his grip, but she seemed strangely floppy. Her eyes were aware, frantic, even, but her body lolled in his arms, and Taya finally noticed the little device the sky raider held near her head.

She knew what she was looking at.

It could shoot out the dreaded white lightning. It could kill.

She crossed her arms in front of her, gripping her sleeves. "What do you want?" It came out as more of a whisper than a challenge.

"Where is the *yrintyh*?" The hiss of his voice chilled her, the light from his bright torch reflecting off the ground and illuminating the underside of his helmet and throwing strange shadows over Ness's face.

"I don't know what *yrin*... what that is."

He jerked Ness in his arms. "I will hurt her. We scanned and we saw two pieces of it, close together. And then when we landed, they disappeared. You are hiding them from us." He shook Ness again. "Where are they?"

The knives.

Somehow they had seen the shadow ore knives from the air and come down for them. And then she'd stored them in their box full of water, and they couldn't see them anymore.

"I'll show you." She walked a few steps backward and then turned, heading for the fire, thinking through her options as fast as she could. Her fingers worked at the thin sliver of the shadow ore needle threaded into her sleeve. She pulled it almost completely out, and then crouched beside the boxes.

The spears were in two of them, the knives, her sword and the sharp-edged circles that hung from her jacket in another, along with the few arrowheads Quardi had made her.

The knives were smaller, easier to throw, but the danger here was the white lightning. He could turn that device on her as easily as he could use it on Ness, and the spears could form a barrier and protect her.

She had used them to block white lightning on the Endless Escarpment and they had shielded her.

She reached for the lid on one of the spear boxes and lifted it. The fire was to her right, and her back was to it, her body throwing a shadow over the box. She hoped he wouldn't see what she was doing until it was too late.

She called her Change, and lifted the spears, lining all six up in front of her.

As they rose up, she worked the last bit of the needle in her sleeve loose and held it between trembling fingers. She looked over her shoulder, as if checking to see if he had followed her.

He was holding Ness at an angle, her head in the crook of his arm. He was open from the chest upward.

She turned, bringing the spears with her, and aimed the needle at where the helmet met the neck of his suit, sending it with force into the thick material.

The sky raider reacted immediately.

He almost threw Ness away from him, lifting his white lightning device with one hand, trying to pull the needle out with the other.

The device spat white lightning at her protective fence of spears. It hit the spears and danced across them, running up and down and then fizzing out.

She started moving toward him.

He shot at her again and again, and then, in panic, turned and ran back toward the sky craft. He tripped over something and fell, rolled to his feet and ran again.

Taya sped up after him.

Her boot glanced off something on the ground but she ignored it, pushing the spears ahead of her.

She rammed them into his back, holding them there for a moment and then pulling them back to a protective barrier again.

He fell a second time, twisting and jerking, and this time, it wasn't because he'd tripped. He was suffocating in his suit. The shadow ore had destroyed it.

She skirted him, kicking the white lightning device away from his hand, and kept moving toward the sky craft, heart hammering so hard she could barely hear the engines over the thudding in her ears.

She drew the spears closer to her, and when white lightning lanced out of the sky craft itself, she wasn't surprised.

She smelled a strange, metallic odor as it flashed out, and heard the spit and fizz of it crawling over her spears.

She ran toward it faster.

If she could reach it, if she could use the spears as a shield but still touch them to the craft, maybe . . .

The sky craft rose straight up, climbing so high, so fast, when she looked up, she couldn't tell where it was.

She stood, watching, for a long time. Trying to get her breathing under control.

When at last she did, there wasn't a sound to be heard, except for the chuckle and splash of the stream and the sighing of the trees.

The sky raider was silent.

She didn't want to look at him, but she forced herself to.

While she was running at his ship, he'd gotten his helmet off. She could see from the way he lay he had convulsed as he breathed the air of a planet he should never have stepped foot on without permission.

From the way he lay, the light on his suit shone a path toward the fire, and she edged around him and headed toward it to get to Ness.

"Taya, what's happening? Was that Garek?"

Damin's call from the hut almost frightened her into a scream.

She blew out a breath, shaking her head at herself. "No. An

attack. Sky raiders." She looked up at the sky again, but the sky was silent.

"An attack?" His hushed horror forced her forward.

"They hurt Ness, but I chased them off. One of them is dead." She jogged to the fire, crouching down beside Ness. She lay exactly where she'd been thrown, on her side, one arm above her head, the other resting on her stomach.

Taya gently moved her to her back, and looked into eyes that were clearly aware, frightened, and angry.

"They're gone. And the one that did this to you is dead."

Ness blinked her eyes in acknowledgment.

"Just relax. It'll wear off." Taya smoothed Ness's hair off her forehead, keeping her expression calm. She didn't know what had been done to Ness, but she didn't think Ness had been able to blink earlier, so she was already improving.

She rose up and walked over to the hut. Damin had crawled to the doorway, and he used the doorframe to help him stand.

"Can you pass me a pallet? I can't carry her to the hut, and neither can you with that injury, but we can roll her onto a mattress so she can sleep by the fire."

Damin leaned in and grabbed two, one for Taya, one for Ness. "What did they do to Ness?"

"I don't know." She looked back at the fireplace, and then turned to him, keeping her voice low. "She can't move, but she seems aware of what I'm saying so I think she can hear and see. It will hopefully wear off, like the effects of white lightning."

Damin took the first step down, favoring his side. "What did you do to them?" He was looking at her with speculation in his eyes. "I didn't understand what I was seeing at first, but that sky raider was running away from you. And when you charged the sky craft, it flew away. Like they were afraid of you."

Taya's lips twisted. "It's shadow ore they're afraid of, not me." She turned with the pallets and walked back to the fire, setting them down on level ground and then looked up when Damin joined her.

He was breathing hard, but he helped her lift Ness up onto the mattress, his face a grim mask.

"I'll stay out here with you," he said when he had his breath back, so Taya walked to the hut and got blankets for all of them and another pallet for Damin.

They lay on either side of Ness and Taya rose up on her elbows, head tipped back, to search the sky again.

She must have fallen asleep while she watched, because the scream of engines woke her with a heart-pounding snap.

She was up and running, a spear in her hand, before it landed, but this one was backing into the waterfall and she slowed as she approached the river bank.

Her boot connected with something, stubbing her toe, and she stopped and looked down at the thing that had tripped the sky raider, and which she'd bumped into twice. It was a box, attached to a very long rod.

She nudged it to one side when it appeared to be harmless, watching and listening over the sound of the stream and the whisper of the trees.

"Taya?" Garek's call carried over the water, and she felt such relief her knees gave way a little.

"I'm here." She cleared her throat. "On the bank." She waved, although they probably couldn't see her.

She hesitated, then dropped the spear and jumped into the water, wading across to meet Garek half way.

He had left Aidan to close up, powering through the thigh-deep rapids to snatch her up, lifting her so she was the same height as him.

"What is it?" One arm lifted her a little higher. "Are you all right?"

She nodded.

"Where is the Guard?" Kima called out.

"Gone back to Juli."

"Really?" Aidan sloshed across, Kima and Rig right behind him.

"Yes." She traced a line from Garek's brow down to his chin. "You had trouble, didn't you?"

He nodded and then started walking again, lifting her onto the bank and then pulling himself up beside her.

He went still at the sight of the dead sky raider.

Kima drew in a sharp breath as she scrambled up behind them, and Rig and Aidan spread out, slowly circling the body.

Garek looked down at her. "What happened?"

"We thought they were you." She suddenly remembered the spear she'd dropped by the river, then relaxed when she saw Rig was holding it. "Ness walked straight up to them."

"Why did they come down? Why now?" Garek looked up at the sky, and the expression on his face was frightening.

"They said they saw shadow ore as they were flying past. Their equipment must register it now somehow. I think they saw my knives. When they landed, they set down by the river, but I thought it was you wanting to find out where the Guard was before you settled the sky craft under the waterfall, so I put the knives back in the water box." She waved her hand toward the fire. "They did something to Ness. I couldn't see what happened in the dark, but she's paralyzed, and they threatened to kill her if I didn't give them the shadow ore."

"How would they have safely taken it?" Aidan wondered.

"There's a box on a long stick back there." Taya glanced in its direction. "We can look at it in the light, but I think that's what they were going to use."

"How did you . . . win?" Kima asked, her eyes still on the sky raider.

"I opened the box with the spears, and I shot the shadow ore needle I had in my sleeve into his suit. I didn't know if one would be enough to destroy the suit or not. I've used them to bring a sky raider down before on Shadow, but I used all ten of them that time. I needed the spears to block the white lightning. He had one of the little devices that shoots it." She pointed in the general direction she'd kicked it. "I blocked the shots with the spears, and then when he realized the white lightning wasn't going to hit me, he ran. They tried to shoot me from the sky craft as well, but the spears shielded me and I ran straight at them."

"They shot up into the sky so fast it hurt my ears." Damin's voice had them all turning, weapons out.

"Damin?" Rig asked, frowning as he stepped closer to the fire. "What are you doing here?"

Garek rubbed a hand over his face in a gesture Taya had come to learn meant he was exhausted. "It sounds like we've all had a very interesting day."

"Can it end now?" Taya asked. "Let's talk when it's light. All I was worried about is whether you were safe, and you are."

Garek looked like he was going to argue, but when he studied her face, he gave a nod, turned to the hut and brought out a pallet to lay next to hers.

He drew her to him, and she closed her eyes with a sigh of relief.

Tomorrow could come with all its troubles and burdens attached, but for now, she was safe, warm, and in her lover's arms.

SEVENTEEN

"WHY DO they take the helmet off?" Ness asked. She stood over the sky raider who had hurt her, and stared down at him. "Even if the breathing system in their suit is gone, the air outside is poisonous to them."

Taya looked over at her, finding it hard to keep her relief hidden. Ness had woken fully mobile. At some point in the night she'd fallen asleep and when she woke, she was back to normal.

"It seems to be instinctive. I have a feeling I'd do it if I was suffocating."

Ness nodded. "I think I would, too. Does that mean we have something in common with them?"

"I would guess we have more in common with them than we'd like to acknowledge." Taya crouched beside the body and tried to find the needle lodged in the fabric.

She called her Change, and it flew out and hovered over the sky raider's face. She plucked it from the air and began threading it through her sleeve, thinking through the chain of events the night before.

Had a single needle had an effect on the suit?

She was sure that touching the spears to his back had finished the suit off, but he'd reacted so quickly when the needle pierced his suit, it had to have done something.

It was dangerous.

Instead of threading the needles back in, she worked the one in her other sleeve loose and then headed back to the now bright, leaping fire.

Rig added another load of sticks onto it, and watched her as she opened the lid of a small box full of water and added the needles to the others inside.

Garek, Kima and Aidan were crouched over the box the sky raider had brought with him last night. It appeared at first glance to have only three sides, but at the end of the stick to which it was attached, there was a lever that could be turned, and a fourth side slid across to close the box off.

"So, they put the box over the shadow ore, and they can do that at a distance, because of the length of the stick, and then they turn the dial and close the box up, with the shadow ore inside." Aidan opened the box and closed it with interest.

"It seems like something that could be created on Barit," Kima said. "Not like the almost magical things in their ships."

"That's because shadow ore stops their systems working. They had to get back to what is probably basics to them." Garek took the box from Aidan and extended the stick, gauging the length of it.

"My guess is this is the closest they think they can come to a small piece of shadow ore without it affecting them."

"Small because the box won't take that much?" Aidan asked.

Garek nodded. "They've been reduced to picking up what they can find lying around, because they've lost their miners."

"But there isn't any of it lying about here." Taya knew that to be true. She scanned for shadow ore a few times a day, almost without realizing it. "When I was in the Dartalian Range I could feel ore, but it was in tiny amounts, even if it was quite evenly spread through the rock."

"They are probably searching everywhere. They don't know where to look, so they're patrolling the whole of Barit. It was just bad luck they saw your knives." Garek looked up at Shadow. "Although I don't know why they aren't doing their prospecting on Shadow. They'd have a lot more luck there."

"Maybe they've gotten everything they could off Shadow." Taya lifted her gaze to the planet, hanging low on the horizon. "It's been over two weeks since we escaped."

"Or maybe Shadow isn't safe for them anymore," Aidan mused.

"You're talking about the other group of sky raiders." Taya didn't know whether to share Garek's feeling that a second group was good for them, or not. It just seemed like more trouble, to her.

"So what now?" Ness asked. She was sitting down, elbows on her knees, and Taya thought she was probably not as recovered as she wanted them all to believe. As she needed to believe herself.

"Now, we take Damin back to Garamundo, fetch Nostra, and then head for Juli. Let everyone see we have a liege again, and hold a council of war."

Aidan gave a wide grin. "Let's go."

THEY CAUGHT up with the Iron Guard on the winding road through the low hills about a day's hard run from Juli.

They set down in front of them, and Garek opened the ramp.

He glanced at Aidan. "Go make up with the general. You know you have to. And it'll be a lot better if you're friendly when we get to Juli than if you're at each other's throats."

He didn't need to point out that a united front would be the balm the city needed after suspecting they were leaderless.

Aidan set his shoulders and walked out the pilot's cabin into the back.

Taya leaned against the front window of the sky craft, arms crossed over her chest, and watched him through the open door.

He thought back to last night, to the moment he saw the dead sky raider lying at his feet, and the icy fear that had doused him when he realized Taya had faced it on her own.

He had to keep reminding himself she had triumphed. She had overcome. And they had the interesting shadow ore containment box into the bargain.

If he needed something to trade for favors with the new group of sky raiders, he had a feeling they would be very interested in that box. Very interested, indeed.

They also had another of the small white lightning devices. He had taken four from Shadow, and had left two of them in Pan Nuk, with Kas, and given one to Falk to study. He had the fourth in his bag, but he kept forgetting about it.

The only chance he would have had to use it was against the three armies, when he'd stood with Susa and Dix.

He knew first hand the pain it caused, and he felt it was . . . wrong to use it against his own people.

Taya wouldn't touch them.

She'd been hit more than once by white lightning, and she wanted nothing to do with something that made it.

But not everyone thought like they did, and he could imagine what some lieges would do to have a weapon like that. It would be better for everyone if they were destroyed when this fight was over, but until the sky raiders were gone for good, he didn't dare do it.

"You look like the weight of Barit is on your shoulders," Taya said, and he looked up to see she was watching him, now, rather than what was going on outside the sky craft.

He shook his head. "What's happening out there? I assume they aren't killing each other?"

She studied him for another beat, then glanced back outside. "No, they're obviously not thrilled with each other, but it looks like Hanson's ordering her guards into the sky craft, so at the very least, the liege will return triumphant, with the Iron Guard in tow."

"It's a good thing." Nostra spoke up from her corner of the

cabin. She looked tired, but from the moment they'd landed in Gara and she'd seen Aidan, alive and well, she'd been coolly satisfied.

"Gara giving you any trouble?" Garek asked. He had walked the walls there for two years, he knew what she was up against.

"The way the old town master and guard master were so publicly exposed as having done a deal with the enemy helped." She gave a wicked smile. "No one feels brave enough to admit to supporting them, so they've had little choice but to pretend to be fully behind me."

Garek chuckled. "That must almost physically hurt some of them."

Nostra's grin widened. "I can see the pain in their eyes. And then the confusion and disbelief as I sideline them."

She straightened, and Taya stood up from her slouch as well, so Garek wasn't surprised to turn his head and find Hanson and Aidan stepping into the cabin.

"Is everyone in?" he asked.

Aidan nodded, and he lifted the ramp, and when it closed, he rose up into the air.

"Kima tells me—" Hanson had turned to Taya, but when she caught sight of Nostra, she stopped.

They stepped toward each other and hugged each other close.

"It bolsters me that my welcome is still warm," Hanson said.

Nostra drew her even closer, held her tighter, before releasing her, but she said nothing. Garek had the sense that since Nostra had heard why Hanson had left, and why she'd taken Aidan, she was in the camp that felt more should have been done for the general when she'd used the proper channels and asked politely for what was nothing more than the right moral choice.

Aidan must have guessed the same, because he looked at his feet and said nothing, either.

However right the princeling was to refuse to sign anything under duress in Hanson's camp, he would still have to grapple with the fact that his father had made bad decision after bad decision, and he would have to own them, and put them right.

Hanson's attention was suddenly riveted on the horizon, and Garek saw the tips of the palace towers rising above the hills.

Hanson pressed her hands against the window as the palace seemed to rise up from the hills, and then the river was below them and Garek followed it toward the city.

The palace, with its high walls and towers, spanned the top of the waterfall, a sentinel guarding the city from the north.

Fine mist swirled up from the massive waterfalls that fell on either side of Juli, forced left and right by the walls of the palace. It made the palace look like it was floating on clouds, and then the sky craft passed overhead, and the city itself was revealed, terraced down from the top of the cliff in row after row of high buildings. The city was bracketed by the waterfalls—the Plaits of Corinnda's Hair—its roofs thick with gleaming green moss, the colors of its walls jewel-like against the black of the rocks and the white of the water.

He saw Hanson close her eyes for a moment.

She was happy to be coming home.

And it was best that everyone knew she and her guards had returned.

He went low, flying down at an angle so they were just above the roofs, and then leveled out where the waterfalls fell into the deep, placid lake that lay at Juli's feet.

The engines screamed as he flew a little way out into the center of the lake and then turned back, lifting up to circle the palace one more time and then landing not on the walls, as he had before, but in the massive courtyard.

The more people saw Aidan and Hanson were back, the better.

EIGHTEEN

"SO YOU FORCED those bastards to go back through the Range?" Vent, Juli's guard master, rubbed his hands together in glee. "That'll take them over half a week, at least."

They sat around the massive table in what Taya decided must be the advisory chamber. Everyone who'd been involved up until now, including Savo—who believed if Rig and Ness were here, as their commander, he should be too—seemed to have invited themselves. Aidan had obviously decided to allow it.

Garek sat beside her, and now he leaned forward, palms flat on the table. "We need to go to them. The only way out of Harven into West Lathor will put them in the upper highlands, between the Crag and the Dartalian Range. And while there are a lot of hills in that area, there are a few flat valleys that would be good battlefields, and more importantly, nobody lives in that area."

"We'll never get our troops there in time," Vent said. "Yes, we have almost a week, but it'll take days for us to get what we need for a campaign together, and then days again to march anywhere near the Crag."

"We don't let them come into West Lathor further than the high-lands." Aidan nodded in agreement with Garek. "The villagers of West Lathor won't be left to fend for themselves again. We're not going to hunker down in the walled cities and plan for a siege. We stop them before they even reach the first homestead."

Vent blinked, but Hanson was nodding.

"It's all very well to say that, but how do we accomplish it?" Savo asked. "As Vent says, just mobilizing the troops will take time, getting the Gara regiments and the Juli regiments together and then covering the ground we'd need to cover . . ."

Rig made a sound like the screaming of engines, and moved his hand, palm facing down, across the table.

"The sky craft?" Vent's eyebrows rose. "I hadn't thought . . ."

"We can take eighty guards at a time," Garek said. "Or we can take all the equipment and weapons, so the guards can travel light. Or a mixture of the two."

"We could get a couple of units out there, to get the lay of the land, and work out the best places to ambush, to set up camp. And then, yes, get the equipment transported." Aidan stood up.

"The Iron Guard is ready right now." Hanson leaned back in her chair.

Aidan stood, and gave her a short, sincere bow. "I accept. And I thank you."

"What about the sky raiders?" Hanson steepled her fingers together. "Now we have the added complication of a second group, and we're more or less sure that Halbred is in league with the first group. Do you think they'll attack on his behalf?"

"The moment they do, Halbred loses his standing," Nostra said. "There is one common enemy on Barit, and that's the sky raiders. No one will stand with someone who has aligned with them to bring their own people down."

"So far, the cooperation has only extended to not attacking Luf, and in Dartan's case, Juli, in exchange for people to experiment on or capture." Garek looked rough; there was a dark scruff of beard on his lean, bronze face, his hair was messy, his clothes the worse for wear.

A well of emotion, tender and lustful all at once, rose up in her, and she lowered her eyes to keep it hidden.

"We can only hope it stays that way. We've got the sky craft, but Halbred has three armies."

"We also have the Iron Guard. And Garek." Taya kept her voice soft, but when she lifted her gaze, Aidan was watching her, and gave her a nod.

"I have a feeling Halbred will know enough to know that his people will never get willingly into a sky craft piloted by sky raiders. That would go against every instinct, and throw his authority into question. I don't think we need to worry about them having the same ability to move troops as we do."

"The people need to see their liege before we do any of this." Vent gestured out the window. "And we probably need to explain what's about to happen."

Aidan walked to the window and looked down on the cascading terraces of the city. "Once I address Juli, we need to understand whatever spies Halbred has here will report back. And if the sky raiders have spies here, they'll know, too."

"The sky raiders?" Ness could barely speak through the depth of her shock.

"Some of Dartan's guards were reporting to him, and he was passing it on." Garek was sure of that. Taya had killed one of the guards Dartan had sent after her, but he'd questioned the one who'd survived.

"There's nothing to be done about that. We need West Lathor to understand we're going to war."

"Send messengers out to the smaller towns and villages as well." Hanson stood, leaning forward on her hands. "They'll appreciate the information, and they'll be on alert, watching who moves through the countryside."

Vent nodded in agreement. "You've seen the armies, how outmatched are we?"

Garek and Aidan exchanged a look.

"By a lot."

GAREK CIRCLED the valleys and Captain Hanson, along with her two lieutenants, Kima and Nori, debated the various sites below quietly with each other.

"There." Hanson turned to him, and pointed down. "It's not perfect, but it's the best of them."

Taya's hand tightened on his shoulder, and Garek knew it was her way of reassuring him.

She had argued, logically and calmly, that she was better off in the front line on the slim chance Halbred did have some help from the sky raiders.

In Juli or Gara, or even Pan Nuk, she was a wasted resource.

He knew that he would have agreed if she was anyone to him but who she was. And it was hard to concede.

She was soothing him. Trying to make it easier for him.

And he had the self-awareness to smile at himself.

He needed to get over it and focus. Even if the thought of leaving her here in the middle of nowhere made every instinct in him rise up and rebel.

He lifted his hand and squeezed hers, then set the sky craft down lightly on the sloping field that was one of the few that was free of dark gray rocks.

The three armies would have to approach from the bottom of the valley, so the Iron Guard would be sitting above them, looking down.

As soon as the ramp lowered, he heard the guards moving out, and Taya bent and kissed him, a light, sweet touch of her lips to his.

He wanted to grab her close, hold her tight, and sink into her, but that wasn't possible now.

He stood and put his arm around her, and the look in her eyes told him his hunger and his desire were returned.

There was regret and amusement both on her face, a sort of self-deprecating humor that forced a chuckle out of his throat.

"It's good motivation to get this done," she said, and his smile deepened.

He kissed her. Not quite the way he wanted to, but with enough heat that there were a few whistles from the guards around them.

"Look after my intended," he said as he raised his head and caught Hanson's scandalized gaze.

Taya tightened her grip on him for one more moment and stepped back. "Stay safe."

She bent and picked up her pack, slinging it over her shoulder.

He remembered how she looked when he left to walk the walls of Gara; younger, softer. In flowing dresses, with her hair free about her shoulders.

She was a guard now. In the dark brown of a uniform, with her hair tied back in a braid, she looked as competent as any guard he'd served with.

He ran a finger down the side of her cheek and bent to give her one last kiss. "I'll see you soon."

She smiled at him, and walked out the back, and he heard her thanking the guards who were carrying her shadow ore weapons in their heavy water boxes out for her.

They'd decided that she wouldn't take any of the weapons out unless a sky craft was clearly coming in to attack. The weapons could stay invisible in their water and avoid the attention of the sky raiders' new method of finding shadow ore as much as possible.

As Garek lifted the sky craft up, he saw her waving to him, and he tipped the sky craft from side to side to wave back.

"Now on to Gara to fetch some of my troops?" Nostra had taken the place Hanson had occupied on the way here, leaning against the window to look down onto the landscape below.

"To Gara, then to Dartalia to check on how Dix is faring at the border."

Nostra chuckled. "Who would ever have thought just a few months ago we'd have allies, a sky raider ship, and the Iron Guard back?"

"Things can change quickly," he agreed. The problem, Garek knew, was they could also change the other way.

NINETEEN

THE SKY RAIDERS were coming again.

Taya watched the Star's light glint silver off the wings as she crouched low beside the long, narrow, wooden box that contained her shadow ore spears.

This was the sky raiders' third flyover in an hour and she wondered what they were doing.

They couldn't know about her shadow ore—all her weapons were in boxes full of water—so their reason for circling back over and over again was for some other reason.

It was nearly a day since Garek had dropped them off here, and the first time she'd caught sight of the ship earlier today, she'd thought it was him returning. But then she saw it was a small fighter craft, and there could be no doubt now that it was not him.

The Iron Guard stood still, clustered together in small groups as they looked upward.

The biggest group was in the training yard, where moments before they'd been flinging practice spears at each other and dodging and weaving, deflecting the spears by calling their Change.

She'd seen this amazing display once before, when Garek and

Kima had returned to camp with a levik, and spirits had been high. Now they did it with focused, serious intent.

Although it appeared to be a frenetic, chaotic attack, no one was hit, each person dipping and gliding out of the way with a smooth, graceful economy of movement that was a pleasure to watch.

Now, though, their weapons lay on the ground, and all that deadly focus was on the sky.

Taya's fingers gripped the lid of the box, ready to throw it off and grab her spears the moment the sky raiders looked like they were on more than just a reconnaissance mission.

She sank lower on her haunches in relief as it passed overhead again, the scream of the engines deafening, and if she hadn't looked back to see the direction it was taking through the mountains, she would have missed the moment it banked, curved downward, and flew low over the camp, strafing the guards in the training ring with a flash of white lightning.

She didn't have time to wonder why, and what they had to gain, she flipped the lid off, and grabbed two spears out of the water.

She didn't run toward the sky craft, either, it was already on its upward trajectory. Instead, she got up just enough speed and momentum to throw the first spear, and concentrated on aiming it at the back engines.

It must have had some indication that the spear was coming, perhaps whatever new system they were using to track shadow ore sent them a warning, because they tilted to one side.

She changed the spear's course, felt the strain of aiming it as she pushed it higher and further than she had ever pushed shadow ore before. She had to dig deep, but she managed to make contact with the back of the ship.

It was nothing more than a glancing blow.

The engine cut off as her spear fell to the ground, and the whole craft went into free fall for ten meters or more before it coughed back to life and the ship sped away, slightly favoring one side.

The whine of the engine faded into the distance, and then there was silence.

She could feel the headache already banging against her frontal lobe, and she turned and walked back to the box, dropped the second spear into the water and then wobbled slightly as she turned again to face the training arena.

It was a chaotic mix of fallen bodies and guards crouching down beside the injured or lifting friends between them, carrying them toward the tents.

Her spear was out there somewhere, and she needed to get it back. She couldn't afford to lose any of her weapons.

She started walking, trying automatically to reach for it by calling her Change, and winced with pain as the effort intensified the drumming in her head.

The ground seemed to rush up at her, and she put out her hands just in time to break her fall, and then even that was too much energy and she fell sideways onto the ground.

She rolled onto her back, and as she blinked up at the late afternoon sky, she saw with horror that the sky craft was coming back.

She struggled to sit up, collapsed back down again, and then lost consciousness.

AS HE CAME in to land, all Garek could see were the bodies.

He didn't power down, he simply burst out of the back of the sky craft, pushing through the eighty-strong unit of guards he'd brought from Garamundo as they began gathering the equipment and supplies that had been included in the run.

They all came up short at the sight of a line of armed guards at the foot of the ramp.

Everyone was equally surprised, he could see in the way the Gara guards froze and the Iron Guard hesitated and then relaxed, lowering their swords and arrows.

"There was a sky raider attack." Kima was in the front line of guards, and the look she sent him was off, a quick flick of nerves.

He felt a frisson of fear run down his arms. "Taya?"

"Burnt out." Hanson was suddenly in front of him. "Just burnt out, Garek." Her voice was calm.

He blew out a breath, tried to slow his frenetic heart as he followed her through the guards who were stepping forward to help carry the supplies.

Taya was being carried to her tent, and Garek took her from the two guards holding her between them and set her on her pallet.

His hands shook but her breathing was strong and even, her color good, and after watching her for a long moment, he ducked out of the tent to join Kima and Hanson.

"It just happened?"

Kima nodded. "They kept circling, three or four times, and then suddenly they came down and shot the guards while they were training. There are twenty down, but they're all breathing."

"Taya tried to get them with shadow ore?" Of course she did.

"She threw a spear at them. I think she must have at least got close or touched the ship with it because the engine stalled and when they flew away, they were listing to one side."

"Just one spear?" He wondered how high and far she had pushed it to burn out.

"We're looking for it, but it landed far up the valley." Hanson motioned up the hill, and Garek could see a team of four walking in a line, searching for it.

"What do you think this means?" Kima worried her lip.

"Taya didn't pull out the spear until they attacked?"

Hanson shook her head. "She was crouching beside the box, but she didn't take it out until after they shot their white lightning."

She shivered, and Garek realized this was probably the first time the general had seen the white lightning and its effects.

"Then they were doing it to hurt us."

"Why, though?" Hanson looked down the valley to where they

knew the three armies would emerge once they made their way through the mountains. "They couldn't know Taya was here, and they shot randomly. Was it just for fun? Some strange amusement?"

Garek shook his head. "I've observed them up close when I was hiding in their mothership, and they did not seem to me to be cruel for its own sake. Besides, they've never done anything before for no logical reason."

"Then we have to look at who benefits." Kima's eyes narrowed as she, too, looked down the valley.

Garek nodded. "Habred and his three armies."

He wondered what the deal was that Habred had struck with the sky raiders for them to interfere in this way.

"Perhaps they were trying to capture us, take us off to Shadow?" Hanson asked.

It was a seductive option, because it would be more in line with what they knew of the sky raiders' motivations, but . . .

"Were they in a small fighter, or a people-carrier like mine?"

"Fighter." Kima's eyes widened. "They couldn't have been trying to grab us, they had nowhere to put us."

Garek gave a nod. "I think they only have one people-carrier left. We have one, Taya destroyed another, and I think they only ever had three."

"Then yes, they were trying to harm us. But no one was killed."

"That might have been a mistake on their part. From what Taya learned in Luf, they've been playing with the strength of their weapon, and they perfected it to knock us down but keep us alive. All they need to do to kill us is turn up the strength again." And then, the war would be over.

"And if they meant to kill with this strike, and somehow realize they haven't done that, they'll turn it up, you're saying?" Hanson scowled. "How can we fight against something like that?"

"We can't." Garek accepted it, it was the truth.

"We are going to lose this war, and lose West Lathor." Hanson's face was a mask of frustration.

"There must be a way." Kima's stricken gaze was on her general's face.

"First, we need to check on the Dartalian guards barring the way out of Dartalia into Favre." Garek crouched and glanced in at Taya, but she was still asleep.

"You think they might have been attacked, too?" Kima stiffened. "Of course, if this is to benefit the three armies, the biggest boon they could get is having the way through Dartalia cleared for them again. It would be quicker for them to turn around and go back through Dartalia than make their way through the mountains." She looked in the direction of the training area. "Bringing us down was probably a secondary consideration."

Hanson moved, agitated and restless. "If that's what's happened, this camp is useless. We need to go to Dartalia, and if the Dartalian guards are down, help them hold the line."

Garek nodded. "We'll load the supplies back onboard, and I'll take a group of Iron Guard and some of the Gara guards I brought today."

"What will the Dartalian liege think of our presuming like this?" Hanson asked. "It's more for our benefit than it is for hers."

"We'll ask her." Garek crouched, and looked into Taya's tent.

"What can we do to counter this new threat?" Kima was staring across the field where her colleagues were being tended to.

Garek tipped his head up and looked at Shadow. "Maybe there's a way."

It was time to find the new sky raiders, and talk.

TWENTY

BODIES LAY EVERYWHERE.

There didn't seem to be a single Dartalian guard left standing.

Hanson looked at the carnage with a grim line to her mouth, and Garek thought she was probably thinking about the attack on her own camp, and what would have happened if Taya hadn't been there.

She straightened and started calling orders, and the Iron Guard and the Garamundo guards they'd brought with them went to work, carefully lifting the fallen and taking them to their tents.

Everything was orderly and a few of the fires were still smolder-ing, which only made the still bodies of the guards who'd set it up all the more disturbing.

This had happened maybe four or so hours ago.

He tapped Hanson on the shoulder as two guards carried Dix past her. "That's Dix, Susa's general. I'll take her with me."

Hanson nodded, and waved the guards toward the sky craft. "You're going to get Aidan before you go to Susa?"

He nodded. There was no question about that. The lieges would need to be personally involved in this situation.

"Hold the Corridor, General. And we'll be back as soon as we can."

She nodded, and Garek saw the banked rage in her eyes.

No matter who came at them now, they would be met with no mercy.

He jogged back to the sky craft, made sure Dix was comfortable on a pallet in the pilot's cabin, and that Taya was still breathing evenly.

He was halfway to Juli when Dix came awake with an explosive cry.

"You're safe," he told her, keeping his voice matter-of-fact.

She stared at him, eyes wide, and then toppled back onto her mattress.

"Your people are safe."

He had guessed that would bother her the most, and she was quiet for a little while after that.

Eventually, she struggled back up to a seated position. "Why am I in your sky craft?"

He told her, and her gaze went to Taya, still deeply asleep.

"You only lost twenty because of her. We lost everyone." She looked back at him. "And you say she damaged the craft?"

"That's what General Hanson believes. She said it was tilted to one side as it flew away, and the engine was making a strange sound."

Dix drew her knees to her chest, and hugged them to her. "So where are we going now?"

"To fetch Aidan and then fly to Susa."

Dix grunted in satisfaction and lay back down again.

When Garek glanced at her a little while later, she was fast asleep.

Juli came into sight. The last glow of Star's light rimmed the horizon with a thin line of gold and turned the night sky a dark indigo blue. Lanterns had been lit, and light fractured and danced off the fine sprays of mist thrown up by Corinnda's Hair as the water tumbled and fell on either side of the city.

He landed on the wall, and stayed where he was, waiting for Aidan to come to him.

It only took minutes before the liege was climbing the ladder, Vent right behind him.

"Trouble?" Aidan looked at Taya and then Dix, his features hardening.

"Trouble," Garek agreed.

TAYA AWOKE IN AN INSTANT. Her hand lay on the cold floor of a sky craft, and for a stark, terror-filled moment she was thrown back to the day she was first captured.

She went still, playing dead, but then the sound of soft conversation made her aware of Garek's voice, and she heard the boom and hiss of water falling, and she went weak with relief.

She was safe.

She opened her eyes and saw she was lying on a pallet in the pilot's cabin, but she could see through the door to the back of the sky craft. Garek, Vent and Aidan spoke with one another, their voices low, and beyond them, a team of guards stood watch, eyes on the sky.

A sound to her right had Taya turning, and she looked into the eyes of a woman who stared at her with interest.

"I'm Dix, the guard master of Valian," the woman said. "And you are Taya, the one who calls the shadow ore."

Taya nodded, and pushed herself up. "You were guarding the way out of Dartalia."

"I was." Dix's face was grim. "Until the sky raiders took down every one of us."

Taya drew in a sharp breath. "Before they got us, or after?"

"Before, I think." Her gaze was on the small group in the back, and Garek must have heard them because he turned.

Taya lifted her gaze to his, and for a beat he was all she saw, and all she cared about.

Then Aidan put a hand on Garek's shoulder, and he reluctantly turned, said something curt, and then strode toward her.

She held out her hand to him, and he pulled her into his arms for a quick, fierce hug.

"All good?"

"All good." Her voice cracked a little, and he released her, returning with water pouches for her and Dix.

"What's the delay?" Dix asked.

Aidan flicked a look at her. "We are arguing about who is going to come."

Dix frowned. "Why is that such an issue?"

"Because we aren't just going to see Susa," Garek said, his voice low. "We're going to find some sky raider allies."

TWENTY-ONE

TAYA HAD ONLY BEEN to Valian once, and it had been late at night that time, too.

The low, sprawling palace seemed to flow over and down the hill on which it was built and was lit with colored lights that lent it a magical air.

They set down on a flat area beside one of the big entrances, and while the guards that came out to them looked serious, they didn't look afraid.

They were used to Garek coming and going already, it seemed.

Dix climbed out of the craft first, dropping to the ground before she got to the bottom of the ladder. She strode forward, calling orders as she went.

The guards stared at her for a moment in surprise and disbelief, and then half of them scattered to do her bidding.

Taya followed Garek as he swung down, and Aidan crowded behind her.

Eventually, Vent had lost. He'd been the one to stay behind.

Dix waited for them impatiently at the big double doors into the palace, and flicked her fingers at the two guards who stood behind her. "They'll take you to a chamber to wait. I'll track down Susa, and we'll meet you there."

She strode off and disappeared around a corner. Taya heard her call out to someone, the sound was muffled, the tone clear.

Dix was on the warpath.

The room they were led to was massive, a multi-level room of stairs and sunken areas with deep couches and low tables.

The windows looked out down the hill to the city of Valian below, and Taya walked over to see the view.

They were offered food and drink and then left to themselves, although Taya guessed the guards were just outside.

It was only because she moved along the bank of windows, to the far end of the room, that she discovered they weren't alone.

An old man sat in a deep armchair, and when her surprised gaze met his, he gave her an impish smile, acknowledging his rudeness at not announcing himself, but not regretting it.

She guessed that the only reason for keeping quiet was because he wanted to hear some unguarded talk.

"I'm Taya of Pan Nuk." She pitched her voice so that Aidan and Garek would hear her, but kept her tone even and polite. She gave a respectful half bow.

"Danalian Varn." He rose from the seat, and despite his age, he seemed to have no difficulty doing so.

"I'm sorry we didn't greet you, we weren't aware there was someone else in the room."

He smiled at her subtle rebuke and dipped his head.

Garek had moved to stand just behind her, and Aidan took up position at her other shoulder.

"Ah, Aidan." Danalian Varn's eyes sparked with humor and interest. "It has been a long time since I last saw you."

Aidan blinked. "Councilor Varn. Yes. Since my father last attended a council meeting, which would have been . . ."

"Four years ago." Varn watched him with sharp black eyes. "I hear congratulations are in order."

Aidan stepped to the side, and bowed. "Yes. I have written to the council to tell you I've replaced my father. He is ill and can no longer lead."

There was a long moment when the two men stared directly at each other and said nothing.

Valtor's long descent into confusion and bitterness lay between them. But while some of that was Valtor's reaction to his wife's death, Taya now knew there was reason to suspect that Dartan, his advisor, had helped lead the West Lathorian liege into the pit of darkness and despair.

She felt a little less angry with her former liege, knowing that.

"Has the way the council works changed since last I attended?" Aidan asked suddenly, his voice a little deeper. "I have gone through my father's papers and I cannot see any notification from you or any other councilor authorizing an attack on my state."

Varn looked away and down, and Taya realized his cheeks had taken on a ruddy hue.

"No. The rules haven't changed. That's why I'm here." He lifted his head again. "Harven, Kadmine and Favre have not been given leave to take action against you. You know how we work. Your father's . . . illness was well known, but you and your sister are both considered competent replacements, and all avenues are explored before military action is approved. It's what's kept the coalition of the states of the Illy strong all these years."

"And yet, three armies are currently marching toward my people."

"Susa has made the same claim, has accused them of violating her own borders to get to you?" He made it a question, and Aidan nodded.

"I saw them with my own eyes."

"And I." Garek spoke for the first time.

She saw Varn start, as if he'd forgotten she and Garek were there, and his gaze slid over her and up to Garek.

"And you are?"

"Garek of Pan Nuk."

Taya saw he was studying the councilor with interest.

"Which state do you represent on the Council?"

"Kadmine."

Taya drew in a sharp breath. "Then how can you not know what Kadmine is doing?"

"Because they chose not to tell him." Aidan was watching Varn with almost pitying eyes. "They're going to try to take West Lathor, and then appeal to the council to authorize it retroactively. They might have gone the legal route, and put their plans forward for debate, but I suspect that would have taken too long for them."

"And what is the rush?" For the first time, Varn looked his age.

"I don't know." Aidan glanced at her and Garek, inviting their input.

"The sky raiders' ships won't last forever," Garek said, with a shrug. "Maybe the armies are moving while they can count on their help."

"It's true the ships are rusting, but that also means they only have so long to collect shadow ore." Taya slid her hands into her pockets. "Why would they waste precious time helping Habred?"

"Excellent question." Susa stood just inside the door, Dix and Zek at her side.

"Because," Garek's hand slid across Taya's back and curved a hand around her shoulder, "Habred has probably agreed to give them Taya."

"And with Taya, they can go back to Shadow and find all the easily available ore." Zek gave a nod.

It occurred to her that even before Garek told Dix what she could do, Zek would have told his liege everything about her. Her ability to call shadow ore had never been a secret here. Zek had been part of the camp on Shadow, had helped in their escape.

He knew exactly what she could do. And there was no chance he would not have given a full account of what had happened on Shadow and on the Endless Escarpment to Susa and Dix.

"How do they know there *is* easily available ore?" Dix asked.

Zek paused, looked over at her. Opened his mouth, and then hesitated.

"Luci," he said at last.

Taya drew in a breath. "Yes. When Min and I found the cave with the shadow ore, we didn't keep it a secret among ourselves, and the Cassinyans would have told the story in Luf. Why wouldn't they? They thought they were among friends, not traitors. Habred could easily have heard about it. Passed the information on to the sky raiders."

A cold drop of fear ran down her spine. She really was being hunted.

Then she remembered the attack on her and Ness. "But they already have something that can pinpoint the ore more accurately than just the general warning Garek gets over the Dartalian Range. Why would they need me?"

"There must be some drawbacks to the system. Perhaps there is something on Shadow that makes it unreliable." Aidan shrugged. "The fact is, they know there is a place full of shadow ore, and they can't find it, but know you can. Habred has tried to grab you, and so has Dartan, and both those men were working with the sky raiders. Also, in these last attacks, they weren't trying to kill, even though they can. Perhaps they can't risk killing indiscriminately in case they kill you by mistake. I think Garek is right. They're looking for you."

"Whatever the reason, they put the whole of my border guard on the ground." Susa's voice trembled a little with rage.

"I wonder why they did it when the armies weren't right there to take advantage of it?" Dix wondered. "We were struck down, but you arrived four, five hours later, and there was no sign of the three armies."

"They wouldn't want to hit you in view of any loyal Illians," Taya said. "That would be treachery on a high scale. I don't believe most of the people of Harven, Kadmine and Favre would support taking

West Lathor by doing a deal with sky raiders, and I think Habred and the other two lieges know that."

"There could be another, more mundane reason." Garek gave a wry grin. "They simply don't understand how long it takes to get from one place to another without a sky craft. They may have known to hit Dix's troops before any Illians could see them do it, but perhaps they misjudged how long it would take the armies to get there."

Dix gave a strangled laugh. "I can understand how they could make that mistake. I'm becoming very used to sky craft travel myself. But there is a third option." She waved a hand at Varn. "The Kadmine and Favre lieutenants didn't know West Lathor had a sky craft until we set down in front of them. And they were clearly surprised to learn Dartalia hadn't given them permission to cross into our land. So perhaps, if Harven is the only one of the three in league with the sky raiders, they were more than a little resistant to going back after Susa expressly told them she didn't give her permission. I think they might have developed a serious distrust in their partner."

"You think the delay is because of internal squabbles?" Aidan sounded satisfied with that explanation. "Favre and Kadmine balking at destroying their relationship with Dartalia, and starting to get suspicious of Harven?"

"Or a combination of all three things," Taya suggested.

Varn had stood opened-mouthed since asking his question. Now his head lifted with a jerk. "This is the first I've heard of a deal with the sky raiders. The first I've heard of any of this. I cannot believe Kadmine has knowingly gone into a deal with the enemies of the whole of Barit, but if they have been duped into it, I trust they are thinking twice about their involvement."

"And now, we have to make a decision." Garek looked around the room. "We can't fight the sky raiders if they intend to rain white lightning down on us. I've brought a sky craft down a few times, and Taya has, as well, but there are only two of us. It's not enough."

"What else can we do?" Susa's gaze went back to Dix, and Taya knew she was imagining her friend lying unconscious on the ground.

"We do a deal of our own."

TWENTY-TWO

GAREK DID NOT like the nothing that was the space between Barit and Shadow.

He could feel the air getting thinner and thinner as he piloted the sky craft higher, angling toward Shadow as a point of reference, and then they seemed to break free of the last wisps of air and it was as if a part of him went numb.

He glanced across at Taya, standing beside his chair with legs braced for balance, looking out the window with intense focus.

They ran the risk of meeting the wrong sky raiders up here, and even if they met the right kind, Garek wasn't sure of their welcome.

But if they didn't get help, he was sure they were lost, anyway.

Susa agreed with him, and had insisted on coming along. He could see the specter of her people lying strewn around their camp haunted her.

Now she stood beside Aidan, eyes on the stars ahead of them, and the massive curve of Shadow up ahead.

There were two other passengers on this trip; Dix, who had refused to leave her liege unprotected, and Dalanial Varn, from the Illian Council.

Varn stood without speaking, his gaze far into the distance. Garek guessed he was in his seventies, but he was fit and nimble in his movements.

Susa seemed to trust him, even though he must have once been deeply involved in Kadmine's court. Councilors had to represent all Illians. While each councilor was voted on by the people of their state, the understanding was that they ceased to be partisan when they took their place.

Garek hoped that was true.

"What happens if we encounter the group of sky raiders who are trying to harm us?" Varn asked.

There was silence.

Varn turned his head, eyebrows raised.

"We run," Garek said eventually.

Varn blew out a breath, wheezing out a laugh as he did so, and looked even more enthusiastic than he had before.

He'd asked many questions since they'd made the decision to find the other sky raiders.

How they'd come by the sky craft. What they had done on Shadow. What the sky raiders looked like.

He'd listened, rapt, as various members of the group told him what they knew.

Soon, though, he'd see for himself.

Garek curved away to the left, heading around the back of Shadow. If he'd understood the sky raider correctly before he died, the newcomers where hiding there somewhere.

Anything could have changed in the few days since the explosion, but it was a place to start.

What he didn't expect as Barit disappeared from view, and they rounded Shadow, was that a small, fast craft would race right up to their window.

Everyone went still as they stared back at the reflective black circle that sat at the front of the tiny craft, like some kind of blind eye.

The craft turned, moving away, then stopped, turned back, and then faced forward and began moving again.

It wanted them to follow.

"We might as well," Aidan said, quietly. "No matter who they are, they know we're here, and we have nothing to lose."

Because it was true, Garek followed, allowing enough room between his sky craft and the small vessel for him to maneuver away if he needed to.

They may have nothing to lose, but he wasn't prepared to simply roll over if they were attacked.

There was silence in the cabin as they slid through the black nothingness, and eventually something seemed to appear out of the darkness, a massive, gargantuan thing that made even his people-carrier look tiny.

"Can you tell if this is the mothership of the first lot?" Susa asked.

He shook his head. "This is about twice the size of that one."

It made sense, because the ship that had been destroyed the other day had been huge as well. It would take something this big to house it.

"So, this is a bigger, better equipped force?" Dix asked.

"Maybe because this second group is bigger and better equipped, the first lot needed a new way to fight them, and they went out looking for shadow ore." Taya had left his side and she was leaning against the window, looking up at the massive mothership with a tense expression.

He hadn't wanted her to come. Not just because he always wanted her where it was safe, although there was nowhere that was really safe in West Lathor or Dartalia now, but because she could call shadow ore.

The sky raiders had been actively trying to capture her. Now she was going to them.

Admittedly, this was a different group, but Garek had a feeling that they would grasp the value of what she could do as quickly as the first group had done.

And yet, when she had looked at him with a hot, implacable expression, and held his gaze, he had given way.

Because she had a say, too, and she thought she could help in this negotiation.

As she pointed out, they needed every advantage they could get. As she said it, she'd slid two thin needles of shadow ore into a tiny vial of water, corked it and put it in her pocket. The rest of her weapons were in boxes full of water, stacked in the storage area at the back of the sky craft.

They'd considered leaving them in Susa's palace, but in the end, Taya couldn't part with them.

"Let's hope the enemy of our enemy is our friend," Aidan said as the mothership dominated the window, big enough to block everything else out.

"How will we speak with them?" Dix asked. "They can't breathe our air, and we can't breathe theirs."

"I don't know." Garek had encountered walls of light, and other wonders when he'd snuck into the mothership of the other group of sky raiders. He assumed he would see similar things here.

"They may come aboard in their suits," Aidan suggested.

"I look forward to seeing these monsters who have caused us so much suffering with my own eyes." Dalanial Varn sank down on the floor cross-legged to get a better view through the window.

The mothership was now above them, and there was something stifling about flying beneath it and being enveloped in its dark shadow.

Ahead, jutting out from the base of the ship, was a wide, thin entrance, with an extended lower lip, lit with green.

It was the same as the mothership he'd flown into before, but in an order of at least twice the size.

He flew the sky craft through the glow, slowing until they were more drifting forward than flying.

As soon as they were through the curtain of light, a second curtain confronted them. This was the same as last time, too.

And like before, he was suddenly hit with the sensation of air all around them again, although not the air he was used to.

He flexed the muscles of his calling, swirling the air around the ship to test it, and buffeting the small craft that had led them in. It stopped, and then landed, and Garek settled the sky craft down, too.

"We're not going all the way through?" Aidan asked.

"Last time they thought we were one of their own, and paid no attention to us. This time, they know we're coming. I'm happier staying out here."

Susa stared at him. "You flew right into the mothership, without knowing what was on the other side of the light wall?"

Garek shrugged. "It was the only way to rescue Taya."

Taya turned as he said it, and her eyes glittered with moisture. Her face was bathed in green, and he stood up and walked to her, sliding an arm around her and pulling her to him as they both looked out of the window.

They had had no time together for days, no privacy, no rest.

If they were able to win, to get through this victorious, he would take her away somewhere and just be, while they considered what came next.

He sensed something, a change in the air, and the idea he'd had last time, that the walls of light somehow trapped the air between them, and held back the nothingness of the space beyond, solidified.

"Will you come out of the ship to talk?" The hiss of sound came from the arm of his pilot's chair.

"Can we breathe?" Aidan asked.

Garek nodded. "They've matched the air outside to the air in this sky craft."

"Look." Taya lifted a hand. "They're standing just on the other side of the light wall."

He glanced through the window, saw a line of about five figures just discernible through the green glow.

He walked to the chair, and lowered the ramp. "Time to talk."

TWENTY-THREE

SHE'D KNOWN Garek had braved many things for her, but stepping into the wash of green in the strange nowhere land between the vast black of space and the inside of the ship, she realized the full extent of the courage it had taken.

He kept himself a little apart from her, and she understood he wanted his hands free, and room to move if this was a trap, or if it didn't go the way they hoped.

They walked out in a loosely-formed group and then spread out to match the line of sky raiders on the other side of the light wall.

When they came to a stop, she put her hand in her pocket and curled her fingers around the vial with its two thin needles of ore.

"We're amazed to see you here." The sky raider who spoke stood in the center of the line.

"Why amazed?" Garek asked.

"Because you have no training in flying that ship."

Garek knew he used his Change more than he realized when he flew the sky craft. He shrugged. "The sky raider who was killed in the ambush said you wanted to talk, and that we could find you here."

"Yes, he did." The hiss was thoughtful. "Why did you take up the invitation?"

"Because we want to get rid of you." Aidan was blunt. "The group that has been here for a year has devastated our lands and killed and captured our people. We want you gone."

There was a stunned silence for a moment.

"And why would you come to us, if you want us gone?"

"Because we guess, after they blew up your ship, that you are not friends with the first group, and so far, we have no fight with you." Aidan crossed his arms over his chest. "Will we have a fight with you?"

There was another silence, and Taya had the sense there was some communication going on they couldn't hear.

"We have no wish to fight. We would like information. And we are as eager as you to bring the *sevn* to heel."

"Then bring them to heel," Garek said.

There was a laugh, like the choke, choke, choke of a slither. "We would, except it seems they have a new weapon."

"Shadow ore," Garek agreed.

"The weapon they intend to bring home with them, to fight you." Taya spoke for the first time, and she immediately felt the shift of focus onto her.

"What do you know of it?" There was an edge to the voice.

"I was one of their captives, working the mine on Shadow." Taya made herself remain tall and not fidget under that cold, yellow gaze.

"This other one," the leader waved a hand at Garek, "said before there was a place on . . . Shadow . . ."

Their translator had difficulty with the Illian word.

"But there is no one there, now. They concentrate on your planet. Why is that?"

"They can't mine the shadow ore themselves. They tried in the beginning, but your systems can't be near it." Taya recalled the drunken, half-finished tunnels in the mine originally made by the sky raiders' diggers.

"But they aren't taking more captives to continue mining. We can only listen to them when they communicate from ship to ship, we don't have our ears in their mothership. They seem to be looking for someone. Do you know who and why that is?"

Everyone was quiet, and Taya realized they were very carefully not looking at her.

"What if we do?" Garek asked. "What is the information worth to you?"

"What do you want?" The response was candid.

"We want your friends dead or gone. And we want you to leave afterward, never to return." Garek spread his hands in a 'that's all' gesture.

"As we told you before, we find ourselves at a disadvantage in this place. Our friends, as you call them, have something dangerous to us that we don't understand or have ourselves. And they used it to destroy our exploration unit."

"They almost destroyed themselves when they did it. The fighter was damaged as it flew away." Aidan spoke up.

"And the one that attacked the camp yesterday was damaged, too," Taya said. "How many can they have left?"

"At least one, maybe two. And one people-carrier." Garek waved at his own craft. "And they are all at least as rusted as this one. They won't last much longer."

"Then why not just wait for their equipment to get so damaged, they're forced to leave, or it fails on them, and they die on your planet?" The hiss was soft.

That's what *their* plan was, Taya understood with sudden shock. They were panicked by the destruction of their ship, afraid to engage. They'd decided to block the way home and wait their enemies out.

"What happens if they get what they want and slip by you?" she asked quietly. "Can you risk them getting back home armed with shadow ore?"

One of them made a noise, an explosive sound of frustration.

They must have realized by now how corrosive the atmosphere

on Barit and Shadow was to the sky craft. It was only a matter of months before things fell to pieces. But they had to know the risks of holding back and waiting. Every new piece of shadow ore gained was one that could be used against them. Especially if they weren't able to stop their enemy from getting home.

And the other group—that was why they had gotten further into bed with Habred. They wanted her found, so she could help them get as much shadow ore as they could in as short a time as possible. The trip here must be long, and it had been expensive for them. They had lost people and ships. They'd want as much ore in their hold as they could carry before they returned home to fight their enemy.

"We can't wait them out because in order to find the person they're looking for, they've agreed to assist people who are at war with us." Aidan's tone was overly patient.

Susa put a soothing hand on his arm. "With the sky raiders' help, our lands will be taken from us. We no longer have the luxury of time."

"And why should that matter to us?" The sky raider shifted back a little.

"Because if they capture us, then the person they are looking for will be found. And that is a problem for you. This person will be forced to get them more shadow ore. And that cannot be in your interests." Garek kept his voice calm, but Taya could see his fists were clenched.

"How can this one person help them, out of everyone on your planet?"

"There are plenty who could help them." Taya kept her voice absolutely steady. "They only know of one, though. They don't understand there are thousands like the one they seek. And it may be they are looking for her especially because some of those rescued from the mine would have shared stories about a place she found full of shadow ore. And they would want her to take them to it."

"So it will be easier for them to find what they are looking for than they realize?"

Taya nodded. "And more dangerous to them, too. They fear the person they're looking for as much as they want her, because she can take down their ships. They have more to fear than they realize, because she is not the only one."

She sensed the tension from those around her as she spun her lies. Garek alone was relaxed. His hand brushed hers, as if accidentally.

"These people of yours can destroy our ships?" There was that thoughtful tone again. "What's different about them?"

"They control shadow ore. They can make it go where they want it to go. Your friends think their exposure to harm is smaller because they believe there is only one." She let herself give a chuckle. "But there are many."

"If everything you say is true, then yes, it is in our interests to stop the *sevn* before they find someone who controls shadow ore. But it doesn't help to know what we must do, when we don't have the weapons to fight them with."

"What if we can give you some?" Taya asked.

A long, long silence this time. They were definitely talking to each other by some silent means.

"You can give us ore? But if what you say is true, we have no way to work with it without it affecting us."

"One moment." Garek turned and walked back up the ramp, and returned with the shadow ore containment box on its long stick that they'd found after the sky raider attack. He shoved it through the wall of light, and it was snatched from his hand.

"What is this?" There was a great deal of curiosity in the question.

"We took it from a sky raider who attacked us." Garek lifted a shoulder. "His pilot got away. He didn't."

The sky raiders shifted uncomfortably. It was almost as if they couldn't work out how they felt. Glad one of their enemy was dead, or disturbed and angry because some other race of beings had killed one of their own.

"We have never attacked first," Taya said. "We've rescued ourselves, defended ourselves and our friends. If your people had left us alone, they would not have lost a single life."

The sky raiders looked at each other, as if surprised she had picked up on their emotional conflict. The leader shook his head and lifted the box.

"What does it do?"

"It's a box for shadow ore. While the ore is in there, it won't harm your systems."

All five of them gathered round and studied it, and then a sixth sky raider ran up, was handed the box, and then ran away.

"Why did you give it to us?"

Garek held out open hands. "We don't need it. We have other ways to protect our systems."

"What systems?" The leader scoffed.

Garek waved at the sky craft. Gave a slow smile. "We have found our own solution."

"Is it quicker to develop than us taking that box apart and recreating more like it?" For the first time, one of the others spoke. "It will take days at least for us to replicate it."

"Yes. Much quicker." Garek looked them over. "What is that solution worth to you?"

"Isn't anything that speeds up our ability to fight our friends a good thing?" The hiss was a challenge now.

Garek conceded the point with a grin. "Are you going to fight them?"

"If you give us a way to protect our systems and have access to the ore." There was a nod.

The one thing they needed the sky raiders to do was to destroy or incapacitate the other mothership. Taya worried her lip. Without their home base, would the smaller ships even continue their fight? They may even turn themselves in to their fellow sky raiders.

She thought how it could be done. "You would have to find a way to encase the ore in the protective layer we have, but even if you can't make it explode and fragment the way they have managed to do, even if you just shot raw chucks of ore at their mothership, it would damage it."

"Damaging it without destroying it is not a bad outcome." There was interest in the words.

"All right. Let's go then. Can you bring us some boxes with lids?" Taya indicated the size of the boxes with her hands.

"Where are we going?" An arrogant tilt of the head.

"To Shadow. To get you your ore."

The tilt's angle increased.

"You are the person they are looking for, aren't you?"

Taya smiled. "I told you, there isn't just one."

"But they think there is. And they have described you in the communications. The golden hair."

"There are a lot of people with golden hair." Taya nodded to Dix, who had said nothing at all through the whole conversation.

"They can only know you because they have seen you, and you are the one who worked their mine on Shadow." He didn't want to drop it.

Taya shrugged. "Whatever they think, I'm far from unique. There is a whole battalion of people like me, better trained than me by far."

Four sky raiders arrived with boxes, and they pushed them through the light wall.

It was cold in here, Taya realized for the first time. She shivered. Released her grip on the vial and drew her hand out of her pocket. "Time to go."

"What is in your pocket?" The sky raider to one side, who'd been interested in taking the other mothership without destroying it, had locked her gaze on Taya's hand.

She contemplated her answer. "Protection."

There was a hiss from all five.

"I didn't need to use it, so it wasn't used." She lifted both arms. "You no doubt have weapons pointed at us." She looked upward, to the top of the ceiling where the wall of light started. "In any case, if I'd sent shadow ore through the wall, it might have broken whatever is making it work."

"Then you would have been suffocated by our air." They all seemed to relax.

"Maybe." She didn't look at Garek. "Maybe not."

Garek could hold the air together. Long enough for them to make it to the sky craft. Of that she was sure.

"Surely, there is no maybe about it." The woman again. Curious. Very curious. "Or perhaps you don't understand what would happen."

They thought the people of Barit were intellectually inferior. But being less advanced didn't mean being more stupid. It just meant the others had had a head start.

"I think I do understand." She shrugged. "It never came to that, so it doesn't matter."

She knew her lack of concern rattled them by the quality of the silence.

It was yet another chip at the self-confidence the sky raiders wore like a shield.

They were not the natural inhabitants of this place, and they were beginning to understand they were at a disadvantage.

She walked to the sky craft beside Garek, very satisfied.

TWENTY-FOUR

NO ONE SAID a word as they flew away from the mothership.

There was a suspicion amongst them all that they could be listened to, although Garek thought it unlikely.

No point taking the chance, though. And they could talk when they landed on Shadow.

Taya stood beside him, a hand resting lightly on his shoulder for balance.

She had sold a story he had grasped the ramifications of immediately. The more of her there were, the more dangerous it was for all sky raiders to remain.

He had a few ideas on how she would produce this battalion of shadow warriors, but no doubt she'd already thought it through.

"Go to the mine, then head in the direction of that hill where you and Aidan took down the tower," she said.

He angled into Shadow's atmosphere, felt the tug and relief of air around them again. Even the thin, strange air of Shadow was better than nothing.

The massive sky craft following alongside them lit up in front, the glow of heated air flaring.

Garek realized he'd been dispersing the heat automatically. It appeared the sky craft was designed to handle it, but he found the reflex difficult to rein in, even now he was aware of what he was doing.

He had to slow down to allow the other sky craft to keep pace, and then, when they were low enough, he took the lead, heading toward the camp, then over the hills to the mine.

He slowed down as they approached the hill with the tower he and Aidan had destroyed.

"See the hill with the cliff face on one side?" Taya gripped his shoulder a little harder. "That's where it is."

He maneuvered the ship in front of the hill and slowly lowered it down, but the warning bell suddenly sounded, just as he was about to set down at the foot of the cliff, and he swore and moved the sky craft back until it stopped.

"Well, that explains why they need you. Unless you know where it is and you're right on top of it, their way of finding it doesn't work on Shadow." Aidan ran a shaking hand through his hair.

"They must have a new, more accurate way to pick it up. They saw my knife from quite high up, but I think the problem for them on Shadow is that most of the ore is near or submerged in a protective layer." She mouthed the word 'water'. "My guess is they were able to pick up the seam in the mine, but it was too deep to get to easily, which is why they needed us. The easy-to-get stuff was invisible to them."

"And the ore on Barit is mostly like what's in the Dartalian Range. Tiny flecks spread over a huge area." Garek wanted to laugh at how the planet seemed to have protected itself from the sky raiders. Barit would not give them what they wanted.

He lowered the ramp, and they walked out of the back. Garek picked up a box in each arm, and Aidan did the same.

It would be at least a ten minute walk to the cliff face.

While they'd been talking, the larger ship had landed beside them, but no one emerged.

Afraid, he guessed. And why not?

They might not have a way to detect shadow ore, if it was truly unknown to them, but they had picked up enough information to know they were at risk if they got near it.

When it was clear the sky raiders weren't going to step out of their ship, they started toward the cave.

Everyone came along except Dalanial Varn. He looked at the rock-strewn way and chose instead to sit on the ramp and take in the wonder of being on Shadow.

"That was quite a story you told back there," Aidan said to Taya when they were far enough away from the two ships.

"You made sure they realize there is an ongoing danger to them if they decide to stay and take up where their friends leave off." Susa's tone was approving.

Taya nodded. "It can't hurt. I also had an idea that if we can convince the other lot we have lots of people like me, they're more likely to take what shadow ore they have and make a run for their home."

"How would we convince them of that?" Dix spoke for the first time since they'd entered the mothership.

"Get Garek's father to your camp in the Corridor, smelt some shadow ore, and dip the tip of every Iron Guard's arrow in it."

There was silence.

"How would that help?" Susa asked. "They will surely just think we've done exactly what you've just described. Dipped weapons in ore. A flying arrow of shadow ore would be dangerous to them, but not as deadly as Zek tells me your manipulation of the ore is."

Taya glanced over at Aidan, and he stared back. Then he looked at Garek, as if for advice.

Garek nodded. If they had allies, they had to trust them. Besides, if Hanson got her way, and she would, then the secret would no doubt slowly leak out.

"Taya wasn't stretching the truth that far. The Iron Guard *is* like her. Only they call iron, not shadow ore."

Dix, unlike her liege, did not look shocked. "I have long wondered."

There was the satisfaction of having a suspicion confirmed in her voice.

Susa had stopped dead. "I've heard of that, too. Heard it whispered about the Nordren. Never West Lathor."

"Except my mother was Nordren," Aidan reminded her.

"Yes." Susa said the word slowly. "And thinking back, the Iron Guard was hers, wasn't it?"

"My mother started the Guard," Aidan admitted. "But there will be changes in how it's run from now on."

"It is no longer being kept a secret?" Dix asked.

Aidan hesitated. Shook his head. "I would very much appreciate it if you would keep the secret. And I will offer the opportunity of any of your own Changed who call iron to be trained by General Hanson, if you wish."

It was an incredibly generous offer. And a clever one. Dartalia would not share a secret they had a stake in keeping.

"We don't have any iron called." Susa frowned.

"That you or even they, know of." Aidan waved at Taya. "Taya only discovered her calling because she was forced down a shadow ore mine. She's right in that there are probably more of her. And certainly enough iron called to create an entire battalion in West Lathor, and who knows how many in Nordra?"

Dix looked thoughtful. "Perhaps you will allow me to spend some time with General Hanson, and we can see how to find these iron called."

Aidan inclined his head, and Garek felt the mood as they reached the foot of the cliff was very congenial.

Taya went straight to a narrow crack in the wall of the cliff, and slipped through it.

He heard the rattle of falling stones, and set the boxes down to peer in. It was only just wide enough for him to fit through sideways.

The inside glowed.

He crouched down so he wasn't completely blocking the light behind him, and saw the phosphorous glow of what looked like moss gently illuminating the vast space.

"Move away from the crack and I'll send shadow ore out," Taya called from below him.

She had obviously had contact with moss in her scramble down to the lake's shore, and her arms and hands were glowing, too.

She looked like some magical creature, almost alien, until she grinned at him and blew him a kiss.

He stepped back, and large fist-sized rocks floated out and then were dropped. Most of them were gray stone thickly veined with ore, but some were almost entirely ore, as if they had fallen from a rich seam.

He and Dix began throwing them into the boxes, leaving a third of the space for the water that would need to be added.

When all four boxes were packed, he called to her to stop, and then squeezed through the opening and slid down the slope of pebbles to the gently lit rocks of the shore.

The smell was of damp and stone, and a green fecundity from the moss.

"The motherlode," he murmured, looking at the visible seam of shadow ore along the far wall of the cave.

Taya carefully traversed the rocks to stand beside him. "The motherlode," she agreed.

He pulled her close and kissed her, pulling her flush against him. His hands gripped the back of her jacket, and he had to hold himself in check, keeping it as light as he could.

"I know," she murmured to him, pulling back a little to nip along his jawline. "I know."

There was enough pent-up feeling in her words to make him chuckle, and she joined in.

"What's so funny?" Aidan slid down in a clatter of stones, and Garek shook his head and let his arms drop.

"Can you get the water out of this lake and into the boxes?" Taya asked Aidan.

The princeling looked from the lake to the thin sliver of light that was the entrance. "If the boxes are right outside."

"I can stand at the top," Susa called down, "and direct it as it comes out."

Garek lifted his gaze. So Susa had a water calling.

"Let's try it." Aidan sent a stream of water up from the lake and shot it through the crack.

"Wait," Dix called down after a minute.

They heard her grunt as she moved what must be an incredibly heavy box. "All right. Again."

Aidan followed the instructions from above until all four boxes were filled, and then Dix appeared in the crack and slid down, then waited for Susa to come, her arms out to catch her liege in case she fell.

They picked their way across the stones to join them at the water's edge.

"Amazing." Susa looked around. "How did you know this was here, Taya?"

Taya pointed to a low, gushing waterfall that seemed to be the source of the lake. "A friend and I were forced into the cave system by a Kardanx with a grudge against us, and we got swept away by the river and ended up in here."

"And the sky raiders never knew you'd been here?" Dix looked at her with surprise.

"We got out through the opening and walked for a whole day to get back to the mine. They didn't even bother to ask us where we'd come out."

Dix shook her head, trying to work out why the sky raiders wouldn't follow up on something like that.

"They think of us as dumb beasts of burden," Garek said. "At least, they did."

"Well, that's what we're about to be." Aidan started back up the steep incline. "We're going to have to think of how to carry those boxes back."

"Easy." Taya followed him. "Between you, Susa and myself, and maybe with some of Garek's help, we'll call our Change."

Aidan turned to look at her. "You lift the shadow ore, Susa and I lift the water?"

"And I help with a little air." Garek grinned. While the sky raiders hadn't come out of their ship, they *would* be watching. And they were about to see the reason why it was a mistake to underestimate the people of Barit.

TWENTY-FIVE

THEIR TRIP back to the ship must have made for an interesting sight.

With the lids securely clamped down, they had lifted the boxes between them, with only Dix, who called the earth Change and couldn't help, not participating.

It took a while to get used to cooperating with more than just one calling, but there was something satisfying in it, too.

The shared load made for easy work, although the distance from the cliff to the ship was far enough for them all to be feeling it by the time they set the boxes down.

Taya lifted one by herself, and set it on the ramp of their sky craft, beside Dalanial Varn.

Garek glanced at her, eyes amused.

"It's probably our last trip here," she murmured. "If I'm going to lose some ore on arrows for the Guard, I'll need to replace it."

Varn tapped the top of the box with a fist and took up position in front of it.

Taya gave him a smile of thanks for his guard services, and then joined the others beside the much bigger ship, waiting for either a ramp to come down or someone to make an appearance.

After a few minutes, a door opened, and a ramp extended to the ground in segmented pieces that seemed to grow out of each other and then clamp in place. These sky raiders had more sophisticated equipment than the other group, that was clear.

Two sky raiders in blue suits and helmets came down, and pointed little handheld machines at the three boxes.

"Our sensors pick up nothing," one of them said, and Taya recognized the voice of the sky raider who had been so interested in what she had to say on the mothership.

"The water masks it and protects your systems from it."

"How can we know this? Can you prove it?" She bent closer with her device.

Taya nodded. "Do you have a machine you don't mind being destroyed?"

The sky raider looked up in surprise.

"Yes." The silence that followed was strange, because Taya could see the sky raider talking to someone in her helmet.

Another suited sky raider emerged, carrying a small box, and ran down the ramp.

"Where should he put it?"

Taya waved the sky raider back a fair way before she was sure it was safe.

He set it down, and jogged back.

"And now?" The sky raider seemed very interested in what she would do next.

Taya opened the lid of one of the boxes.

"Aidan, when I lift out a rock, can you coat it in water?" They were both tired, she could feel just the edges of a headache looming, but the princeling nodded, and she lifted a small rock the size of her fist out. It was far easier than she thought it would be. After lifting the ore in the boxes, this was like picking up a feather.

Aidan covered it with water about two fingers deep all around as she hovered it over the box.

There was a shocked gasp from the sky raider.

She sent the rock about halfway between the ships and the box and then nodded to Aidan, and he called the water back.

It lifted off the rock and seemed to leap from it all the way back into the box, like a live creature.

Taya slowly moved the rock toward the machine, using a smooth, steady pace.

When it was about five meters away, the machine began to make a warning sound, and when the rock finally touched it, acrid smoke drifted toward them on the cool breeze, and what lights had been on the machine went off.

She brought the rock back halfway, waited for Aidan's water to coat it again, and then together they returned the rock and water to its box.

"Was that enough for you?" Taya had been concentrating on the rock, but she saw the sky raider had darkened the glass of her helmet, and she could no longer see her expression.

"What allows you to manipulate the water and the rock in that way?" There was a little too much avid interest in the voice.

"That information is not part of this arrangement. What do you wish to know about the ore?"

She could see the sky raider stiffen at her rebuff, but eventually her shoulders relaxed again, although Taya still couldn't see her face.

"How did you learn that water shields the ore?"

"I ran experiments." She remembered the fear of walking past the sky raider screens at the mine, holding a tiny piece of shadow ore wrapped in various things; wood, cloth, iron.

"And the *sevn* don't know about the water?"

"No, I don't think so."

The sky raider gave a nod, then looked at the box Taya had taken for herself. "That is ours, too."

"No." Taya shook her head. "It's mine. I've given you plenty.

Although I will warn you that the other group has a lot more. They took everything that we brought up from the mine, although that ore wasn't as rich as in the rock I've given you."

The sky raider hunched, as if she wanted to argue, but she had just seen what Taya could do, and they must have been excited enough by what they had been given not to push it.

"So, what are your plans now?" Garek had moved so quietly, Taya hadn't realized he was right beside her.

"We'll be able to make projectiles of water and ore, and shoot them at the mothership," the sky raider conceded. "And then, when that is done, we will hunt down the smaller craft."

"And then you'll go." Susa's voice was cold.

"And then, we'll go. This is not a hospitable place for us." The sky raider inclined her head and turned, walking up the ramp and leaving the two sky raiders who stepped out with her to gingerly lift a box between them.

The weight of it was clearly a surprise, because they dropped it and leapt away in fear as it tipped over.

Fortunately for them, the lid held.

And it wouldn't do any harm for the sky raiders to understand that they had floated boxes through the air that two sky raiders could barely pick up.

Taya walked up the ramp, lifting the box of ore by calling her Change and setting it down at the back. She knew the sky raiders eyes were on her as she did it, and it was therefore worth the full bloom of the headache that had been skulking around the edges of her mind up until now.

"Even if they do everything they say, we might still have to deal with the smaller craft—at least for a while." Aidan watched the sky raiders struggle with a box as the ramp lifted.

"Then that's what we'll do," Garek said.

Dix glanced at him, and Taya saw the same promise in her eyes she saw in Garek's. They wanted to end the sky raiders with their bare hands.

TWENTY-SIX

PAN NUK LAY, sleepy and golden, in the early morning Star's light.

It was a beautiful sight, but Garek could feel the tug of exhaustion on his eyelids as he turned the sky craft to land facing down the length of the village street.

He would have to catch at least an hour or two of sleep before he could fly again. The last time he'd lain his head down was for four or five hours in Valian before he'd flown everyone to Shadow. And he had called a lot of his Change in between.

He lowered the ramp and didn't know how long he sat, half-slumped in his chair, before Taya came to find him.

She put out a hand and he automatically took it, stumbling to his feet as she pulled him up, and took him a few short steps to the mattress he'd put in the pilot's chamber for her when she'd burnt out.

As he lay down, she pulled off his boots.

He wanted to say thank you, but he simply didn't have the energy.

When he woke, it was to the feel of a cool breeze coming into the sky craft from the still open ramp, and to the sound of conversation.

It looked like it was midday, or perhaps just before, which meant he'd slept at least five hours.

He felt a lot better for it.

He heard a shout of laughter, shook his head as he identified it as his father's.

Quardi lived his life loud.

The sound of footsteps on the ramp finally gave him the energy to pull himself up to sitting, and he wasn't surprised to see Kas was the first person to step into the pilot's chamber.

"I was coming to wake you." Kas crouched down, at eye level. "Taya says there are other sky raiders. That you went to bargain with them."

He nodded.

"Do you trust them?"

Garek shook his head. "I don't think they have any love for us, and I don't know if they have honor or believe in keeping their word, but they'll do what we want them to because their objective aligns with ours. If it didn't, they would have ignored us."

Kas blew out a breath. "That makes me feel better, actually. I trust self-serving motives far more than altruistic ones."

Garek agreed. "I heard my father. Has he agreed to come?"

"You couldn't have kept him away." Kas's lips twitched. "He and Dalanial Varn seem to have hit it off."

Garek made a face. "Well, I'm more or less awake now. We should go."

Kas looked at him, and Garek saw the mentor he remembered from his early days of coming into his Change, rather than his future brother-in-law, in his face.

"Taya is worried. She says you don't get enough sleep."

Or enough time alone with Taya, but Garek decided he wouldn't mention that to her brother. "I'm the only one who can fly the craft, and we're about to go to war." He shrugged. "It won't be long now, either way. If we're right, then the three armies are heading back through Dartalia toward the Corridor, and we won't just be fighting them off, but the sky raiders, too."

"I want to come."

Garek didn't know why he hadn't expected this, but he hadn't. "You have Luca and Pan Nuk to worry about."

"I know, but I still want to go. I want to see them defeated. Have a hand in their defeat." Kas blew out a breath. "Eli wants to come, and Pilar, too."

Garek rubbed his forehead. "I can't stop them, that's on Aidan, I suppose, and Dix. It's her camp, and she's the general of Dartalia."

"I can stop them, I'm town master, but I don't want to. And I want to come as well." Kas gave a short laugh, shook his head. "Luca has been through enough, so I'll be the responsible father and stay. But I'll let Eli and Pilar and whoever else wants to go, go."

Garek smothered a yawn and got to his feet.

Someone—most likely Taya—had put a mug of water and food beside his mattress, and he scooped them up and walked out to the back as he gulped the water down.

There was a small group gathered at the bottom of the ramp. Min and Luca were stuck to Taya's side, each with an arm around her, and Quardi was holding court from his wheelchair with the lieges of West Lathor and Dartalia.

Garek grinned at the sight.

"He can walk pretty well now," Kas said from beside him. "But it tires him after a while, so he keeps the chair handy."

That was good.

His father looked up and saw him standing there, and gave a wave. "Garek. You're awake."

Everyone looked up at him, except Luca, who broke free of Taya and ran up the ramp to fling himself at Garek. He was just able to hand off his plate to Kas in time to catch him.

"You're going to fight the sky raiders."

"Maybe," Garek conceded.

"Aidan says you are."

"They might not attack again, but probably they will."

"Will you fight them in the sky craft?"

Would he? "I can't fire anything at them from the sky craft, so probably not."

"What if you had someone who could call the earth Change onboard?" Kas asked. "You could work with them the way we did on the Endless Escarpment. Blind the sky raiders with dust and create cover for our own people, only this time from the air."

That might work. It would feel better to have the mobility of the sky craft, to keep watch on where the enemy were.

He slid a look at Kas, who sounded like he was trying to talk his way back into going.

"Are you going to help Garek?" Luca must have heard the same wistfulness in Kas's tone.

Kas hesitated, and then took Luca's hand, led him down the ramp and to the side.

"What's going on?"

He'd seen Taya kiss Min on the cheek and then make her way up the ramp slowly, giving him time with Luca, and he drew her into his arms, loosely threading his fingers together to trap her in his embrace.

She didn't seem to mind being caught.

"I think Kas is gauging how much Luca will mind if he comes along."

Taya sighed. "I wish he would stay here. Pan Nuk needs him, and Luca needs him even more."

"He's a protector, and he knows he can't protect anyone if the sky raiders come back. He wants a hand in ending them."

"I can understand that." She pressed her head against his shoulder, and they watched Kas crouch down in front of Luca, who put a hand on his father's shoulder, and waved the other one around.

Min walked up to them, and Kas rose. It was a shock to see him slide a hand around Min's waist and pull her close.

"Kas and Min?"

"You didn't see the way that wind was blowing?" Taya's voice bubbled with happiness. "And to think how rude he was to her when she first came to our side of the camp."

Garek chuckled. "I think she has something to say about his going, too."

But it was difficult to say what, Garek conceded. They all looked very serious.

"You ready to go, Garek?" Aidan came up the ramp, pushing his father's chair in front of him.

Garek bent to give his father a one-armed hug, and Quardi thumped him on the back.

"You'll need equipment," Garek said as he pulled back. "Dix will know if they have some of the things you'll need to smelt ore at the camp, but they won't have much."

"Eli and Pilar are bringing my things." Quardi himself had a hammer on his lap, and a few other tools.

The others started walking up the ramp; Susa and Dix, Dalanial Varn, and then what looked like the whole of Pan Nuk, some carrying equipment for Quardi, others with packs slung over their shoulders.

Kas met them at the bottom of the ramp and gave a nod of permission.

Eli slapped his back in thanks and strode up the ramp, holding one of Quardi's massive pots in each hand, with a pack slung over his back.

The others followed, turning briefly to say their goodbyes before they walked into the ship.

Garek counted fifteen.

Kas turned to look up at them, and Garek, who hadn't yet set foot on the ground of Pan Nuk, walked down to him, with Taya's hand linked in his.

"I'm staying," Kas said. "But we'll get ourselves ready. If things don't go the way we all hope on the battlefield, then the three armies will have a hard time making their way through West Lathor."

Taya threw her arms around Kas, Min and Luca in a group hug, and Garek gingerly joined in.

He saw the flash of laughter in Kas's eyes at that and sent his old mentor the smirk he knew used to drive him mad.

Then everyone not going edged back, and he and Taya walked into the sky craft.

"Your fellow villagers are determined to fight," Dix said as he sat down in the pilot's chair.

"They've fought the sky raiders before, with a lot less going for them, and won." Garek lifted the sky craft into the air.

Dix crossed her arms over her chest. "Well, then, let's hope we can achieve that outcome again."

TWENTY-SEVEN

THE THREE ARMIES SAT, not exactly hunkered down, but not moving forward, either, at least a half day from the camp in the Dartalian Corridor.

Garek kept the sky craft high above them, although anyone with sharp eyes would have seen him.

He hoped the fact that Aidan and Taya had spotted sky raider craft following them three times since they'd gotten closer to Dartalia meant they were one of several sky craft in the air.

When they'd made certain they had accounted for all three of the armies, he turned back to the camp, keeping high, and Aidan made a quiet sound of warning, as if they were walking the walls, not flying high above any harm, and pointed down.

"Three armies scout party," Dix said, following his finger.

"Two," Eli said, pointing to the left.

Garek climbed higher, and hovered. It seemed unlikely the scouts could have come through unseen in the light of day, so Garek guessed they'd slipped in under cover of dark the night before, and now they were trapped until the light fell again.

One group had climbed the hill to the left of the camp and lay flat against the ground, just out of sight.

General Hanson had obviously instituted patrols, but they were in groups of two and as he watched, he saw two guards take a path just below where the scouts were lying, missing them completely.

The guards were following the curve of the path to the valley floor, headed for the camp, and missed the second group, who were hunkered down below the path in the reeds of the river.

"Put down in front of the camp, with the back ramp pointed toward the river, and I'll get them," Dix said, voice grim.

"I'll help," Aidan said. "And Pilar can choose a few others to come with us."

"I'll take another group and go after the ones on the hill," Eli said. There was something in his tone that worried Garek a little.

"You got some pent up anger there, Eli?" he asked as lightly as he could.

"Seems the sky raiders had some Baritan help in my first and second abductions to Shadow. This lot are traitors."

Garek grunted in agreement. The man had a point.

"I don't think they know much about the betrayal," Taya said, sending Eli a troubled look. "The lieutenants and generals must, or they wouldn't have turned around and come back. However much the sky raiders have misjudged how long it would take our troops to recover, and the troops of the three armies to get here, the leaders must surely have been told the sky raiders would clear the way for them to reach the border. But the scouts and the general guard? I don't think they know."

"Why do you say that?" Eli seemed a little calmer already.

"Because, like us, I don't think they'd agree with it. And the Harven particularly wouldn't agree, because we saved the whole village of Cassinya. They were given the Harven Welcome when we returned them to Luf.

"Their liege may have betrayed us all, but his people are victims, too. I was given help from the Harven when I was taken to Luf. I was given a lot of help."

Eli gave a nod, but Garek sensed some reluctance in it, and decided he wouldn't want to be the scouts on the hill when Eli found them, regardless of Taya softening his rage a little.

He put the sky craft down between the camp and the river, and as soon as the ramp lowered, Dix and Aidan ran straight out with Pilar and a group of Pan Nukkers.

Eli's group were right behind them and there was a palpable sense of excitement that they were going straight into action.

Susa followed behind, and Garek rose and stretched.

"Garek." Taya's voice held a tone that brooked no delay, and he ran to the back, saw Hanson racing at them, guards in formation.

"Stand down, General." He barked it, because Susa looked like she was about to be impaled by a knife that stopped suddenly, and then drifted back to the hand of its thrower.

Which turned out to be Etta.

"Garek." Hanson gave the stand down signal, and then looked behind her as a man in Dartalian uniform came running.

"My liege." He bowed to Susa and shot Hanson a horrified look.

"My apologies." Hanson kept her back ramrod straight. "We saw the sky craft, and we were afraid of another attack. I didn't recognize the group of guards who ran up the hill, they weren't wearing a uniform, and . . . oh." She caught sight of Aidan as he, Dix and their team returned with three captured scouts, and Garek could see her color rise.

"Who was on patrol?" She barked the question and no one answered.

The silence stretched out.

"We saw the scouts from the air. I don't think they would have easily been found by a patrol." Taya's attempt to to smooth and soothe seemed to have the opposite effect.

Hanson shook her head, disgusted. "There is an issue of cooperation here." She looked at the man beside her. "Lieutenant Criss has been suspicious of us since he came back from unconsciousness, and the disappearance of Commander Dix has disturbed him greatly. I tried to explain she'd been taken back to Valian, but . . ."

"But it was difficult for me to believe that. And I see now that every word you told me was the truth. My apologies, General." Criss thumped a fist over his heart. "Sincerely. You stood watch over us while we were down, and then we didn't thank you for it."

Plenty of guards had run up behind the two leaders, and Garek noticed more than a few winces.

Hanson, caught short by the apology, gave a nod of acceptance. "Who ran up the hill?" she asked, turning her gaze to Garek.

"A few former guards from my village. There's another group of scouts on the hill." As he said it, a shout rang out from that direction and then the distant sounds of a fight drifted down to them.

Hanson seemed to grow grimmer at the news, and Etta, who'd run up beside her, looked a little sick and edged away, moving toward the sound of the fight, and using hand signals to call two others to come with her.

"How far away are the three armies?" The way Hanson asked, he realized she'd been expecting a full assault at any time, and he couldn't blame her for being a little jumpy.

After all, it didn't make sense to knock everyone down and then give them time to recover and get back up before an attack.

"Half a day away." He saw her relax a little. "We think they made a mistake with the timing, and also, that maybe Favre and Kadmine aren't as happy with the idea of sky raider help as the Harven."

"And even with the Harven," Taya said, "I think it's just the senior officers. I don't think it's the guards themselves. I believe they haven't been told."

Aidan and Dix reached them, striding ahead of Pilar and a few others marching the three spies toward the camp.

"General." Aidan gave Hanson a respectful bow, and she returned it. No sign of any cracks between them in front of their allies.

"General Dix, it's good to see you are well. We were worried."
Criss bowed as well.

Something in his tone made Dix frown. "Surely General Hanson
told you I'd been taken home to give a report to the liege?"

Criss cleared his throat. "You have to understand we were all
disoriented by the attack. When I came to, it was to find you missing
and the camp being run by General Hanson."

"Ah." Dix thought it through. "How much apologizing do I need
to do, Lieutenant?"

Criss sent Hanson a sidelong look, and Dix's face grew stony as
she noticed the fidgeting of some of her guards.

"A lot, it seems."

Hanson gave a sudden grin. "I'm a stranger, you were missing,
and they woke up after a very unnatural attack." She let it go with a
shrug, and everyone seemed to breathe out in relief.

"Is it safe to come out?"

Garek looked back to see his father at the top of the ramp.

"Seems like it."

Quardi rolled down in his chair, and looked around. Pointed to a
flat spot near the river.

"Then let's get started making shadow warriors."

TWENTY-EIGHT

EVERY TIME A SKY craft flew overhead, everyone in camp went still, watching it, tense and ready to dive for the special cover the guards calling an earth Change had built.

Taya knew how they felt; that strong, almost overwhelming fear of being hit by white lightning. Of being prepared to do almost anything not to be hit again.

But first, she checked to see if it might be Garek.

It never was.

The ships that patrolled the skies were all small fighter craft.

Garek had taken Susa back to Valian, gone to fetch the rest of the Iron Guard from their original camp in West Lathor and brought them to the Corridor camp, and then gone on to Gara and Juli for more guards. He wouldn't be back with them until late in the night, and it was only dusk now, but she still felt a flutter in her heart and a quick frisson of excitement, until she confirmed it wasn't him.

"Why don't they attack?" Dalanial Varn asked.

He'd taken up a seat beside Quardi, seemingly fascinated by the process of smelting the ore.

They were still waiting for the fire Quardi had started to reach the heat he needed, but as the Star had almost completely set, the firelight was comforting, the flames spreading a warm glow over the camp and drawing those who were off duty.

Taya watched the sky craft move away in the darkening sky high above them, and then looked over at Varn. "They don't want to make the same mistake again. Until the three armies are within sight of us, I don't think they'll hit us again."

"What's the delay, then?" Quardi stoked the fire hotter and Pilar wiped sweat from his forehead and threw on more fuel.

"The top leadership will have to break it to their troops that they're working with the sky raiders. I think some are probably resisting doing that. As soon as the sky craft swoop down and hit us, that secret will be out."

Whoever was leading those armies would have to concede at some point that they had to either advance, and let the sky raiders knock everyone out so they could find Taya unscathed by arrow or sword, or retreat, and end this whole thing.

"So when Dix or General Hanson's scouts let us know the armies are on the move, we have to look to the skies for the attack, not to the end of the valley?" Pilar's disgust was palpable as he tossed more wood on the fire.

Taya saw Varn wince, and she guessed he knew that Pilar would not be alone in the feeling of betrayal, the loss of respect, and that it would taint Kadmine for a long time.

A shout from the head of the valley stopped all conversation, and while they waited for whoever was running toward them, the Star slipped beyond the horizon.

Taya moved with a few other guards to the trail the lookouts would be using, and Dix was suddenly beside her.

She said nothing as the first scout reached them, sides heaving.

"Small group of maybe sixty are moving," he managed to get out.

"Oh." Dix took a step back. "Clever. They're coming under cover of darkness and with a small, hand-picked group. What do you bet they're going to pretend the group coming this way somehow managed to capture us all by themselves? No one but them will see the sky raiders and their white lightning."

Taya sucked in a hard, painful breath. That *was* clever. It was better than she had assumed they would come up with. But after all, they were motivated. The three armies wanted West Lathor, and the sky raiders wanted her.

"What do you suggest?" Hanson must have been just behind her, and it took Taya a moment to realize the general was speaking to her.

Everyone turned to look, some with eyebrows raised.

"Taya defeated a group of sky raiders on Shadow. And did it at least twice more here on Barit." Hanson didn't look at anyone but Taya as she said it. "What would you do?"

Taya looked around the camp. "They can see us even in the dark. They have a machine that sees the light inside us, or maybe it's the heat of our bodies, I don't know, but they used it on Shadow. But they can't see us if we're underground or in the water. In the mines they had lights in the passageways that I think also had the little devices that could see our body heat. They don't have that here. I think everyone should get into the tunnels the earth Changed made this afternoon, and if there isn't room for everyone, the rest should go into the river, keep low, and duck under the water as often as possible."

"Hide?" someone asked incredulously.

"The choice isn't hide or fight," Taya said. "It's hide or get hit with white lightning."

"And once we're hidden?" Dix asked, intrigued.

"Then they have to land, and come after us with the small, hand-held white lightning devices. They can also shoot the white lightning from the sky craft when it's on the ground, but they'd need a target."

"So we're already better off forcing them to land." Hanson nodded.

"And once they're on the ground, I can come out of the water, and hit them with shadow ore. Hit their ship." All her shadow ore weapons were in boxes of water now, as was the ore they were waiting to smelt—no sense in calling more attention to themselves with the sky raiders.

"Would you allow me to wield one of your shadow ore weapons?" Dix asked. "My lieutenant, Criss, calls the water Change. He can hide us in the river until it's time to attack."

"I would very much like to join you," Hanson said.

"Then I suggest bringing in another water Changed from my unit. Tuin can shield you and himself, General." Dix turned to Taya, waited for her to agree.

She nodded, and then orders were barked all around her, for everyone to crawl into the shallow tunnels that had been dug that afternoon, or get into the river. All the water Changed they had were spread equally among those who were assigned the river.

She heard Quardi arguing with someone, and she jogged over to him.

"They want me to hide, but I need to keep the fire hot. If it goes down now, it'll be hours more before I can smelt the ore." He looked furious, but she could hear the distress just under the surface.

"Quardi was shot in the legs by the sky raiders on Shadow. That's why he's in this chair," she told the guard looming over him, Pilar and Varn. "He knows better than you do the danger to himself if he doesn't hide."

The guard blinked.

Hanson and Dix stepped into the glow of light, and Dix frowned.

"Quardi makes a good point. We need this fire to get hotter. If Quardi and Pilar hide now, we'll lose time."

"Quardi and I will stay, and if they come for us, I'll push him and his chair into the river." Pilar's face was hard in the light, and Taya knew he was thinking of Shadow. Of everything he'd been through since they'd been taken.

"I'll stay and help." The guard's tone had changed from annoyance to respect.

"Good." Dix slapped her man on the shoulder. Then she looked over at Taya. "Your weapons are here?"

Taya crouched down in front of the wooden boxes beside Quardi's equipment. Opened the lids. "What would you like?"

Dix chose the sword, and Hanson, Criss and Tuin chose spears. Taya took out her knives, slid them into the hilts attached to her belt, and then took two spears as well.

Criss kept them all coated with water as she lifted them out of their boxes.

"Taya. You keep safe." Quardi's voice quavered a little.

"Always. And you, too." She turned, flashed him a smile, and then ran behind the other four and jumped into the river.

THE SKY RAIDERS knew they were endangering themselves.

Taya wondered if they would even land.

They flew over the camp four times, something she could only just make out as she followed the lights on their sky craft with a water mask over her face.

Criss had coated every inch of her that was out of the water. He must surely be straining himself, because he had done the same for himself and Dix.

The effect was that whatever machine the sky raiders used to see them in the dark had been rendered blind.

They seemed to know it, too.

They had been looking at a camp of over a hundred people, and now it would look like there were only three. Even that must be difficult, with Quardi, Pilar and the guard so close to the roaring fire.

Eventually, they lowered the sky craft on the flat field beside the camp, and as soon as they touched down, Taya rose up out of the water.

Dix and Criss stood with her, and as they stepped up the bank, Taya realized she was still completely coated in water. Criss was shielding them for as long as he could.

Hanson and Tuin appeared beside them, and Taya saw Tuin was doing the same for himself and Hanson as Criss was doing for her.

She ran toward the sky craft, spears in one hand, keeping her other free to pull one of her knives.

A sky raider was climbing down the ladder that dropped from underneath the fighter craft, and she smiled to herself. There was a time they would have both gotten out, secure in their ability to conquer.

Now one remained at the pilot's controls, ready to fly them away at the first sign of trouble.

It was progress.

The sky raider turned as he reached the ground, looked straight at her.

She felt the stab of disappointment at losing the element of surprise. It was dark, but she was running full out and he must have sharp eyes.

He shot at her without even lifting his arm, but she'd let go of her spears the moment his head turned her way, and crossed them in front of her.

The white lightning from his device hit the spears with an explosive thump that reverberated through her bones, making her ears ring and blinding her.

She stumbled and fell to her knees, eyes closed, and sent her shadow ore knife straight at him.

Water. There had been water coating the spears.

White lightning had never reacted like this to shadow ore before. It was clear it didn't mix well with water.

She shook her head.

All sound had stopped. The roar of the sky craft engine, the rush of the river behind her, all silent. And purple and blue lights danced in front of her eyes.

She tried to blink them away, but they swam back.

She had the sense of someone running past her and she managed to get one knee up, managed to make sure her spears were still shielding her.

White lightning shot out again, with the whomp and bone shaking reaction that told her water was involved again, although she wasn't sure what the sky raider was aiming at.

Disappointment gripped her that she must have missed him when she threw her knife. She had been so sure . . .

Someone was suddenly behind her, a white lightning device pressed against her forehead.

She heard the sky raider say something, but it was too indistinct and her ears were ringing too loudly for her to make it out.

The belt on which her knife hilts hung was cut from her, and while it was, the device was jammed even harder into the skin of her temple.

She didn't need to hear to understand the meaning. They would kill her if she called her Change. Perhaps not just her, either.

She couldn't see who else they had.

An arm, encased in dark blue, came around her chest, clamped hard, and lifted her off her feet.

She was on the short side, and the sky raiders were tall. She dangled from his arm.

She was shaken like a tree in a hard wind, and something more was shouted, and she realized her spears were still floating above the ground, and she let them drop.

Her eyes were clearing, and she caught a glimpse of Tuin, lying on the ground, and Dix, Criss and Hanson, teeth bared, watching helpless as she was carried to the ladder and lifted up.

She felt the water fall off her, its protection no longer needed.

She looked down, desperate to make eye contact with either Dix or Hanson, but instead she saw a sky raider lying on the ground, her knife in him, and as she was grabbed from above and hauled up, she saw the sky raider below her fall back, a sword through his chest.

The reaction of the sky raider who was lifting her into the sky craft could only be described as panicked.

He threw her across the chamber, threw himself at the pilot's chair, and shot the sky craft straight up. Taya was thrown to one side, hitting the wall and then, as the circular opening in the floor closed up, she tumbled to the back of the craft.

The pilot held a white lightning device in one hand and piloted with the other, and she knew every second that passed was one less chance of getting back down to Barit.

She rammed her hand in her pocket, hauled out the vial she'd never removed from the trip to the mothership, and pulled the stopper off with her teeth.

She sent both needles flying together, nervous that one wouldn't be enough, and flattened them against the white lightning device.

She still couldn't hear well, but from the horror on the sky raider's face through his helmet as he turned to look at her, she guessed he had heard the unmistakeable fizz and pop of it dying. He let the device go, and she hovered the needles in front of him.

"I want to live, so I'm going to let you land. But if you don't do it in five seconds, I will break this ship anyway I can. It's up to you. Land and let me out, or both you, me and this ship go down."

She could barely hear herself, and she hoped whatever translator they had had caught everything she'd said.

She lifted her hand and spread out her fingers, then she brought them down one by one.

At three, she felt the familiar sensation of the sky craft dropping down, had to brace herself as they came down hard, in what she assumed was a clumsy attempt to hurt her, or knock her out.

She danced the needles in front of the sky raider's face. "Open the door."

The hatch slid open, and she saw the ladder was gone. Either he wasn't extending it for her, or something had happened to break it off during the fight at the camp.

Never mind.

She slid to it, lowering herself, eyes still on the sky raider.

"You take the needles with you." The words were hissed.

"No." She lowered herself further down the opening. "If you try to shoot me when you take off, I'll send both these needles around the interior of this ship like dervishes, touching everything inside they can. So you take your chance. Head straight up and away, and they'll drop on the floor and hopefully won't touch anything important, or try to get me again, and lose your sky craft, and then suffocate."

She kept her face and voice confident, but he could best her, and he had to know it. The needles were small. They could inflict damage, but it would take some luck to hit something important without being able to see what she was doing.

"No. Take them with you." The words were panicked.

"I'll take one." She called it to her. "If you try to shoot me, then I'll have one to send into the opening where the white lightning comes out. If you don't, you have one less needle to worry about. And let me explain. My control is based on proximity. The closer I am, the more damage I can inflict. The faster you leave, the safer you'll be."

She hung down from the hole by her arms for a moment, trying to get a sense of where she was.

Her hearing was still wrong, she had barely been able to hear her own voice when she spoke, but she just made out the sound of flowing water.

It was either really close, or really big.

There was no choice, she had to go.

She dropped down to the ground and the sky craft shot straight up, the sky raider taking her seriously, and probably deciding she was far more trouble to him personally than she was worth.

She landed in a crouch and stayed there, waiting for her eyes to adjust to the almost pitch black of the night after the lights in the sky craft.

She was vulnerable out here because she didn't know where he'd set her down, and she still couldn't hear properly.

She needed some height, some way to get the lay of the land.

She rested for a moment more, threading the shadow ore needle through her sleeve.

It was so dark, she couldn't see a high point to head to, if there even was one. She might walk toward the enemy, not away from it if she set out now.

And why wouldn't the sky raider have set her down amongst the three armies, where she was likely to be caught up again?

He had nothing to lose.

But the thought of waiting, and possibly being scooped up, was just as unappealing.

She was resting one hand on the ground for balance, and she felt the soil beneath her palm begin to tremble in rhythmic bursts.

Zanir. Ridden fast enough their hooves shook the ground.

A moment of cold panic froze her in place, and then she shot to her feet.

The river was her only option. She ran toward the sound of it, tripping and stumbling over rocks and uneven ground. She bit her tongue as she fell down the bank and landed hard on her backside, but she let the tears of pain flow down her cheeks without making a sound as the blood filled her mouth.

The water was icy, a shock after what she now realized was the unreasonably warm water at the camp.

Criss had something to do with that, she was sure. He'd taken the chill off the water, and when he'd called back the water coating Taya while she was being dragged into the sky craft, he must have drawn it out of her clothes as well, so she'd landed in the sky craft dry and comfortable.

She crouched low in the river, opening her mouth, letting it fill with water, and then spitting it out to get rid of the blood.

She could hear the zanir now, but they slowed, and lantern light proceeded them, throwing long shadows forward.

Taya let herself drift closer to the bank, crouching even lower, and hugging herself against the freezing caress of the water.

"It came down here, or close to here. I'm sure of it." The person spoke Illian, but with an accent that told her the speaker wasn't West Lathorian.

So the sky raider had set her down close to the three armies.

"What does it matter if it did? Who knows why the sky raiders do what they do?"

"You don't think it matters?" The comment was incredulous.

"No, I don't. What can we do about it if they did land here? If they're still around here somewhere?"

"Well." Surprise in the tone. "I saw them fly away, so they aren't still around, but I wanted to see if we could work out what they were doing here."

"For all we know, they could have stopped to take a quick toilet break."

Laughter.

"Could be. You know, it could be."

"Let's head back to camp. I heard they sent the top fighters from all three armies to see if they could take the Dartalians."

"I heard that too. Don't like the idea of fighting any Dartalians, though. My aunt lives in Valian."

There was silence. "No. I don't either. Don't think most of the guards do, either. In fact, I'm still trying to work out what in the shadow pits we're doing here."

Their voices faded, and Taya crept back onto the bank, her whole body shivering.

They were headed downstream, which made sense if this was the same river that ran through Dix's camp.

All she needed to do was follow it up through the valley to end up right next to Quardi's roaring fire.

Of course, she'd also have to avoid the crack team of guards who may or may not have been told they were going to the camp to deal with a hundred unconscious Dartalians. If that was the information they'd been given, they were about to find some very conscious, very angry, Dartalians, Iron Guards and West Lathorians waiting for them.

The thought cheered her up, and she set a path close to the river bank, and tried to stop her teeth from chattering.

TWENTY-NINE

THERE HAD BEEN three sky raiders.

Taya started thinking about the confusion of her capture as she concentrated on what little of the ground she could see in front of her.

There had been three, because she'd seen the body of one, Hanson had gotten the second, and the third had flown off in the sky craft.

Which meant the sky raider who'd come up behind her had dropped out of the sky craft before it landed. Or had been dropped off in a second sky craft.

She remembered Garek telling her he'd seen a sky raider fly with something strapped to their suit before, so perhaps they'd done something like that. However they'd accomplished it, they'd snuck up behind her.

It had worked really well.

While the sky raider hadn't touched the knives hanging from her belt when he'd cut it off, his suit hadn't gone fizz pop because of the proximity, so they must have found a way for their blue suits to be insulated from the shadow ore.

It didn't seem to stop the sharp point of a knife going in, or a sword going through, though.

Fortunately for her and Hanson.

But now the sky raiders knew that, they'd probably adjust again.

She would have to make sure they didn't have time to do that.

They *had* lost her again. Had nearly lost another sky craft.

They had to be getting near their tipping point. And surely, with the new sky raiders working on a way to lob some shadow ore at their mothership, things would start to become too uncomfortable to make it worth their while.

Surely.

She'd been looking down, watching where she put her feet so she didn't fall down a bank again, when the high sweet song of a night wag cut off abruptly.

She froze. Her first thought was who might be up ahead. Her second was that her hearing had returned. She hadn't consciously registered the bird song, but she had been listening to it for more than five minutes.

Someone coughed softly, and she heard the scuff of a boot.

She waited, trying to work out which way they were moving.

After a while, she realized they were staying put, and closed her eyes in frustration.

She had to get around them. She couldn't stand here all night.

She started forward again, plotting a course that went around the guard, putting him between her and the river.

She went slowly, listening carefully and testing each step before she put her foot down.

Whoever it was, they moved restlessly, and she guessed they were a sentry of sorts.

The question was, sentry for what?

When the cough came again, behind her this time, she started again on her route beside the river, the one sure path to the camp.

She was tempted to move faster, to not take as much care as she had when skirting the sentry, but she forced herself to keep as quiet and slow as possible, and stopped as a prickle of fear ran down her arms when someone sniffed just a few meters in front of her.

She took a step to the side, then another, grateful for the utter darkness of the night.

She maneuvered around the sentry in tiny increments, and was expecting it when she came across a third roughly the same distance apart as the first two had been.

They must have set sentries all down the river.

Lucky for her, they weren't expecting anyone to be coming up behind them, but it was taking a lot of time to get around them.

When the sky craft had come down into the camp, it hadn't been that late. They hadn't even eaten supper yet. But the journey back from where she'd been set down was not turning out to be quick.

She had very little idea how long it would take her to get back to camp and she could not risk being caught out here at Star's rise.

A sky craft screamed overhead, coming in low and following the river toward where the three armies were camped.

She heard an exclamation behind her, and used the distraction and the noise to move a little faster.

The sky raiders were looking for her. Fair enough—she expected them too. She almost wondered why it had taken them this long.

She fingered the needle on her sleeve, wondering if they had the ability to see something so small from so high.

She felt her pockets, and found she still had the vial, but the stopper was gone.

She crept to the river's edge, and had to lower herself down onto a rock to fill it.

She dropped the needle inside, and then held it carefully as she pulled herself back onto the bank and started forward again.

There was no sentry where she expected to find one up ahead, and she stood still for a long time, listening carefully.

Perhaps she'd reached the end of the sentry line.

Eventually, as the sky craft came roaring back and then peeled away to the right, she forced herself to move, her heart hammering in her chest as she followed the river bank, eyes and ears straining for any sound of a sentry who had stepped out of his or her position.

There was no one.

She was cold, tired and hungry, but she forced herself to keep alert.

She noticed the moment the flat escarpment on either side of the river began to give way to low hills.

She was entering the mouth of the valley.

Her heart beat a little faster, and she forgot the bone deep chill for a moment at the thought that the camp was just through the narrow gap between the hills.

She sped up, hoping that the proximity to the valley entrance was the reason there were no more sentries.

The river made a sharp turn, and in the distance she could see the glow of Quardi's fire.

A sob tore from her throat and she stopped and swallowed, forcing herself to breathe, to calm down.

She wasn't safe until she was in that camp, and she'd most likely have to contend with Dix's own guards as well as Hanson's before she made it to her own bed.

The first shouts reached her ears as she moved into the narrowest part of the gully. The path was narrow—it would take no more than two people abreast—and in places it skirted huge rocks that looked as though they'd tumbled down the hill.

The sounds came from in front of her, from the direction of the camp, and she wondered at first if someone had seen her, a lookout perhaps. She sped up, jogging along the path as it wound between rocks taller than her.

And suddenly, she made sense of the calls.

The Illian was thickly accented to her ear, Kadminian or Favrean, and it was panicked.

This was the clean-up crew. The team sent in pretending to the rest of the three armies they were going to subdue the Dartalians, but in truth expecting to deal with unconscious guards.

And they were on the run.

She could hear the thud of running feet, the shouted orders, and looked around wildly for a place to hide.

There was no time to go anywhere but up.

She was still holding her vial, although less carefully than when she started, and realizing she'd need both hands to do any climbing, she propped it behind the nearest stone.

She ran to the rock closest to her, felt for hand and footholds in the dark, and hauled herself up. She scraped her fingers as she got them caught in a crack with sharp edges, banged her knee as her foot slipped, but she managed to gain some height.

She wriggled and pulled herself up, scraping her stomach and her forearms and then with a final heave, she lay sprawled—inelegant and gasping for breath—on top.

She swung herself around, careful to get a good grip because the top part of the rock angled sharply downward on one side, and then perched uncomfortably on the very tip, legs bent at the knees to brace herself, as the first of the guards ran past.

They were focused on getting away, and they didn't look up. She had a feeling they wouldn't have seen her in the darkness even if they had raised their eyes.

She kept still and quiet, and mostly they did, too, saving their energy and their breath on running.

She tried to count them as they came past her, and put the number at roughly twenty. She wondered how many more were captured or dead in the camp.

Because of the dark, and the lack of conversation, quite a few of Dix and Hanson's guards ran past her in pursuit before she realized she was among friends at last.

She opened her mouth to call out, and then paused, mouth still open, as she pondered what might get their attention, but not get her killed.

"It's Taya," she decided on at last, and it got results.

There was the sound of bodies slamming into each other as a number of guards slid to a halt.

"I'm up on this rock, wait a moment and I'll climb down."

"Where did you come from?" She recognized the voice of the guard asking as one she'd practiced with at Hanson's camp in the forest.

"The sky raider set me down right near the three armies camp, so I had to make my way back from there."

There was silence as she swung down and felt for footholds, and then hands reached up for her, and she was lifted down.

"Thank you." She leaned back against the rock for a moment, her knees suddenly weak. "I nearly got caught in the stampede of the three armies guards running back to safety."

Someone chuckled, and then everyone started to laugh.

Taya wipe tears off her cheeks, and she couldn't tell if they were from laughing or crying, but it didn't matter. She felt better for it.

She reached out with her Change, called the thin needle from where she'd left it, so small and fine no one even saw it as it flew into her hand.

"Can you take me back to camp, or do you need to go on?" she asked when her legs felt they could support her again.

"We'll take you." The guard's tone was fervent. "The sooner you're back, the safer for everyone."

She touched his arm to get his attention in the dark. "What does that mean?"

"It means Garek of Pan Nuk is a very scary man when he is upset. And right now, he is very, very upset."

THIRTY

IT WAS ONLY a half hour walk to camp, and she was met by a contingent of people, including Dix and Hanson, because one of the guards in the group helping her had run ahead.

They were carrying lanterns, and in the glow, she saw Hanson's face sag with relief at the sight of her.

"How did you get free?" Dix strode forward, and gripped her shoulder in what Taya guessed was the guard master equivalent of a full hug.

"Never mind that, we need to signal to Garek that she's safe." Hanson looked up.

"Garek is looking for me in the sky craft?" Maybe that had been him overhead earlier. She had been so sure the sky raiders would try to find her and take her again while she was cut off from allies and on her own, she had never even considered it could be him.

Hanson nodded, then pointed to one of her guards. "Bring the whirly." She turned and headed for the fire, and Taya followed her, eager to get warm, and to see if Quardi was all right.

"I'm sure we all have some interesting stories to tell," Dix said as she fell into step with Taya.

"There must have been three on that sky craft, or a second ship dropped someone nearby who snuck up behind us."

"The scouts on the hill saw a second craft landing nearby. They were more wary of an ambush than we gave them credit for." Dix looked grim.

"I think they also reinforced their suits with something that shielded them from shadow ore. I wouldn't have expected an attack like that from behind because I didn't think they could get that close to me."

Dix looked over at her in surprise. "That's interesting. But you were able to kill one, and Hanson another."

Taya nodded. "But that was because the suit was pierced. I don't think they've managed to counter the hardness and sharpness of the ore, but before, just resting ore against the suit would destroy it. Now it has to be penetrated."

"They're adapting to compensate for our own strengths."

"Yes, and the longer they're here, the better they'll get."

They arrived at the fire to find Hanson crouched over a steel receptacle of some kind, like a shallow flower-shaped dish with a hinged lid.

The lid was open and one of the guards was carefully carrying coals from the fire on a flat spade and then tipped them into the dish.

Hanson shook it, to evenly spread the coal, closed the lid and secured it with a lever.

"Everyone back."

The guards in her unit moved back immediately, and Taya followed their lead.

She saw no sign of Quardi, but before she could ask Dix about him, Hanson called her Change and shot the whirly up into the air, and then spun it as she sent it high into the sky.

Flames shot from what seemed to be vent holes at the tips of the 'petals' of the flower.

It was a signal all right. A signal Garek would see if he was looking this way.

It shone bright and clear, and beautiful in the way it created a flickering light show.

"I will definitely be taking up your liege's offer of instruction from General Hanson," Dix murmured. "Just having someone in my unit who can do that would be invaluable."

Hanson kept the whirly high and spinning until the coals winked out, and then brought it back down.

Taya walked back to the fire, looking more earnestly for Quardi.

Her mistake was she was looking for a man in a chair, but when she moved around the massive blaze to the other side, she saw him bent over a large pot, Pilar with him, both their faces fierce with concentration.

"Don't you need help with that?"

They both looked up, blinking.

"Taya?" Quardi took an unsteady step, and she ran the last few yards to put her arms around him.

He hugged her until her bones creaked in protest. "We thought they got you for good this time." His words were choked.

She shook her head against his shoulder. "They keep underestimating me. In the end, they couldn't get rid of me fast enough."

He gave a sudden, loud, Quardi laugh, one of the deep belly laughs she realized she hadn't heard for too long.

"You're right, we do need you. But you look done in."

"I'm cold and wet and hungry, but if you'll give me time to change, and get some food inside me, then I can separate the ore for you."

They were running out of time. She wanted to sleep, but she wouldn't have to shape the ore, just separate out the impurities. Quardi and Pilar could dip arrow heads into the smelted ore without her help.

When she returned, clean, dry and with a bowl of stew in her hand, Hanson had sent the whirly up a second time.

No one had asked her for information about what had happened, and she hadn't asked what had happened in camp, either. It could wait until after she helped Quardi.

She didn't think she was imagining the real sense of relief from most of the guards that she was back. It made her wonder what had happened with Garek when he'd arrived to find her gone.

That he had brought new guards to camp was obvious. There was almost double the number there had been.

"Taya." Eli was suddenly beside her, enveloping her in a crushing hug that almost caused her to drop her stew.

He set her back a little, shook his head. "I saw that crazy signal, came back to camp. A few of us are keeping watch on the hill. I didn't see you come in, but they told me you walked in through the valley?"

She nodded. "The sky raider set me down near the three armies, so I had to walk. Fortunately he set down near the river, so I had a path back."

If he'd dropped her off somewhere out on the plain, she would have been truly lost.

"How'd you get him to let you out?" Eli hugged her close with one arm, and walked with her toward Quardi.

She lifted her arm, pointed to the needle threaded onto her sleeve.

"That?"

She grinned. Nodded. "Well, I had two of them. I left one in the sky craft, told him I'd stab him and his equipment with it if he tried to shoot me with white lightning as he flew off."

He gaped at her.

Pilar waved and she took a last bite of stew, set the bowl down, and joined him and Quardi at the massive pot.

"It's at temperature." Pilar indicated the smelted ore. A second pot sat in the fire, empty and waiting for the purified ore.

Taya called her Change, lifting the molten ore out, and sending it in an elegant, glowing arc into the second pot.

Everything that wasn't shadow ore stayed behind in the first pot.

"All done."

"That's interesting."

Taya looked up to see Hanson had been watching them.

The slag she'd left behind in the first pot rose up, glowing red and viscous, and Quardi swung his gaze to her.

"You can call it?"

"It's mostly iron." Hanson shrugged. "Enough that I can work it."

"Why don't you just call the iron and leave the rest behind?" Pilar asked her.

"Iron is too soft to make a good blade. Usually we add limestone to make steel, but I want to see how this mixture works." She fashioned a blade in the air over the pot, her manipulation of the ore far more practiced and assured than Taya's had been when she'd created the blades for her sword and knives. Quardi had had to work on them for a while to improve them, whereas this . . . Taya could see Quardi would have barely anything to do.

And then the roar of a sky craft descending on the camp had her head jerking upward.

It set down, and she was running before the engines had even cut off.

Garek appeared in the pilot's door, and she waved as she ran toward him.

She suddenly found herself flying, and she let out a laugh of delight that died as soon as she got a good look at his face.

He stepped back, and grabbed her as she reached him, and the door closed behind her.

His face was stark, his eyes almost wild.

She didn't say anything, she simply took him in her arms and held him.

He shuddered, his arms coming tight around her and he buried his face in her hair. "How?" He cleared his throat. "How did you get free?"

"The needles. I still had the vial in my pocket." She didn't say anything else, just let him breathe her in.

"Did you bring it down?" When he finally spoke, there was a dark edge to his tone. A vicious edge.

She shook her head. "I threatened to, but I was inside it at the time, so I got him to let me out instead."

"Good." He gripped her even tighter. "That's good." He drew back, frowning. "Where did he let you out? It was hours after you were taken that Hanson sent up that signal."

She hesitated and his eyes narrowed.

"Where, Taya?"

"Near the three armies."

He drew in a deep breath. Straightened.

She put a hand on his chest, holding him in place. "Before you go level the lot of them, how about this first?" She went up on her toes and kissed him. "I don't think anyone is going to dare interrupt us for a while. You seem to have terrorized the camp to the point they almost wept with relief when they stumbled across me. And I am tired, Garek. I am tired, and I want a break from this for a little while. We can talk about what happened, and who did what tomorrow. Let's close the world off for a few hours."

He looked at her, and she saw him slowly come back to himself, to the calm, thoughtful man he was most of the time.

He sighed. "I thought they had you. That this was the end."

"I know. But once again I turned out to be more a thorn in their side than the prize they were looking for." She smiled up at him. "Lucky for you, I take a different approach when it comes to those I love."

He smiled back, heat rising in his eyes. "Oh, I know how lucky I am."

He lifted her up and pressed her back against the wall. And showed her just how lucky.

THIRTY-ONE

GAREK OPENED the pilot's door sometime in the night, uneasy with being deaf to what was happening in the camp. It meant the Star's morning light poured in, waking him, and he heard the low murmur of guards stirring around the camp fires.

"Time to talk?" Taya lifted a sleep-tousled head off the pallet and hid a huge yawn behind her hand.

"Time to talk." Anger still rode him, and the panic-inducing fear that he had lost her for good still lingered.

That she had overcome the odds, and walked out alive and unharmed, was a testament to her, not a point in favor of his enemies.

And they were now all his enemies.

Before last night, he'd hesitated to think through the more destructive options in dealing with the three armies, but now those options were on the table.

He could walk through their ranks in the inbetween, and destroy swathes of them. And if they didn't lay down their weapons and concede the fight, he would do just that.

"Where'd you go?" Taya was crouched beside her pack. She held a comb in her hand, but her eyes were on him.

"Nowhere good."

She rose and tied her hair at her nape. "Let's go talk to Hanson and Dix, see if we can work out a way to turn this around."

He nodded, but he realized he had no problem going down the roads he was considering.

Harven and its allies started this; they were the trespassers, not him.

And he protected his own.

He bypassed the ladder, jumping to the ground, and held out his arms.

Taya jumped after him, and he called his Change and caught her in the air, sent her tumbling to the ground in careful somersaults the way she used to love him doing when they first fell in love, before he was sent to walk the walls.

He protected his own, and no one was more his own than Taya.

They walked to the big fire, found Quardi and Pilar fast asleep on thick pallets, blankets covering them, and big wooden vats of water with feather-tipped arrows standing in them like strange flowers in even stranger vases.

They turned away, leaving them to sleep, and Hanson waved them over to where she stood with Dix, Kima and Dalanial Varn.

"You look better," Dix said, her focus on Taya, but Garek had a feeling she was also talking about him.

He had been a little . . . crazy last night when he'd arrived back from a round trip of Juli and Gara with troops and supplies to find the camp under attack and Taya abducted.

He'd dealt with some of the three armies' attackers before he'd flown off to find the sky craft that had taken Taya—he remembered that much—but he hadn't waited around to see what had become of them.

"Thank you." Taya accept two bowls from a guard who'd run over at a signal from Dix, and she handed one to him.

The bowls were full of hot porridge, and he realized he hadn't eaten anything since yesterday afternoon. He decided it might be better for everyone if his mouth was too full to take part in the conversation. At least initially.

Dix looked around the group, and everyone fell silent, waiting for her to speak. "So, as we discussed last night, there were two sky craft, and one dropped a sky raider off just outside the camp, and he came in on foot, while the second ship landed here.

"Taya's theory that they've added a layer of protection to their suits so they can get close to shadow ore without it affecting them makes a lot of sense, but fortunately for us it isn't foolproof, because it can still be pierced."

Garek looked up from his bowl at that. "The suits were different?"

Taya nodded. "They didn't look different, but the sky raider got right up behind me, put one of those white lightning devices against my head and cut my belt off, and my shadow ore knife definitely touched his suit without effect."

"How did he get the jump on you?" Dalanial Varn asked.

Garek looked over at him, and the councilor raised his hands in a placating gesture. "I'm just curious."

"I wasn't expecting him, for a start," Taya said. "I thought there were only two of them, but it was mainly because Criss had coated my spears with water so we could sneak right up on top of them, and when the sky raider saw me and shot, the white lightning reacted with the water. It exploded, and my ears were ringing and my eyes were blinded. Even if I'd known he was behind me, I couldn't have done anything about it."

"They shot at Tuin, and it had the same effect on him, but some of it also jumped off his spear and caught his body and he went down." Hanson rubbed a hand over her face, and Garek noticed she looked haggard.

He felt a fleeting moment of guilt for his and Taya's night off. But it only lasted a second.

"Is Tuin all right?" Taya asked and Dix nodded.

"So, the question we're all dying to ask is how did you escape?" Dix's gaze was riveted on Taya's face.

Garek looked at her himself, and tried to see her through the eyes of a stranger. She was of medium height, slim in build. She looked more dangerous that she used to, with her guard's trousers and jacket rather than the dresses she used to wear, but still, not very imposing.

"I thought Eli would have told you," she said, and tapped her sleeve.

Hanson and Dix bent forward, trying to see what she was pointing to.

"What is that?"

"It's a shadow ore needle. It was in that vial of water I took onto the mothership. I still had it in my pocket. I destroyed the sky raider's white lightning device with the two I had and then threatened to bring down the sky craft unless he landed and let me out."

"Just like that?" Hanson breathed.

"Just like that." She grinned. "The device going pop and dying was all it took. And, to be honest, I think I could have brought the ship down, and he knew it."

"And he let you off between us and the three armies?" Hanson asked.

"Yes. Nearer the three armies than this camp. Some guards came out to investigate from the camp when they saw the sky craft land and then take off again, so I had to go into the river to hide. It made for a chilly walk home. And there were sentries all along the river. I had to edge past them on my way."

Thinking about it, thinking about what could have gone wrong, Garek felt the anger rise up in him again. Taya must have sensed it, because she leaned into him, the warmth and vitality of her centering him.

"So how long after I got taken did the clean-up crew arrive?" Taya threaded her fingers through his, and he suppressed a grin at the way she was managing him. It was working, too.

Hanson's gaze focused on their clasped hands, and then lifted her gaze to Garek's, humor lighting her hazel eyes. "Not long. Maybe a half hour. By then, we were ready and waiting for them."

"How many did you capture?" Garek had landed in the middle of the fight. Had been told of Taya's abduction, and had lashed out at the invaders.

"We have twenty dead, thirty prisoners."

"How many did I kill?" Garek didn't really care, but he decided it was best to acknowledge his part in it.

"Ten." Hanson shrugged. "You're a potent weapon on any battle-field, and I would have you in my unit any time."

Garek inclined his head, taking her words as the high praise they were.

"You did to them what you did to the Harven lieutenant who tried to attack Susa." Dix was watching him. Like Hanson, there was no censure on her face, only interest.

He nodded.

"But you did it faster. It was like you ripped the air out of their lungs."

"I was making a point with the Harven lieutenant. I was just trying to kill the attackers."

Hanson cleared her throat delicately. "Well, we can thank you for that, because they came a lot quieter after seeing their fellow guards collapse and suffocate. Some ran, and we got a few of them, but when the guards found Taya, they gave up the chase and came back."

"It's always good to let a few escape anyway," Dix said. "Myste-rious deaths and a total routing always add a nice flavor of fear to the enemy camp."

Garek grinned in agreement.

"I've spoken to the Kadmine prisoners." Dalanial Varn had been standing to one side until now, but he stepped forward. "They were told the Harven had some secret weapon that would lay everyone in the camp out, and all they would have to do was deal with uncon-scious guards." He looked down at his feet. "I had to walk away from them at that point." He breathed in deeply through his nose, rubbed his eyes, and then looked up. "One of them has been asking to speak to me again since then. Do you want to hear what he has to say?"

"Always good to hear what your enemies have to say," Dix said, and Garek saw Varn wince at that.

The councilor was in the uncomfortable position of representing Kadmine on the state council, and yet having no control over the Kadmine liege and his army. He obviously wanted to believe the Kadmine cohort had been duped by Harven and didn't understand what they'd gotten into.

Whether that was true or not, they would have to take responsibility for what they'd done so far, and one of those consequences was the disrespect of their neighbor, Dartalia.

They had less to lose with West Lathor, because since Valtor had become more self-involved, West Lathor's relations with the other Illian states had fallen away. But Garek guessed the loss of Dartalian goodwill would hurt Kadmine. And they deserved it to.

While they waited for Varn to fetch the prisoner, Garek looked up into the clear blue sky.

He was expected back in Juli this morning, to fetch more troops and to coordinate with Aidan and Vent, but he wasn't leaving Taya again. The princeling would just have to wait.

There was no sign of a sky craft anywhere, but that could change in moments and as he scanned the skies, he realized that Taya was doing the same.

"How long have you been able to draw the air out of peoples' lungs?"

He looked to the left, saw Hanson was standing watching him with a hint of fear in her eyes.

He moved away from Taya, stepping closer to Hanson. "For a while."

"You could have done that to me, to anyone in our camp." Hanson made it a statement of fact, so he nodded.

"Aidan knows this?"

"The princeling knows," he agreed. "And what I did to the trees in that forest, I can do to people, too."

She sucked in a breath. "I'm only standing here because you wanted the Iron Guard back, aren't I?"

"You're standing here because Taya wanted to see if you could teach her how to better call her Change, and because if it were iron she called, not shadow ore, then she would be in the same position as your recruits, and I'd want someone like you to stand up to someone like Valtor for her."

Hanson gave a slow nod. "I thought I knew why Aidan insists you are going to be his general . . ." She paused. Frowned. "Are his general. But it's more than your tactical acumen. You're—"

She fell silent as Varn arrived back. Beside him was a large Kadminian, arms restrained behind him.

Dix looked over at Garek, and he gave her a nod of acknowledgment. He'd bring the prisoner down if he tried something.

She waved the two guards who'd brought him away, so they had some privacy.

"You wanted to speak." Her words were cool.

"I wanted to speak to Councilor Varn." He looked around the group suspiciously, and when his gaze fell on Taya, he couldn't help the widening of his eyes.

Garek's hands twitched. "See someone you were supposed to hand over to the sky raiders?" he asked neutrally.

"What?" The man's gaze snapped to Garek, eyes even wider than they had been. "Not the sky raiders, the Harven . . ." His voice trailed off as he looked at the faces around him. "They were going to give her to the sky raiders?"

"Who do you think was going to knock everyone here unconscious?" Varn asked him, disgust in his tone. "What do you think the Harven's 'secret weapon' was?"

The man was shaking his head. "No. It was some herb. They had a spy who was going to put it in the food and . . ."

Dix snorted. "And in a small, tight-knit team, we wouldn't notice someone sneaking in and dropping something in each pot? And then everyone was going to collapse and lie helpless?"

"What is your name?" Varn asked him, and there was a weariness to the slump of his shoulders.

"Fredic." The guard looked around the group again. "What went wrong with the plan?"

"The reason the sky raiders want Taya so badly is because she is dangerous, and she proved that last night when she foiled their attempt to hit us all with a weapon that shoots out lightning." Varn folded his arms over his chest. "They flew off in panic, and I can only assume the communication between the sky raiders and the traitors in the three armies isn't instantaneous, because no one warned you we were waiting for you to arrive."

"The traitors—" Fredic blinked.

"What would you call Baritans who collaborate with the sky raiders?" Garek asked softly.

"I—" He swallowed. "I didn't know about that. I swear, I didn't know."

"Well, now you do." Varn shook his head.

"What about you, you have a sky craft?" Suddenly defiant, Fredic pointed to the ship.

"That's because I stole it from the sky raiders up on Shadow, while I was rescuing Baritans who'd been abducted. And that surely is common knowledge." Garek held his gaze, and eventually he conceded the point with a nod.

"I had heard that, but some of the Harven are whispering about it not being true."

Taya made a sound of such outrage, all eyes turned to her.

"That they would do that, when they saw us bring back a whole Harven village worth of captives to Luf." She shot a look of horror at Garek. "This is Habred trying to rewrite history so he can go after West Lathor even though he owes us for saving his own people."

"I've seen the camp on Shadow where the sky raiders kept their captives." Varn looked Fredic straight in the eye. "I've spoken with Dartalians who were captives as well, and with some West Lathorians who were taken not once but twice, and I can confirm this is all true."

"So the Harven have lied to us." Fredic's gaze was fixed to Varn's face.

Varn shrugged. "Nothing would make me happier than if the Kadmine liege and commanders are all innocent dupes. But why did they not get Council permission for this war, if that's the case? And why have they insulted Dartalia, one of our closest allies?"

Fredic shook his head.

There was silence; a crushing, heavy silence.

Eventually Dix waved at the guards and they took the Kadminian away.

"What do you think is keeping the other sky raiders?" Dix looked up at the sky.

"Maybe they're still working out how to use the shadow ore on the enemy mothership. Maybe they betrayed us." Garek had known it was a gamble. It might still pay off, but they had to forge ahead as if it wouldn't.

"What's next for you?" Hanson asked, looking at Garek with that direct gaze.

"Taya and I are due in Juli, and then if you like, when I come back with troops, I can go to Valian, bring more of your people back here?" He had turned to Dix as he spoke.

She nodded. "I think that's a good idea. I'd like more Dartalians here, and it would be good to get word from Susa."

"Don't you think I should stay here?" Taya looked between them. "If the sky raiders come back—"

"We have shadow ore arrows," Hanson interrupted her, perhaps a little too quickly.

Taya frowned, looked at Garek, then sighed. "You won't go without me, will you?"

He simply smiled, and held out his arm.

She took it, shaking her head, and walked with him to the sky craft.

He had Taya safe and by his side.

It was as good as it could be in the current circumstances. And Garek had learned to take whatever good he found with both hands.

THIRTY-TWO

THEY WERE BEING FOLLOWED.

Somewhere between Dix's camp and the Dartalian capital of Valian they'd picked up a small sky raider fighter.

Taya kept her gaze on the burnished glint of light off the silver wings of the craft and ignored the glorious colors of a sky lit up by the setting Star.

"They want to stop us from landing, maybe?" She glanced at Aidan, standing beside her, but his gaze remained fixed on the sky raiders following them.

Garek hunched forward. "Maybe. Or they just want to know what we're up to."

"Unless they're waiting for us to land so they can blow us up like they did those other sky raiders." Despite his dark words, Aidan looked rested and energized. When she and Garek had arrived in Juli earlier today, he had been ready to go with the troops he'd assembled for Garek to ferry to Dix's camp. Ready to fight.

Taya put out a hand to steady herself as Garek tilted the sky craft to the right, and Aidan did the same.

"You're changing course?" Aidan looked down at the ground far below them.

"Even if we lose them for an hour or so, that would give me time to talk to Susa, load up some troops." Dix spoke from her pallet on the floor. She half-sat, half-lay, slumped against the wall. Taya thought the general probably hadn't slept in nearly two days.

Even when Taya had first picked up sky raiders following them, she hadn't moved, and now she closed her eyes and slid all the way down so she was lying flat.

The sky craft suddenly moved faster, and Aidan turned to look at Garek. "Where are you—?"

"Those storm clouds." Garek pointed, and Taya noticed what she'd in truth been looking at for minutes—a bank of dark purple clouds hanging low on the horizon.

"How will that help?" Dix asked, eyes still closed.

"Water," Taya said, shooting Garek a wide grin. "The clouds are full of water. They can't track us in there."

"Huh." Dix forced herself up onto her elbows.

Aidan tapped the window with a fist. "I could coat the craft in water from the clouds."

Garek gave a slow nod. "That should make us just about invisible to their systems. Although they could still see us with their eyes."

"It's nearly dark. If we can hide in there until the Star sets, we can sneak off without them any the wiser."

"I think that is going to be a little harder now." Taya pointed, and Aidan's lips thinned in disgust.

"A second sky craft."

"They seem to be working in pairs since the night they took Taya." Dix lay back down again.

"Maybe these are the only two they have left. We've destroyed at least four of them, and a few have been damaged. How many could they really have had to begin with?" Taya leaned against the window, looking out at the two ships flying parallel to each other.

"Time's running out for them." Garek's face was fierce with

concentration. "The longer they're here, the worse their ships are corroded, and now their fellow sky raiders have arrived, they'll be wanting to get back home with their shadow ore before the bigger ship catches up to them."

"That means they'll probably be prepared to sacrifice everything to protect the ore on their mothership." Aidan nodded. "So what we need is for the other sky raiders to make good on their promise. So far, they've done nothing."

"It was always an outside chance." Garek shrugged.

Taya had thought it was more than that. The sky raider who'd watched her shadow ore demonstration on Shadow had seemed focused. Taya had believed her.

She forced herself to let it go. Time would tell.

She turned to face forward and watched the clouds swallow them up.

The light dimmed to almost nothing in the swirling dark gray, and she sensed a shudder as wind buffeted them.

And then she could barely see at all, as a thick layer of water coalesced across the window.

"And now, we're invisible." Aidan smiled.

Garek gave a hum of agreement and lifted the sky craft up, slowing almost to drifting speed.

"Let's hope they don't hit us," Dix said from the floor. She didn't sound as if she cared much, one way or the other.

They waited, letting the minutes slip by. Taya had to force herself to unclench her fists, and she looked at Dix, astonished, when her breathing changed, becoming deeper, steadier.

The general of Dartalia was fast asleep.

She grinned at the sight of it, caught Garek's gaze, and had to force down a laugh as he held a finger to his lips.

Below them, very close below them, she heard the whine of engines, and Garek went very still.

"I can feel the disturbance in the air. They've passed beneath us."

"Then let's turn around and get to Valian." Aidan blurred just a little at the edges. "I've added to our layer, I'll see how long I can hold it for. Let's go."

Garek eased them around and gently moved them back out the thick cloud cover.

Night had fallen when they emerged, and it took only two hours for them to reach Valian.

A tiny makeshift camp seemed to have been set up near Susa's palace.

Taya looked down at it as Garek circled and then spiraled down to land.

There were perhaps ten tents around a single campfire.

Dix woke as they landed, and though Taya knew she had only gotten a few hours sleep, she stood up and strode down the ramp as focused and upright as ever.

She slowed to a stop at the sight of the camp. "I wonder who—?"

A group of people emerged from the palace entrance. Some were guards, but one was Zek and the other . . .

With a cry of surprise and delight, Taya raced down the ramp, overtook Dix and flung her arms around the town master of Cassinya.

"Luci!"

Luci hugged her back. She seemed to struggle to speak for a moment. "We got your note."

It had been over three weeks since Taya had nailed a note to a tree trunk at the end of the path through the woods, warning the Cassinyans that the sky raiders were watching and waiting to recapture them and take them back to Shadow.

"We also saw the wreckage of a sky craft. Did you bring it down?"

Taya nodded. "They were waiting for you, but unfortunately for them, they got me instead."

Luci gave a strangled laugh. "The thought of going back . . . after everything, after being free, to be dragged back . . ." She gulped in a breath. "And to know Habred was behind it."

There was a cold, hard kernel of hate in Luci's voice. "Our liege wasn't being generous, giving us those leviks, he was delaying us so the sky raiders would have easy pickings, taking us on the open road."

"I'm so sorry." Taya gave her a last squeeze. "But what are you doing here, in Valian?"

Luci stepped back. "Zek sent word for us to come. He told us Habred is going to war with West Lathor. And we're here to stand in his way."

She looked up, past Taya, and Taya turned to see Aidan, Garek and Dix approaching.

Aidan and Garek both bowed to her.

"It's good to see you." Aidan gave her a respectful salute.

"You, too." Luci smiled at them all. "I'm here with a few old guards. If it suits the general, then we thought you could drop us near the Harven side of the three armies, and let us . . . waylay them."

"You're Harven?" Dix tilted her head to the side.

"These are the villagers we were captured with." Zek spoke for the first time. "They welcomed us into their group, and we became like family. After they arrived in Luf, and spoke to their liege, Habred told the sky raiders when and where they were going to be on the road back to their village, so the sky raiders could get their old, skilled mining crew back. Taya stopped them, but if she hadn't been there, they would have been taken, and no one would have been the wiser as to what had happened to them."

All around them was silence as everyone absorbed the depth of the betrayal.

Luci almost hunched her shoulders and then forced them straight. "We are Harven. And we deserve better than the liege we have."

There were murmurs all around of agreement.

"How many are there of you?" Dix flicked her gaze to the tents.

"Ten."

Dix nodded slowly. "You're going to expose yourself to harm if you put yourselves between the three armies and us and try to shame them. It's my experience that commanders don't like to look bad, or admit fault."

Luci gave a wry smile. "I know. But if we don't, I can't see a way my village can remain part of Harven. There has to be a reckoning."

It was a reckoning Habred deserved. But Taya wondered how much his own troops knew. And whether they would believe the word of a small village town master over their own liege.

THIRTY-THREE

THEY WERE A CROWDED SHIP.

Garek knew they were overloaded, but he was able to call his Change, keep them going despite the extra weight.

Susa had insisted on coming, and since Zek and Aidan had sent letters to the council, two more councilors had arrived in Valian. One from the far eastern state of Landau, and Dartalia's own councilor.

Neither would hear of staying behind, and Dix was determined to bring as many of her guards as would fit.

Luci nearly had to leave some of her villagers behind, but in the end Garek decided to risk it.

He was paying for it in energy, but if Luci was able to divert some of the Harven contingent and get them to abandon the field, it would be worth it.

"Where do we set Luci down?" Susa was looking out the window, and Garek saw the three armies hadn't moved since he'd last seen them.

"Out of sight," Luci said.

Garek raised an eyebrow.

"It will muddy the waters if we're seen getting out of a sky craft.

We're going to accuse Habred of conspiring with the sky raiders, but we arrive in a flying ship?" She shook her head. "Better we come with no question marks over us."

Garek nodded, turned the sky craft over the three armies camp, flying high, and when the camp was obscured by hills, he turned and came back, slower and low to the ground.

He set down as close to the rear of the three armies camp as he could without being seen.

"Might take you half a day's walk," Dix said as Luci headed to the back to collect her small team.

"Beats walking all the way from Cassinya," Luci replied, and Dix laughed, a hearty laugh that told Garek she was back on form again.

"Don't I know it. I've become spoiled by my current mode of transport." She sent Garek a quick grin.

They had spent the night in Valian, had all rested, with teams of guards who called the water Change holding the skin of water that Aidan had formed in the storm clouds in place over the sky craft.

And now, between Aidan and the water Changed guards Dix was flying to the camp, they were still keeping it up for this journey.

To the sky raiders, it would seem as if they had simply vanished.

Taya followed Luci to the back, and Garek heard them saying their goodbyes.

He walked to the doorway that separated the pilot's chamber from the back and leaned against it. Taya was stepping back from Luci, and he caught the Cassinyan's eye.

"If you need me to fetch you, shoot a burning arrow toward Dix's camp. If I can, I'll come for you."

"Thank you, Garek." Luci grimaced. "I hope it doesn't come to that. I'd hate for you to have to rescue us again, only this time from our own people."

"Me, too." He gave the West Lathor guard salute to her and she returned it, then walked down the ramp with nine other Cassinyans in tow.

They all seemed to know Taya, either nodding to her or hugging her as they passed, and Garek guessed the months they'd spent together up on Shadow had formed bonds like the ones he had with the guards he walked the walls with in Gara.

"Her accusation against her liege is a serious one." Cyna, the Landau councilor, followed Garek back into the pilot's chamber, watching with fascination as he raised the ramp again.

"There is no way the sky raiders could have known to wait on that road for the Cassinyans without being told. Habred knew when they left, and if they hadn't taken an alternate route, they would have been captured again." Taya walked past Cyna and went back to her spot at the window.

Garek lifted off, and felt the slight relief of being rid of some of the extra weight he'd been carrying.

"Many others would have known when the Cassinyans left for home," Cyna countered.

"Yes. But only one has been linked to complicity with the sky raiders."

"Who told you Habred is colluding?" The Dartalian councilor, Arne, stepped closer.

"Two guards from Luf. They saw evidence with their own eyes."

There was a stunned silence from both councilors.

"Witnesses?"

"Witnesses," Taya agreed. "And I'm another one. When the sky raiders who were waiting for Luci and the others came down in front of me, two of Habred's guards from Luf blocked my escape. They threatened to kill me unless I let myself be taken, and they admitted they were there to help the sky raiders."

"You have their names?"

"The name of one and I know both their faces." Taya nodded.

Garek forced himself to loosen his grip on the arm of his pilot's chair. He knew the name, too. He would never forget it.

He skimmed over the hills and Dix's camp was suddenly below them. It had swollen to four times its original size with the addition of the Iron Guard and the troops he'd brought from Gara and Juli.

They were still far fewer than the numbers in the three armies, but the odds were getting better.

"A nice little force," Dix said with satisfaction, and her gaze went to the back of the sky craft, where another eighty of her troops with all their gear sat waiting to be let out.

Garek set them down gently, and the relief as he was able to let go of his Change was overwhelming.

"You're burnt out." Taya was crouched beside his chair, and he opened his eyes to find everyone else had already gone.

"We were overweight. I had to work a little harder." He gave her a crooked grin, and slowly her frown of worry softened.

"Rest for a bit." She leaned forward and brushed a kiss on his lips, then stood and got a mattress out of the back and laid it beside his chair. "Hanson has been trying out the arrows, and she's got some of the air Changed to work with her guards. I'm going to help them."

He nodded, forcing himself out of his chair to watch her go, and when she stepped off the ramp, he closed it up and lay down.

He shouldn't have let himself become so drained. The hammering of a headache was discordant in his head, and he reluctantly closed his eyes.

He'd left himself and Taya vulnerable, and there was nothing he could do about it but sleep.

A HISS of sound woke him in an explosive rush.

His hand knocked a jug sitting next to his head but it didn't tip over, and he fumbled for the cup he could see beside it, pouring out water and gulping it down while he tried to make sense of what he'd heard.

Taya must have been here, because aside from the water, there was food wrapped in a cloth.

He leaned back against the wall of the sky craft and drank another cup of water, trying to work out the time.

The hiss came again, and he flowed up onto his feet, staring at the pilot's chair.

A sky raider wanted to talk.

He knew the communication between other sky raider ships and his must be two way, but he didn't know how to do it. So far, they had spoken to him, but he couldn't reply.

An overloud string of words, interrupted by static, made the hair on the back of his neck stand up.

He couldn't understand any of them.

He looked out of the window, found the view was obscured in some way, and then, when his brain finally caught up with his eyes, he ran to the door, opened it and thrust himself through the layer of water that was covering it.

A guard stared up at him, eyes wide with surprise.

"Can you call the water to you for a few minutes, and then cover the sky craft with it again?" He looked between her and her partner, and they both nodded.

Water lifted up, each guard taking roughly half, the water coalescing around the guards themselves, so just their heads stuck out, the bulk of the volume held in what looked like a massive water droplet that encased them.

"Thank you."

He heard another hiss and pulled back into the craft, dripping wet. This time, he understood the words that came next.

"Very clever of you. The water shield makes you completely invisible to us. If we hadn't been able to actually see your ship, we wouldn't have known where you were."

Garek sat in the chair, looking for some clue as to how to respond.

"That you removed the water after we hailed you tells us you can hear us." There was a pause, and Garek got out of the pilot's chair and crouched beside it, hunting for a way to answer.

"Perhaps you can't reply. It might even be likely." The hiss came again and then after a moment, the voice forged on. "This is a warning. There is an imminent attack planned on your camp. A coordinated attempt by your enemies and ours. We tell you this to confirm our cooperation. We are preparing to incapacitate our enemy's mothership, and the communications we've picked up from them indicate they are about to engage you. Our efforts are concentrated elsewhere, but we felt this warning might give you the edge in the coming fight." There was a long hiss, and then the broadcast cut off.

Garek leapt for the door, then stopped as Aidan hauled himself up the stairs.

He stepped back to let the princeling in.

"What's happening? You ordered the water shield off the ship."

Garek moved to the window. "Our new sky raider friends were trying to hail us, but their message couldn't get through the water."

"Ah." Aidan's eyes gleamed, and he joined Garek, looking upward to try and see where they were. "And?"

"They've overheard communications that we're about to be attacked. A coordinated effort by the three armies and their sky raider friends."

"How long do we have?" Dix spoke behind them. He turned to see her stepping from the ladder into the craft.

"They said imminent." Garek moved his gaze from the skies to the camp, looking for Taya. He saw his father, sitting near the fire, talking to Eli, but Taya was nowhere to be seen.

Neither was Hanson.

"Let's go up, see what's going on." Aidan gestured with his hand.

Dix stepped deeper into the chamber, nodding.

"Where's Taya?" He was starting to feel the first light touches of worry that he couldn't find her.

"Over there." Aidan pointed, and Garek saw a group of guards halfway between the camp and the valley mouth.

He tried to make out Taya in the crowd. Couldn't.

"The best thing we can do for everyone is go up and have a look. Otherwise we're blind." Dix's words were blunt.

She was right.

He turned to Aidan. "You going hold the water shield on, or do you want the guards outside to join us?"

"I'll do it." Aidan jogged back to the door, called out to the guards, and water started climbing up the window.

Garek eased them up in a smooth move that was almost equal parts his Change and the engines, and then let the engines take over as he skimmed over the troops.

Taya, Hanson and the Iron Guard were ranged out in a loose line, and as he flew over, they looked up in surprise. Taya waved at him, although he couldn't see her face clearly through the water covering the window.

He kept the sky craft directly over Taya, but rose higher, giving them a view of the escarpment beyond, which was made clearer when Aidan pulled the water back to form a water-free porthole.

It looked as if the three armies were still camped where they had been early this morning.

"It doesn't look as if they've moved an inch." Dix frowned. "And that's what I'd expect, because our lookouts on the hills haven't reported anything unusual."

"I don't think our friends would have lied about this."

"You trust them?" Aidan asked.

Garek snorted out a laugh. "No. But they know we're cooperative, and we've given them real help. If it comes down to choosing a side, they'd prefer us to prevail over the three armies. But they also want to make sure Taya is telling the truth. That there really are many like her."

"You think they could easily intervene and help us, but won't because they want to see if we have the shadow Called we say we do?" Dix leaned against the window and looked over her shoulder at him.

He nodded. "They don't want us taken by surprise, but they're not extending all the help they can. They want to see exactly what they would be facing if they decided to stay and mine more ore, and we turned against them."

"You sound satisfied," Aidan said.

"Because I don't think they'd have told me this if they hadn't worked out a way to bring down the other sky raider mothership."

"You think they're preparing to attack?"

Garek shrugged. "It's a guess, but yes."

They watched the escarpment for a while.

"I think I see something odd." Aidan pointed. "Can you fly over that area, near to the valley mouth?"

Garek eased them over the hill and hovered over the spot.

"What's that?" Dix cupped her hands on either side of her face. "It's like the ground is flapping."

"Can you stir some air down below?" Aidan asked, and Garek called his Change, swirling air just above ground level.

"It's cloth. A large piece of cloth—" Dix gasped. "There's a group of guards underneath that cloth. They're holding it over their heads. It looks exactly like the ground around them."

"Yes." Aidan sounded awestruck. "There's about fifty guards hiding underneath."

"Where there's one, there's probably more." Garek flicked his gaze to the skies. "Just keep watch for sky craft, too. They told us it was going to be a coordinated attack."

He swooped the sky craft down the escarpment, feeling the joy of gathering air beneath him and then he sent it flying toward the three armies camp.

Three pieces of ground lifted up like lids on some strange box, to reveal the troops beneath.

"Three." Aidan shook his head in disgust. "And what is that cloth? Could they really have made it themselves?"

"You think the sky raiders gave it to them?" Dix's gaze was fixed below.

Garek circled the troops, most of whom where protecting their eyes from the wind-blasted dust by turning away.

"That's right." Aidan's voice was grim. "We see you."

One of the fabric coverings ripped loose and flew away, and

Garek caught it on an updraft, lifted it up higher, and then drew it back over the hill with the sky craft so he could hover over Taya again.

He let the fabric drop near the camp.

"They're running for the valley mouth now." Dix studied the terrain. "They're not backing down."

"Time to get back on the ground." Garek moved back to the landing spot, but he kept high so Dix and Aidan could see as much as possible.

Aidan swore.

"What?"

"I just saw something move. I think a battalion is already through the valley mouth. That's why the others didn't give up, they know a team already snuck through."

Garek tipped the sky craft forward and went back to where Taya stood. There seemed to be nothing and no one between her and the valley mouth.

"I'm sure I saw something." Aidan scanned the ground.

Garek forced himself to hold back, to preserve energy, because he wanted to send a gale down the valley, but instead he used the same swirling, circular wind he'd used on the escarpment.

And then he punched a little more power into it.

A large piece of cloth fluttered, then was ripped up by the wind, and a group of forty or so guards were exposed in the open, about halfway between the camp and the valley mouth.

About five hundred feet from where Taya stood with Hanson.

"How many of the Iron Guard are down there?" He moved to a point between the three armies battalion and Taya, ready to set down and block the way.

"It looks like most of them. Maybe seventy?"

The panic he was feeling subsided a little. Hanson could prevail with much worse odds than that.

And they certainly looked ready to take on anything. They'd seen the battalion, and their weapons were drawn.

The three armies team weren't faring as well. Some were moving back, as if to run, others were moving forward.

Whoever was in command took a few minutes to get them back in a cohesive group.

"Sky craft." Dix was looking up, face grim. "Two of them."

A frisson of fear for Taya ran down his spine, but there were multiple threats here, and Taya had proven over and over again she was up to a fight with the sky raiders.

He made the only sensible choice. "It's better for Taya and the Iron Guard to deal with the sky craft. We'll tackle the three armies group."

"Just the three of us?" Aidan stared at him.

Garek sent him a grin. "No. Just Dix and me. We need you to keep the water shield on the sky craft."

He flew low over the three armies battalion and turned the sky craft to face them as he landed in front of them, barring their way to Taya.

Dix looked down the valley toward the camp. "My people are coming."

Garek locked gazes with her, and she nodded in understanding.

They would have to assume help wouldn't come. If the sky raiders were overhead, most of the guards could be taken down by white lightning.

He opened the door and Dix swung down, face already set.

He followed her, jumping out and landing lightly beside her.

Aidan watched them from the door, pulling the water from their clothes and hair and leaving them dry.

Garek was sure he was wishing now he'd brought the other guards to hold the water shield so he could join them.

The princeling would have to sit this one out.

The scream of engines overhead grew louder as the sky raiders dipped low.

A jagged flash of white lightning blinded, despite the Star still being in the sky, however low it had sunk.

In the wake of the strike, a whole group of Dix's guards went down.

Garek saw the reaction to the attack of some of the three armies group.

Shock.

The swirl of air and dust around him, the beginnings of guards in the group calling their Change, cut off as their attention switched to the fallen Dartalians.

"Traitors." Dix must have seen their hesitation too, because she capitalized on it. She moved right, and Garek moved left.

She had her sword out, but Garek preferred to work without weapons.

"Look long and hard at the result of your betrayal, traitors. You will never look another Baritan in the eye when this is over. How could you ever describe the day you collaborated with the sky raiders to bring down fellow Illians? What could you say about this that will bring you even a scrap of glory?" Dix lifted her sword double-handed, brought it up in front of her.

Her words were having an effect, and then a second lightning strike made almost everyone flinch as the other sky craft dived down.

As another tight unit of Dix's guards fell, some of the three armies started looking a little wild-eyed.

"Time to pay the price of betrayal." Dix was getting relentless. Garek could hear the fury and the outrage in her voice. She raised her sword, and as she did, she called her Change and tore loose the soil from under the guards' feet.

Garek caught it in the air and exploded it in all directions.

There were screams and cries as eyes were blinded.

Dix looked over at him, and he saluted her, and then with a cry, they both ran straight at the battalion.

THIRTY-FOUR

IT LOOKED like Garek and whoever was with him in the sky craft were planning to take on the three armies group that had managed to sneak their way up the valley by themselves.

Taya forced herself to only glance at them as Garek landed, because overhead sky craft engines were whining.

"I think our practice session has become real." Hanson's eyes were trained upward.

"Grab an arrow." Kima was standing by the big water-filled wooden drum that held the arrows, and she started handing them out.

"Your spears are still at the camp?" As Hanson turned to her, one of the sky craft dipped down and a flicker of intense white light blinded her.

Taya closed her eyes to clear them and felt for her knives. Pulled them out. It would be better to have her spears, which *were* at the camp, but she had brought down a sky craft with less.

Dix was shouting something at the guards in the three armies battalion, and when Taya opened her eyes, she saw whatever the Dartalian general was saying had some of them all but spinning;

turning to look at the downed Dartalian guards, turning again to face the sky craft and Garek and Dix.

The second sky craft blasted across the valley, and Taya thought she sensed the air compress a moment before a thin flicker of light seemed to split the sky.

"More of Dix's guards are down. Aim and fire." Hanson had already notched an arrow in her crossbow, and she fired as she shouted her order.

Taya heard the whistle as thirty arrows arced upward and chased the sky craft that buzzed overhead, but it was going very, very fast.

She turned, saw the first craft was on a second run, coming down the valley, low and fast.

She threw both knives straight upward, focusing on height and speed, rather than power, so she could intercept the ship as it flew over her.

She was much better at this game now.

She didn't aim to pierce the skin of the craft. Without Garek giving her an extra push, she didn't think she could.

Her timing was just right, the knives intercepted the ship and she pressed them up against the bottom of the craft.

It tipped left suddenly, then right, the movements panicked rather than smooth, the pilot desperate to change course.

The shadow ore warning bells in the ship must be ringing.

She couldn't see what was happening behind her with the Iron Guard, but she heard a second round of arrows being released, and then the engines on the sky craft they were targeting cut off, sparked again, cut off.

At least some of the small shadow-ore coated arrow heads must have pierced the ship. It should never have taken another run at them.

The sky craft she'd targeted faltered, and she pulled on the knives, sliding them along the undercarriage, hopefully damaging every system, every part of the engine close enough to be affected.

The sky craft had righted and was now climbing at a steep angle, but she held on, feeling the strain of manipulating the ore from so far. By now, she was happy just to keep the knives in contact with the ship, and then, from one moment to the next, there was silence as its engines cut off.

She called her knives back, and as she waited for them, she caught sight of the ship the Iron Guard had targeted trying to gain height and heard its engines misfire.

The weight of her knives falling into her hands snapped her attention back to her own sky craft.

It was coming down.

It had stalled at its steep angle, and now if fell, silently and end over end, like a coin falling from a toss.

"Run." Etta pushed her and she stumbled to the side, turned and ran toward Garek and Dix.

The Iron Guard was scattering, some of them running beside her, eyes up.

She tripped, and forced herself to look ahead, narrowing her eyes to work out what she was seeing in front of her.

There was a cloud of sand hanging in the air, and inside it she could see bodies flailing, falling, staggering.

"It's coming!" The shout right beside her ear made her heart leap, and she turned her head, stumbled to a stop as the ship hit the ground just north of where they'd been standing.

It crumpled on impact, the dull thud as it hit the ground rattling her bones.

She turned away as a massive spray of earth shot up and rained down on them, crouching and putting her arms over her head.

There was a high-pitched screech of metal and rock, and then the ship toppled over slowly, and a second, less intense, thump vibrated the ground beneath her feet.

She stood, put her knives back in their sheaths, and brushed off the dark, rich soil of the valley which coated her from head to foot. When she turned back to the strange sand storm, the dust had cleared.

Garek was looking over at her, face streaked with dirt, standing amongst a pile of bodies. Some were groaning, some were very still.

Dix walked up to him, her eyes wide as she took in the sky craft, upside down and completely destroyed.

Her sword was bloody, and there was dirt and blood on her face.

She said something, and Garek turned his head to her, gave her a salute, and then they clasped hands in a guard handshake.

"They destroyed that whole unit. By themselves." The guard beside her spoke in a hushed voice.

"That's the general of Dartalia, and the general of West Lathor," Taya said. "Of course they did."

THIRTY-FIVE

IT WASN'T OVER.

Garek spun away from Taya to face the oncoming threat—the three other units he'd exposed on the escarpment.

They'd made it through the mouth of the valley, and the way they stood, frozen in place, told him they had seen Taya bring down the sky craft.

To his right, the engines of the second sky craft finally shut off completely and it slammed into the side of the hill in an explosion of orange, green and purple flames.

Satisfaction welled up in him. He had vowed to bring them all down, make them all burn, for taking Taya.

The throat-catching smell of strange materials burning was like the sweetest perfume.

One of the guards at his feet turned a little to see the carnage, but most of them lay still. He'd warned them what would happen if they tried to move, and he'd only had to make good on his promise once to have complete compliance.

Dix had been a little more . . . vigorous . . . with her half of the unit. More lay dead on her side, but then, this was her land to defend.

There was movement behind him, and he glanced back to see Taya striding forward, Aidan just behind her.

Susa and Varn, along with the other two councilors, were walking down, too, accompanied by six guards.

Dix glanced back, frowning, but Susa must have signaled her determination to come to the front, because she subsided, taking a wider stance beside him, her focus back on the enemy.

"Your liege is safe," Garek murmured to her. "We've got Taya, the whole Iron Guard, and you and me."

Her lips twitched.

She must be near burn-out—he certainly was—but he would dig deep for a little more energy to take on the guards in front of them. Especially the pinch-faced man who broke free of the huddle and strode toward them across the wide space of flat field.

Taya reached his side, her face serious, her movements business-like, but her hand brushed his lightly in hello. She was lightly sprinkled with the dark soil of the valley. He looked down at where their hands touched.

So was he.

The man storming across the open space toward them stumbled, and Garek saw it was Taya he was focused on, his gaze fixed on her face.

Taya stiffened and drew herself taller.

"You!" The three armies commander pointed at Taya, and then bent low and scooped something off the ground, reaching for the bow strapped to his back as he straightened. "I thought we were rid of you weeks ago."

He notched an arrow in a fast, practiced move, and Garek saw him shimmer around the edges as he called his Change. It had to be an air Change, because the arrow shot forward far faster than it should have been able to and it was aimed straight at Taya.

Garek lunged into its path, already calling his Change to knock it aside, but it stopped in midair just in front of his face.

He blinked. Stepped to one side and angled a look at Taya.

She shook her head at him, clearly irritated he had stepped into the arrow's path.

A gleam of dark purple reflected off the arrowhead and he realized it was one of the Iron Guard arrows dipped in shadow ore that had fallen to the ground during the attack.

He started to laugh.

Taya turned the arrow around, spinning it like a weathervane so it was facing back the way it had come.

"Let me?" Garek asked.

She flicked him a sidelong look.

"Please?"

She nodded, and let go of her hold.

Garek caught the arrow as it dropped, and sent it straight back.

The man was staring, mouth open, at the arrow, but when he realized what Garek intended he started to turn, to run.

The arrow slammed into his shoulder.

"Who is that?" Garek asked her as the commander cried out, hand going to where the arrow protruded from the join between his arm and chest.

"He's one of the guards from Luf who was working with Habred. He and his partner were the two guards on the road out of Luf who forced me to get into the sky craft with the sky raiders."

Garek felt a far-off roar in his ears.

Things were coming together.

He had wanted to be face to face with the two who had forced Taya to put herself back into sky raider hands since he'd heard about it.

He looked across at the commander, caught his eye, and began to starve him of air.

He choked, and Garek could see the shock on his face. He was already in pain because of the arrow, and it took him a moment to counter with an air Change of his own.

When that didn't work and he was desperate, the troops around him started to raise their weapons in panic, pointing them in all directions, and Taya brushed her hand against his again, to get him to stop.

He did it reluctantly, but she was right. Someone else might get hurt with so many armed and on edge. There would be plenty of time later for revenge.

He waited for the commander to wheeze in a few breaths and stagger back to his feet.

"Your allies are defeated." Garek gestured toward the burning wreck on the hillside. "Your way is still barred. Surrender."

Shocked faces stared at him, mouths slack.

A man stepped out of the crowd around the commander. "We have a larger army than yours on the escarpment. Why would we surrender?"

"Because half that army has disbanded." Susa had reached Garek and Dix's position, and she spoke with cool assurance. "My lookouts tell me there appears to have been a disagreement, and most of the Harven contingent have left, along with small groups from Favre and Kadmine."

Luci and the other Cassinyan villagers had come through. They'd turned the Harven against their own liege.

"The Harven?" The commander coughed it out, his face white with pain, his fingers pressing on either side of the arrow in his shoulder.

"There was a reason you never told them you were allied to the sky raiders." Taya glared at him. "Because you knew they'd revolt if they knew the truth."

There was a shocked gasp behind them, and Garek flicked his gaze back, saw one of the councilor's pointing upward.

Two massive ships, so huge they defied the imagination, chased each other above the clouds, the Star's light shining off them in glittering bursts as they moved.

It was a dance made in silence, and then the smaller of the two ships was engulfed in a massive, catastrophic explosion.

Huge pieces of mothership began raining down over the far hills.

It was a beautiful sight.

Someone moved, a sort of shiver of awe and fear, and Garek forced his attention back to the threat in front of them.

But the three armies guards were still staring at the sky.

Dix tapped his arm, and when he looked over at her, she nodded toward the enemy.

He looked behind him for Hanson, gave the signal for surround, and she grinned, and nodded.

Dix turned, giving signals to her own troops, and quietly, with no fuss or sudden moves, the guards from the camp formed a ring around the three armies battalions.

One or two of them worked out what was happening before the others, but by the time they'd shouted a warning, it was too late.

"What are you going to do? Slaughter us?" The guard who'd stepped out of the crowd and challenged him before curled his lip.

"We charge you with trespass and unprovoked attack." Susa looked back to where the fallen lay, and when she turned to face forward again, anger was visible in her expression. "You will all be imprisoned for your crimes against this state."

"That wasn't us," one of the guards murmured, pointing to the guards struck by the white lightning.

"They were your allies. They did it on your behalf, so yes, it was you." Dix gripped her sword a little tighter. "And what, exactly were you planning to do once you snuck in here with your sky raider fabric anyway?"

"We were going to try to get past you. Continue on to Favre and then to West Lathor."

"There is no Council dispensation to attack West Lathor." The Landau councilor's voice was clear and carrying. "So even that is a crime."

There were murmurs of shock and uncertainty, and the guards began milling around, unsure of themselves.

A cry from behind them, from one of Dix's guards, cut through everything, though.

The woman was pointing up, and everyone's focus went back to the skies.

A small sky raider ship was dropping like a stone toward them. As the smaller mothership had gone up in flames, it had to have come from the bigger one, and Garek wondered if they had been trying to hail him from the sky craft and had finally given up.

It fell so fast through the sky he felt the air compress. A crack reverberated like a whip as the craft sped toward them.

It came to a sudden, shocking stop overhead, and then seemed to float gently down.

This wasn't over, he reminded himself. One group might be gone, but a bigger, better equipped group was still here.

It was time to make it clear they weren't welcome.

THIRTY-SIX

TAYA GAVE Garek some room as a sky craft settled on the field.

She could see a faint blurring around his silhouette, and she got a grip on her shadow ore knives.

"We will not be stepping out." The hiss of a voice seemed to reverberate around them and some of the guards crouched low on the ground in fear. "The *sevn* are defeated."

"We saw." Garek inclined his head. "Have a safe journey home."

There was a moment of bemused silence.

"The journey home is a long one. We will not be coming back."

Taya liked the sound of that, but she saw Garek was not relaxing.

"But?" he asked, voice hard.

"But we would like four more boxes of shadow ore. It makes sense for us to gather more while we have the opportunity."

Taya drew in a quick breath.

"That was not the bargain we struck." Aidan had joined them, and he stood beside Garek, hands fisted.

"We are striking a new one. We don't want to use threats, but we could, right now, level you all and take the one who knows where the ore is on Shadow."

"I could, right now, destroy your ship." Taya lifted both knives.

"You could."

She was sure the voice was that of the sky raider who'd joined her on Shadow and participated in the experiments with shadow ore.

"We knew you might threaten to do so, and we have taken precautions. If anything happens to this ship, we have another nearby that can and will level everyone here and simply take you. However, we'd prefer you unhurt and not affected by injury, so I am sorry to say that as a first option, we will hurt your family unless you come with us. We have been watching you since we met on Shadow, and we followed you to your village. I believe your family means a lot to you, and we have a ship above Pan Nuk, ready to kill them all right now unless you do as we ask."

Taya felt as if she'd been hit by white lightning again while holding a water-covered weapon.

It was as if the sound and the air had been sucked out of the world.

She gasped, and put a hand up to her chest.

Her heart actually hurt.

"I see this is an effective threat." The voice sounded pleased.

Taya threw her knives down and walked toward the ship.

A hand clamped on her shoulder, holding her back. "I'll take her to Shadow." Garek's voice was hoarse.

"No. She comes with us. We'll return her as soon as we have the ore."

"Her people are my people, too. There's no risk in my taking her."

"If you do not let her go, we will send a message to our ship to start attacking the village." There was an implacability to the tone, and Taya looked back at Garek, eyes wide with panic.

Garek wrenched her around to face him, bent his head so his lips brushed her ear. "I will follow. I'll be right there."

She nodded, the numbness lessening as the world righted itself a little.

He pulled her close, squeezing her tight, and then stepped back, and she caught the look in his eye—fury and cunning.

The strange ramp that seemed to fold out of itself came down and she climbed it.

She looked over her shoulder, saw the faces lifted up to her, friend and foe alike, and then the door closed behind her.

"WE ARE HERE."

The disembodied voice broke through Taya's doze and she used the wall of the sky craft behind her to pull herself to her feet.

She was surrounded by a light curtain, and she guessed it had been rigged just for her, so she could be transported without wearing a helmet.

The hours had blurred into one another, and she rubbed at her eyes, tired and jumpy at the same time.

The curtain shifted, creating a passageway to the door, and she walked forward and stepped onto the ramp as the door slid open.

Shadow was in darkness but to the left Barit was lit up by the Star in a glow of blue and green.

She stared at it for a moment, and then sensed sky raiders coming up behind her, so she ran lightly down to the ground.

They had landed in the same place as last time and the cliff face was just up ahead.

She turned back to look at who was coming behind her, saw four sky raiders, each carrying boxes. They stood waiting at the bottom of the ramp.

"How are we going to put the water in?" she asked.

There was a startled double-take. "How did you put it in last time?"

"Using two people in the group who have an affinity for water." She refused to say more than that.

"What do you need?" The scientist was either one of the sky

raiders carrying boxes, or more likely, transmitting her voice through a helmet, but sitting safely elsewhere.

"A bucket, at the very least." It would take her much longer to fill the boxes this way, but there seemed to be no choice.

She turned and started walking toward the cave, uninterested in how they sorted the problem out.

After a moment, the sky raiders followed her, keeping up with her easily.

They stopped a short distance from the cave mouth, though. Too nervous to get any closer.

"You will have to take the boxes from here," one of them called to her.

She sighed and went back for a box, then lifted her gaze to the sky.

Garek was out there somewhere. He said he would come for her, but even if he hadn't whispered it in her ear, she would have known it.

She let her gaze swing slowly across the sky, her heart beating a little faster, but there was no sign of him.

Eventually the weight of the box forced her to move, and she staggered with it to the cave entrance and left it to one side, squeezed through the crack and slid down the scree to the lake.

She stood looking around her for a moment, and then sat suddenly, massaging her heart, head bent.

It was her first moment alone since she'd been forced to enter the sky craft, and she curled over her knees and closed her eyes, breathing deeply.

The clink of a stone falling down the slope made her straighten and stand, but when she looked back, there was no one there.

She'd felt the shadow ore since she'd begun walking to the cave, and she let the feeling of absolute rightness flood her senses.

She would likely never feel this again, be this immersed in her element. She needed to savor it. And it buoyed her. Helped to bolster her.

She called the ore to her, and small pebbles and larger stones rose like a swarm of insects over the marshes, rumbling a little as they rubbed together.

Most of the ore was on the opposite side of the lake to where she stood, where the vein was visible in the rock and pieces had dropped off onto the cave floor over time. They skimmed over the dark waters toward her.

She funneled them up the slope and through the crack, hoping some would land in the box.

When she thought she had enough, she scrambled up the incline and was forced to move some of the ore aside to clear enough space to get out of the entrance.

The sky raiders had been joined by someone holding a bucket, and they had moved back considerably.

She saw the reason was the wide arc of shadow ore that she'd funneled up. Some of it had rolled down the incline and lay spread out in front of the cliff face.

At the sight of the work ahead of her, her shoulders drooped. She was deathly tired. She'd been awake more than a full day and she'd already been close to burn-out after the confrontation with the sky craft on the battlefield.

She sat down and leaned back against the rocks beside the cliff, in the same spot she'd sat with Min all those weeks ago after they'd been flushed out of the cave system.

She'd been just as exhausted then, and cold and wet, too.

She closed her eyes and remembered how she'd lain on the warm stone and told Min about Garek.

It had been a bittersweet memory, because she'd wondered then if she'd ever see him again.

Now, she knew she would. He was out there, thinking up a way to help her.

He would never leave her behind.

She opened her eyes and forced herself to her feet, moving slowly.

She could see the sky raiders watching her nervously from their position, and realized they must be wondering what she was doing.

She squared her shoulders and put one foot in front of the other, filling the boxes with ore, then sliding back down to the lake with the bucket to fill them with water.

When she was done, she called on the ore and got the boxes as far from the entrance as she could before the headache beating behind her forehead became a full blown burn-out, and then she abandoned them, stumbling more than walking back to the cave.

She had devised the plan earlier, but as she slid down the scree and landed in a heap at the bottom, she knew she might not have thought it through properly.

She was too tired to know whether it was a good idea or not, and too exhausted to care.

They couldn't get her here. They couldn't touch her.

And that had to be a good thing.

Maybe they intended to take her home. Maybe not.

They were good at changing the rules, and this way, they would have to leave without her.

Somewhere close to her, something hissed.

She turned her head, heart hammering, icy chills running down her arms as she tried for slow and calm. No quick moves. She had never once come across a slither in all her time on Shadow, but that had definitely been a hiss.

What looked like a smooth stone the size of her fist glowed an arm's length from her head.

She remembered the skitter of a rock falling earlier, and narrowed her eyes at it. Some kind of sky raider spy device, watching her while she worked in the cave.

It had blended in to the scree earlier, so she hadn't noticed it, but now it throbbed with a dark blue light.

"What are you doing in here?" The hiss turned into words.

"Hiding from you." She closed her eyes again.

"We'll take you home. We gave our word."

She made a rude noise. "How is this thing working in here? It's lying pretty close to shadow ore."

"There's a thin film of water coating the outside." The hiss faded then got louder.

"Go away. You got your ore."

"How will you get back?" There was interest in the voice now.

"I'll find a way."

The device was silent for so long, she almost fell asleep.

"If you think your people will come for you in the sky craft you stole from the *sven*, you're wrong. It was destroyed."

She blinked. Turned to look at the device. "How?" She kept her voice scornful, but her heart was fluttering erratically.

"They tried to bring down the sky craft that was watching your village."

She closed her eyes again, trying to keep her face relaxed. "They shot at your sky craft?"

"Yes." Something about the word, the hissing sound of it, chilled her to the bone.

"Go away."

"We don't want you stuck here. Come out and we'll take you home."

They had to be lying about Garek shooting their ship, he didn't know how to, so it was a good bet they were lying about taking her home, too.

Taya raised herself up on her elbow, reached out to grab the device, and threw it into the lake.

It sank immediately.

She watched the ripples in the phosphorescent light for a while, and hoped she had made the right choice.

THIRTY-SEVEN

GAREK TOOK THE TIME, time he didn't have, and swung past Pan Nuk.

There was no sky craft there.

If they'd been telling the truth about having a ship watching the village, it had returned back to the mothership the moment they had what they wanted—Taya in their sky craft.

He flew low over the village, and saw Kas and a few others step out to watch him, uncertain if it was him or the real sky raiders.

He waggled the craft from side to side to let them know it was safe, but didn't stop to talk.

He flew straight to Shadow.

He couldn't get there fast enough.

The fact they wouldn't let him take Taya, that they'd insisted they take her themselves, niggled at him. Worried him.

It could be they were nervous about letting her out of their sight when they needed her so badly, but still, he sensed something off.

He wondered if he should have insisted on bringing some help, but he had wanted to go without delay, and Aidan and Susa were surrounded by a foreign army.

It hadn't seemed an opportune time to pick a team.

He'd simply run to the sky craft the moment the sky raiders disappeared into the dark blue sky with Taya, and taken off.

She knew he was coming.

She just had to keep herself safe until he did.

And they wouldn't hurt her while she was useful to them. He used the thought to keep himself calm and focused.

He came at Shadow from a new angle, slipping into the air around the planet with all the tricks of his calling and heading for the mine, flying low and keeping directly over the river.

He dipped so low that the sky craft touched the water and flung waves up over the craft.

It couldn't hurt.

He reached the mine, and landed in front of it, not bothering to hide it from sight. They obviously had ways of tracking it he didn't understand.

If he was lucky, they wouldn't be looking out for it at the moment, their attention would be on Taya and the cave.

He jumped down and got a line of sight between the mine and the hill where the communication tower used to be.

He stepped into the inbetween, and felt a tug of interest at how it differed from the inbetween on Barit.

It was slower, more deliberate.

If this was any other time, he would have tried to understand it better, but he stepped out of it just before the rocks on the hill, and turned to the larger hills in the distance where Taya must be.

His throat constricted a little at the thought that they might already be gone.

He shrugged it off. Stepped back into the inbetween and stepped out again a little way away from the cave.

The sky craft was there, more or less in the same spot it had been before.

It looked as though sky raiders were carrying boxes between them from near the cave back to the ship, and he tried to see Taya.

He couldn't.

He was concentrating so hard on finding her, he didn't notice the small craft flying toward him, like the one that had led them to the mothership when they'd first reached out to the sky raiders, until he heard the whine of its engine.

The round, eye-like circle at the front of it started to glow a little.

Something told him that wasn't good.

If Taya was in the sky craft, he would have to get her out, and they knew he was coming now. He had nothing to lose.

He stepped into the inbetween, and ran straight at the machine.

He ploughed into it with a spark of curiosity.

He knew he could bring down buildings and trees, even people, but he had never encountered a metal object.

It didn't disappoint.

He was past it and heading straight for the sky craft when the explosion bloomed behind him.

The inbetween protected him from the falling debris, and then he was past the big sky craft and stepping out between it and the cave.

Taya was either inside one, or the other. He couldn't see her anywhere.

There was a long moment of silence as the sky raiders who were out in the open, struggling with their boxes, stared at him, and then the burning hulk of their machine.

He'd made a mistake, he realized, as something on the big ship swivel in his direction. He had made himself an easy target.

He stepped into the inbetween again, just for a moment, as white light bloomed, then stepped out again, to find the sky raiders flat on the ground.

They were either dead or unconscious.

He stared, perplexed. It seemed they had not cared that they would hit their own people. Unless his being in the inbetween caused a ricochet of the white light.

"It appears you have more secrets than we realized." The hiss came from some source on the outside of the sky craft. "We won't fire on you again, given the effect it has on our own. Let us take our people and the boxes, and we'll be gone."

Garek gave a nod. "Where is Taya?"

"She's hiding in the cave where we can't get her." There was a shortness to the tone. An irritation.

He grinned. "So let me get this straight. You can't shoot me, and you can't get to her. What is stopping me from destroying this craft and your boxes of ore like I did to the little machine?"

"Because our mothership can still wreak some havoc on your planet in retaliation. Or on the ship that's your only way off this planet, for that matter."

"As long as we understand that we both have something to lose." Garek stepped into the inbetween and then pulled out just before the cave entrance.

"Fascinating." The same voice spoke again, but this time from the helmet of an unconscious sky raider. "I would also like to know how Taya worked out we planned to take her home with us, and not return her as we promised."

"You'll have to ask her." Garek sent the sky raider a bared-teeth smile. He called over his shoulder, "Taya?"

From within the cave he heard her call his name, and relaxed a little. She had kept herself safe. She had trusted him to come for her.

His satisfaction kept him focused and strong, even though he wouldn't be able to stand upright much longer.

When he turned to look at the ship, a number of sky raiders were running down the ramp.

Some grabbed their fallen, others the boxes, and they started carrying, and in one case dragging, both to safety.

One of the sky raiders approached, walking past her colleagues without attempting to help them. When she got near the entrance, a piece of shadow ore flew over Garek's head and landed near her feet, and she danced back.

Taya was just behind him, he could hear her moving just beyond the cave entrance.

"Stay out of sight," he murmured. "They seem to really want you. Seeing you again might just inspire them to try again."

Another piece of shadow ore flew out, although Taya kept herself hidden, and the sky raider jogged back a little more.

"Peace, Taya, we're going. We would have looked after you. We discovered from their communications that the *sven* had found a small deposit of ore on the planet near our own, but it was too difficult to get to. It would have been easier to get it with you, but I understand you might not have appreciated such an outcome."

"How considerate of you." Taya's voice was a little husky.

The sky raider's translator gave a hiss, hiss, hiss, as if she were laughing.

"This was interesting. And surprising. You may not believe this, but I wish you well." She made a gesture with her hand, if Garek were any judge it was some sort of salute, and then she turned and walked at a fast pace back to the ship, overtaking some of her colleagues hauling the boxes.

Garek watched them with narrowed eyes until they were all inside, and then waited until they lifted off in a blast of gritty, cold dust before he turned to the entrance.

Taya stepped out and into his arms, all phosphorescent light and glittering eyes.

"Is it over?" she whispered.

"Yes." As his lips came down on hers, he hoped for the whole of Barit's sake that it was true.

THIRTY-EIGHT

THEY WOKE to the sound of strange birdsong.

Taya blinked, saw Garek was stirring beside her, and pulled herself to her feet and went to open the door and look out.

She stood, riveted by the sight, until Garek came up behind her and pulled her close, looking over her shoulder.

"Where are we?" She hadn't been in a state to even see where they'd landed last night, she only knew they had to land and sleep, or they would crash.

Now the lush green, and the flashing glimpses of red and yellow birds darting through the foliage, entranced her.

"I think we're in the Southern Sea. I saw a small island, thought it was probably a safe place." His voice rumbled against her ear and she smiled and turned, kissing his neck and winding her arms around him.

"A very good strategic move, General."

He smiled against her cheek. "So I'm the general now, am I?"

"How could you be anything else, after everything that's happened?"

He hesitated. "And Pan Nuk?"

"Isn't that far from Juli. I'm sure there are places in Juli where a person could establish her wool dyeing business."

"I'm sure there are." He had maneuvered her back toward the mattress. "Can it be possible that at last there is nothing stopping us from living together in the same house?"

"If anything tries to prevent it, I will destroy it." She whispered the words as she pushed his shirt off his shoulders.

"You will have to get in line."

THEY WANTED TO DALLY, but they were both aware there were people waiting for them, worrying about them, back in West Lathor.

They found a small pool to wash in, and while it was shallow, the water was much warmer than the chill water of a West Lathor stream in autumn.

They got underway with no delay, and when they reached the Corridor, Taya thought the battlefield looked tidier, but that's all she could see had changed since she'd stepped into the sky raiders' ship yesterday.

They landed near a large group of people standing in the open, and from the zanir surrounding them, banners flying, she guessed there was a negotiation of some kind going on.

Two people detached themselves from the crowd and strode toward them.

Dix and Aidan.

Garek jumped down and she jumped after him, feeling the light touch of air before his hands caught her and set her down.

"Taya!" Aidan gave her a hug. "All right?"

She tipped her head in a side to side movement. "Sort of. What's happening here?"

"Are the sky raiders gone?" Dix looked up at the sky.

"They left directly from Shadow. As far as it's possible for me to be certain, I think they have gone," Garek said.

Dix cut a look his way, gave a nod. "That's good enough for me."

"And me." Aidan's expression said he knew there was more to tell, and he would ask them later.

"Who is here?" Taya craned her neck to see if she recognized anyone in the group up ahead.

"Habred, the lieges of Favre and Kadmine, the full Council, Luci, Susa and Zek. And Dix and I. And now you." Aidan grinned. "That was quite good timing on your part. There were mumbles about where you'd gone, whether the sky raiders had killed or taken you. Some dispute about accusations you've made against Habred."

Garek wasn't listening to him.

Taya could see his gaze was on someone in the group.

It had to be Habred.

"If you want a diplomatic solution with Harven, you might want to rethink letting Garek anywhere near that group." Taya put an urgent hand on Aidan's arm.

He gave her a startled look. "What are you talking about?"

Garek began walking forward, and Taya saw Habred's hand flutter up to his throat, a slight frown on his face.

"I'm talking about Garek killing Habred."

"Hmm." Dix had turned, her bright gaze taking in Garek's easy stroll toward the group.

Habred rubbed at his chest, and then looked over, and Taya saw him narrow his eyes at Garek.

"You will live to regret the lies you've spread about me." He tapped his fist over his heart twice. "You will be brought down for them."

He coughed, hit his chest again, and then started choking.

Taya jogged a little to catch up. "This isn't our peace settlement," she murmured to Garek. "You could kill him later."

Aidan had caught up to her, and he sent her a shocked stare. "Garek, perhaps . . ."

Habred fell to the ground, writhing.

Some of the people around him were kneeling beside him,

looking for ways to help him, but Taya noticed Zek and Susa had simply stepped back and were watching.

Susa sent them a quick, curious look.

Suddenly, Habred whooped in a breath, coughed, and pulled himself up on an elbow, head bent as he sucked in air.

"Taya and Garek, welcome back." Susa greeted them with a bow, and now that Habred appeared to be recovering, all eyes turned to them.

Garek bowed back deeply. "As I have informed my liege, the sky raiders are gone for good." He looked down at Habred, who was still lying on the ground. "Habred. I think you were about to tell us all about how you worked with the sky raiders and betrayed your people to them."

More than one person gasped.

"No. I—" His hand went back to his throat, his eyes went wide.

Taya could see the sudden understanding in his gaze. The horrified knowledge of what was happening to him.

He heaved in a new breath as Garek released him again. "I didn't—"

He fought, desperate this time, kicking his legs, trying to kick out at Garek, although only those who knew what was happening could see who he was aiming at.

When Garek released him again, he lay, panting, for long minutes before he spoke again.

Even the most oblivious of the group had now realized this wasn't an illness. Taya could see a few of them nervously looking around, but most had accurately guessed who the culprit was.

"Do you not have the power to insist this stop?" The liege of Kadmine asked Aidan.

"Why would I stop the questioning of a traitor not just to his own people, but to the whole of Barit?" Aidan asked. "We were not getting very far up until now, were we?"

There was a sudden stillness that descended.

The Favrean liege lifted a hand. "I will admit there is truth to the accusation he had some dealings with the sky raiders, although I don't know all the details. We didn't know about it at all until just a few days ago, and this story from the town master of Cassinya—" she glanced at Luci, "—that he sold his own people to the sky raiders for financial gain, is entirely new to me." Her voice was soft. She was a short woman who looked like she wished she was anywhere else.

"And you?" Garek lifted his gaze off Habred for the first time and focused on the Kadminian liege, who stepped back nervously.

"My commander discovered his dealings with the sky raiders, and sent word to me. By the time I got here, the battle was already over."

"They knew about it, then, and yet, they pushed on." Susa's voice was grim. "Through my lands."

There were a few winces.

"I think Harven's liege is sufficiently recovered." Garek's focus was back on Habred. He was still lying flat, but he was no longer fighting for breath. "Tell us what the deal was."

"They were going to leave Harven alone when it came to their raids, so we prospered, and in exchange, they wanted a few people who no one in the kingdom would have missed."

There was an even deeper silence at his words than there had been before.

"But that changed," Aidan said.

"They wanted a woman. They were desperate for her. Thing was, my people caught her, lost her, then got her back by chance, and they handed her over. Actually watched her get into the sky craft. Then the sky raiders lost her, don't know how. They came back with a new deal. Sounded like the perfect plan to me. They'd knock the West Lathor and Dartalia troops down, and we could advance with no resistance, as long as we looked for the woman amongst the fallen, and let them know when we found her." Habred said everything with a smug little smile on his face, eyes closed, still lying on the grass.

"Except it didn't work out like that." Dix looked like she wanted to swing her boot into his ribs.

Habred opened his eyes, and his lips twisted in a wry smile. "No.

It failed, and somehow my little secret doesn't seem to be so secret after all. But what are you going to do about it? I'm the liege of Harven."

It seemed he had already forgotten Garek.

He remembered him again extremely quickly, though, where his air cut off again.

This was it.

Taya closed her eyes.

Garek wouldn't stop this time.

It took what seemed hardly any time at all for him to suffocate.

"That was . . ." When the liege of Kadmine spoke, Taya opened her eyes again. Saw the look of horror on his face.

"That was justice," Susa said.

Everyone stood mute. This was Dartalia. Susa was liege. Habred had invaded her country.

Her word was the final one on the issue.

"And so," she looked over at the Kadminian and Favrean liege. "I think we have new treaties to negotiate."

Taya slid her hand into Garek's and he looked down at her. There was nothing haunted in his eyes. He simply stared back, serious and focused as always.

"He would have tried to take revenge." He said it quietly, but with absolute conviction. "That's what the double tap over the heart means."

She nodded. "Well, he won't anymore."

"No." He drew her away from the group, and she saw that Quardi, Pilar and Eli were waiting for them a little way off.

"I think all the obstacles have been overcome." There was a light-ness to her that she hadn't felt in a long time.

"And if not . . ."

If not, they would tackle them together.

ABOUT THE AUTHOR

Michelle Diener is an award winning author of historical fiction, science fiction and fantasy.

Michelle was born in London and currently lives in Australia with her husband and children.

You can contact Michelle through her website or sign up to receive notification when she has a new book out on her New Release Notification page.

Connect with Michelle
www.michellediener.com

ACKNOWLEDGMENTS

Thank you to the team of awesome readers, editors and authors who help me make my books as good as they can be. This journey would be a lot more lonely without you. Thanks to Lana for the awesome cover.

www.ingramcontent.com/pod-product-compliance
Lightning Source LLC
Chambersburg PA
CBHW021231250626
47155CB00008B/2955